Veronica Stallwood ~~was~~ ~~born~~ ~~in~~ ~~London,~~ educated abroad and now lives near Oxford. In the past she has worked at the Bodleian Library and more recently in Lincoln college library. Her first crime novel, *Death-spell*, was published to great critical acclaim and became a local bestseller, as did the novels which followed, *Death and the Oxford Box*, *Oxford Exit*, *Oxford Mourning*, *Oxford Fall*, *Oxford Knot* and *Oxford Blue*, all of which feature Kate Ivory.

'Stallwood is in the top rank of crime writers'
Daily Telegraph

'Not only plausible, but in my view, absolutely compelling'
Scotsman

'Novelist Kate Ivory snoops with intelligence, wit and some nice insights'
The Times

'One of the cleverest of the year's crop [with] a flesh-and-brains heroine'
Observer

The Rainbow Sign

Veronica Stallwood

HEADLINE

First published in 1999
by HEADLINE BOOK PUBLISHING

First published in paperback in 1999
by HEADLINE BOOK PUBLISHING

10 9 8 7 6 5 4 3 2 1

ISBN 0 7472 6064 8

Printed and bound in Great Britain by
Clays Ltd, St Ives plc

HEADLINE BOOK PUBLISHING
A division of Hodder Headline PLC
338 Euston Road
London NW1 3BH
www.headline.co.uk
www.hodderheadline.com

For Lorna Rainbow
with love

ACKNOWLEDGEMENTS

With grateful thanks to Audrey, Carlo, Chris, Jane, Lorna, Sally, Diana and Michael for their encouragement and practical help, and to Dr Simon Gates for the dreadful joke about the orchestra.

God gave Noah the rainbow sign,
No more water, the fire next time.

Home in that Rock (Anon.)

1

Beatrice Markland ambles home from school beneath a sky of polished blue enamel. Her school uniform is blue too – a harsh royal blue – with a white piqué collar and cuffs. Although this is only the beginning of June, the temperature is nudging into the nineties and the humidity sucks the energy from her body so that she feels limp and drained. She wears grey cotton socks and brown leather Clarks sandals whose weight glues her feet to the ground.

It takes fifteen minutes to walk from her school to her home, an interval punctuated by the sounds of Arab music wailing from open doorways, the shouts of street traders, the blare of car horns. She can smell donkey droppings on the dusty roadway, and cumin and garlic from nearby cooking. She sniffs the clean, fruity smell from the watermelons heaped up on the stall on the corner, then moves on and wrinkles her nose at the sweet, putrid stench of a dead dog that no one has bothered to clear from the pavement. All the sounds, all the smells, seem to bounce off the dome of the sky and concentrate themselves on to the spot where Beatrice is standing. She never grows used to them; they define both the foreignness of this place, and its familiarity. Turquoise and peridot, lapis lazuli and crystal. Raucous voices, guttural language, the quarter-tones of a haunting contralto, dark masculine eyes that skim her blonde looks and gauche English gait and dismiss her as irrelevant.

There is sweat trickling down her back, forming an oval patch of dampness on her dress. The waistband is chafing, and she wishes she were wearing the loose, lightweight cotton rags of the children playing in the gutter. She wishes she could take off her sandals and feel the dust and grit between her toes. She wishes, too, she could have her ears pierced and wear gold hoops like the women bargaining at the fish stall. She knows that all these things are impossible.

Beatrice's dress does not suit her colouring. Those with dark hair and olive skin merely look sallow in this blue; Beatrice's English fairness is drowned by it. Her skin looks painfully pink, her freckles livid, her hair mousily brown under the dazzling sky. Her mother has considered removing her from the English school run by the Misses Hapsted and sending her somewhere where the uniform is more, well, *refined*, but this would mean putting her daughter in the care of those wily Roman Catholic nuns, who would teach her goodness knows what superstitious nonsense. Beatrice sees the groups of convent girls in their cream shantung tunics, their cool white sandals, their Swiss straw hats with the wide brims and floating ribbons, and it doesn't even occur to her to envy them, for they live in a different world. At fourteen they are adults, and marriageable; at fifteen she is still a child.

From a doorway a young man whistles at her and calls out something she doesn't understand. She turns her head away, embarrassed. So, on she walks, under the burnished dome of the sky, an insignificant girl in a bright blue dress and ugly brown sandals.

Beatrice (who has married Jack Waring in the intervening thirty years, whose mousy hair is professionally streaked with amber and russet, and who has long insisted on being called 'Beech') leaves the sleeping house behind her and steps into her back garden, ignoring the rain that falls on her bare head and spots the shoulders of her grey sweatshirt. The year is turning its back on the dreary days of January and February, though the mornings are still bitterly cold, and at last green shoots are appearing like curled fingers through the sodden earth. By the back door, leaning for support against the wall of the house, stands her ceanothus. Its dark green leaves look dusty and tired after the winter, but the flower buds are visible and will soon be opening to display their fluffy blue heads.

The garden centre tries to call it American Lilac, but it is nothing like a lilac, thinks Beatrice: the flower heads are so much smaller, their colour so much more intense. This one is called 'Italian Skies', and it will bloom a deep, singing blue with a flash and sparkle about it that reminds her, not of Italy, but of somewhere further east. The tree has grown nearly a foot since last year, and broadened out nearly twice as much. In time it will form a dome, the shining, glittering blue of lapis lazuli, and she will stand underneath it and imagine that she is in a country far from Oxford. She looks upwards to the leaden clouds and dreams that she is once more under the blue-and-gold sky of her childhood.

Eventually she sighs, tucks an undisciplined strand of the ceanothus back into its restraining wire and returns to the kitchen to start on the preparations for breakfast.

Water dripped down from the clogged gutters and hit the dustbin lid with a regular *tock, tock*. So regular was the sound that he found himself waiting for the next drop to fall.

Tock.

It had been raining ever since Henry got up that morning, smearing the view of grass and trees, fields and clouds into an impressionistic mess of green and brown. Now the rain had slowed to a drizzle.

Henry Markland took his tray, with the plate of half-eaten toast, into the kitchen. He would do his washing-up later, but first he would treat himself to a second cup of coffee. He filled a cup with water from the tap and then poured it into the kettle.

3

The element hissed with annoyance at its skimpy measure. While he waited for it to boil he went into the hall and dialled his daughter's number.

'Beech?'

'Yes, Henry. Is everything all right?'

'Yes, of course it is. Why should you ask?'

'It's just that it's quite early in the morning, rather early for a casual phone call, and I hoped that nothing was wrong.'

Why was Beatrice sounding so concerned? Anyone would think that he was the child, Beatrice his mother. But he wasn't in his second childhood yet. 'There's no need to worry about me. I'm fine, although of course I am getting a little stiffer in the joints.'

'Is there anything special?' asked Beech, her voice still anxious.

'There was something,' he conceded. 'I wondered whether your mother had told you where she was going today.'

There was silence for a couple of beats at Beech's end. 'Well, yes,' she said. 'She's here with Jack and me. She came over yesterday to stay for a couple of days. She's not down yet but I could give her a call if you want to speak to her.'

'No, I don't think so. I noticed she wasn't here and I was just wondering where she was. I'm glad she's safe at your house.'

'Quite safe. I'll ring you later and I'll ask her to speak to you then.'

'And Jack? Is he well too?'

'He's very well. Blooming, in fact. He sends his love.'

'How kind of him. And yes, ask your mother to phone me later. That would be a good idea,' said Henry. 'But I must go now. I can't stand here gossiping, the kettle's boiling.'

'Goodbye,' said Beech.

'Just one thing before you go.'

'Yes?'

'I just wondered whether it was raining in Oxford.'

'Yes. It's pouring. Goodbye, Henry.'

'Goodbye.' And Henry returned to his kettle, his small cup of coffee, and his contemplation of the rain that streamed down his kitchen windows.

As she replaced the telephone, Beech wondered at what point their roles had reversed so that it was she who played the part of the parent, protecting him from the pain of real life. Or maybe it had always been that way, even when she was the child, and in need of protection herself. She and Nicholas had tried to spare their parents the pain of reality: that was their tragedy.

Beech waited until she had poured the tea, watched Jack take his first spoonful of muesli and Rita spread marmalade on her toast, before saying, 'Henry was on the phone a little while ago.'

'I thought I heard you speaking. I wondered who could be ringing this early in the morning. Is he all right? What did he want?' Her mother paused with her toast poised halfway to her mouth.

'He was asking after you, Rita.'

'He probably woke up, found me gone, and forgot that I'd come over to visit you and Jack,' said Rita, and crunched large, strong teeth into her toast.

'I think Beech is worried that he's getting a bit forgetful,' said Jack.

'He's been like that for ages,' said Rita. 'It's quite normal at his age. But you don't think he's getting worse, do you?'

There was a short pause while the word 'senile' popped into all their minds, but nobody liked to say it out loud.

'Of course not,' said Jack heartily, doubtless fearful that he would be expected to drive up to Chipping Hampton and check on his father-in-law's wellbeing if the women started worrying about the silly old bugger.

'He does seem to concentrate on just two or three things and let everything else go,' said Beech.

'One, rainfall. Two, his sheds. Three, that dreadful dog,' said Rita succinctly.

'He's really very knowledgeable when you get him on to his own subjects,' said Jack.

'But *are* they his subjects?' asked Rita. 'They never used to be. He was interested in *everything* in the old days. Music, art, all those industrial whatsits he was building, the local culture. Everything.'

'Was he?' wondered Beech, who didn't remember that her father was ever interested in her own painting. Perhaps, though, it didn't count as art.

'I suppose we all change as we get older,' said Jack with the smugness of a man who is still in his forties and who doesn't wish to imagine what seventy-eight will be like. 'It's simply that Henry's interests have changed over time. Once he was interested in architecture, books and plays and so on, now he's fascinated by rainfall and—'

'Compost,' said Beech.

'That dog,' added Rita.

'It could be worse,' said Jack. 'Is there any more tea?'

Beech poured tea, hoping it was still hot enough and not too stewed.

'I know I should be more patient with him,' said Rita, 'but every now and then I just have to escape. Why can't he collect stamps, or play golf, or go fishing even, like other men?'

'He always hated killing things,' said Beech.

'He should put the dog down,' said Jack. 'It's well past its sell-by date.'

'Poor old Gunter,' said Beech. 'He is getting a bit smelly.'

'I try to keep that animal out of the house,' said Rita. 'Goodness only knows what Henry's letting him do on my linen chair covers while I'm away.'

6

'I'm sure he won't let him spoil your covers,' soothed Beech. 'And perhaps we are worrying about Henry unnecessarily. Just because his interests aren't the same as other people's doesn't mean there's anything strange about him. He has an original mind. What's wrong with that?'

'Original? Yes, I suppose he has always had an original mind,' said Rita. 'Both of us were imaginative and creative people when we were young.'

Jack said, 'I reckon Henry's original and artistic mind will be all right for a few years yet, just as long as no one confuses him. He doesn't need any upsetting new ideas at his age.'

'He's only five years older than me,' said Rita.

'But he's not quite as well-preserved, is he?'

'That's true enough,' said Rita.

Beech looked at the clock. 'Is it really that late? You need to leave soon if you want to get to the museum in time,' she said to Jack.

'It doesn't matter for once,' said Jack. 'I'll go in after the rush hour traffic. They owe me a morning off.' (The Fyne Museum library owed Jack very little, having provided him with an unstressful job and an unusually large salary for some twenty years.) Jack sighed again. 'But I suppose I should telephone my assistant and tell him I'll be a little late in to work today.'

Although the Fyne had given Jack a very good life, and had demanded so little from him in return (and most of that consisting of his presence at various fund-raising occasions) still the work had been less rewarding than he had hoped, so that he was left with a niggle of frustration, and an underlying grumble of resentment that might well have evaporated with a few weeks' hard graft but which had not had the opportunity to do so. And although he had always tried to appoint young and attractive women to junior positions in the library, believing that by doing so he was helping advance the cause of feminism, he had been frustrated by other members of the Appointments Committee who insisted on appointing promising young men, or women of uncertain years and forbidding looks. And then, the very few attractive women who did come to work at the Fyne, and who should have looked up to him as he sat in his glass-fronted office, authoritative and yet approachable, turned out to be married, or if not married, then 'attached', or somehow not interested in the opposite sex, or if interested in men, then not interested in *him* . . . For a few minutes Jack brooded upon the general unfairness of life, and then he telephoned his assistant, Alan, and felt no guilt at all when he announced that he would not be in to work that day, and gave no excuse for his absence.

He returned to the kitchen a couple of minutes later, frowning. Alan did not seem to be as put out by his superior's proposed absence as Jack thought he should be. Still, there was no chance that his assistant could nudge him out of his enviable position. He was too well-entrenched for that. He had started further up the ladder than most men of his generation: good-looking, athletic and an easy liar, he had brains and enough money in a trust fund to make sure he would never go hungry, however little work he did. Once he had graduated from university he found that people stepped forward and offered him a helping hand. When Jack turned up for his interview at the Fyne, he encountered a man from his cricket team. When he applied for promotion, it was to the eldest son of his own godfather that his application was sent. Jack came to expect the friendly smile, the conniving nod of the head wherever he went, and he was rarely disappointed.

'No problem,' he said, sitting down again.

'Why are you fidgeting like that?' asked Rita. 'What is wrong with you, Beatrice?' Rita had always refused to call her daughter by anything but her unabridged given name.

'I'll have to be going out myself,' said Beech. 'One of my

boring committees. I'll be back later in the morning, after I've done some shopping. You two can have a cosy chat while I'm gone.'

'There is something I wanted to discuss with you,' said Rita.

'Yes?'

'But I wouldn't want to hold you up when you're busy.'

'What is it?' asked Beech.

'Thirty years,' said Rita.

'What?' Beech couldn't think what her mother was talking about for a moment, but then, with a sudden empty feeling inside, she understood. 'Ah,' she said. 'I see.'

'You've forgotten, haven't you?' accused Rita.

'Of course not. How could I?' said Beech. 'Though I had forgotten that it was actually thirty years. But can we talk about it later? I'll be able to give you my full attention then.'

'I really want to make this anniversary something special,' said Rita. And behind the primped, tautened face, Beech saw another, older and sadder Rita.

'We have to mark it in some way,' insisted Rita. 'I think we should produce a memoir.'

'A memorial perhaps,' said Jack.

'Don't be ridiculous,' said Rita. 'He needs no memorial while he is still alive in our hearts.'

'I think a memoir is an excellent idea,' said Beech. She gave Jack a perfunctory farewell kiss on the cheek, which he appeared not to notice, and left the room.

'Where do you suppose she's going?' asked Rita.

'Some committee meeting, she said,' and Jack turned to the financial pages of his newspaper.

'I don't believe her!' said Rita.

'Why not? It's the sort of worthy thing she does with her mornings. It'll be the arthritics or the Alzheimers, I expect.'

Beech, now dressed for outdoors, opened the kitchen door, called, 'Goodbye! I'll see you both later!' and disappeared again.

They heard the front door close with a firm *clunk*.

'There you are! That's what I was talking about!' said Rita. 'Why was she wearing that hat?'

'Doesn't she always?' said Jack, who had lost interest in the subject.

'A smart new green hat,' said Rita. 'Tipped rather rakishly over one eye.'

'And her old black coat, the one she wears for Sainsbury's shopping,' said Jack. 'The coat is because she doesn't care what she looks like, and the hat is to make the other old biddies on the committee jealous.'

'If you say so,' said Rita, and closed her lips in a manner that indicated she could say a lot more if she cared to. Jack, quite satisfied with his own analysis, returned to his newspaper.

'I think you should look into it,' said Rita, as though speaking to herself. 'You shouldn't be so trusting. I think that girl is behaving in a very odd way. Perhaps it's her age, but then again, perhaps it isn't.'

2

Beech slammed the garden gate closed behind her and walked down the street without a backward glance. If her mother had been more observant she would have noticed that not only was Beech wearing her new emerald-green felt hat and smart black shoes with a modestly raised heel, but also had added lipstick to her usually unadorned face. She strode along a road where the houses were set well back – comfortable-looking houses, but with their gardens depressingly bare of colour. Her feet slapped down on to the wet ground, for Beech usually wore boots or heavy walking shoes with deeply ridged soles. The soft leather shoes she was wearing today felt unfamiliar – light and airy – and so she lifted her feet a little too high and set them down a little too solidly, as if walking on the moon. Hedges poked wet black fingers at her coat sleeve as she passed. She pulled up her collar to create a shield between the outside world and herself. Ahead of her two crows stared down from a rooftop. Corvine eyes blinked, bulbous beaks pointed down at her. If she had a shotgun she could slaughter them. One! Two! Bang! Bang! Gone for ever. Nothing left but two dead bodies bleeding into the wet grass. She smiled to herself and quickened her step. The crows flapped wings like black rags and flew off to perch in a skeleton tree. As she watched them, the smaller crow twitched its tail and crapped, adding a fresh glutinous patch to the well-spattered pavement.

Beech crossed another road, turned another corner. She had always loved these north Oxford streets. They were broad and tree-lined and even the cars that were parked the length of the kerb were less obtrusive than elsewhere. She hummed to herself, aware that it wasn't just the pleasant neighbourhood that was making her feel so happy. She had turned towards the east, and the sky in front of her, although still thick with clouds, was brighter. Opalescent, she thought. The light reflected off the greasy footpath and shone on the puddles, transforming them into liquid mercury. Usually at this time of year she would gladly have swapped all the rain and the resulting juicy green vegetation for blue skies, hot sun and the dry, scorched leaves of her childhood. Today she was content to be here, in this particular place.

She turned into Lewis Road. Not far now. In a few minutes she would arrive at Fergus's.

Then, as she turned the last corner, she saw walking towards her a woman, perhaps her own age, but dressed in that shade of beige which does not flatter the English complexion, and with her light-coloured hair set into curls like wood shavings. She was pulling something along on a lead. If it was a dog, it was a very large one. But instead of barking, the animal made bad-tempered *mnyeh mnyeh* noises and bobbed its head up and down in an undoggy way.

It was a goat.

A fat-bellied English goat, with patches of curly hair like a grubby bathroom rug, and it stared at Beech with rectangular devil's eyes.

The pavement was narrow and the three of them had to negotiate their passage, with Beech standing back against the fence, while the woman in the beige coat cajoled the goat past. But the goat was inclined to stop and inspect Beech, and butt its head against her arm, and then nibble at some evergreen plant which overhung the fence. While the woman pulled at its halter, the goat turned its head towards Beech, and jutted its wispy beard and sneered with its sensitive nose. Its breath was hot and dark-smelling. *Gamy*, thought Beech. She had to inhale the goat smell, gaze into the long yellow eyes and stop herself from falling headlong into the past.

'There's no need to be frightened of her. She's only playful. She won't hurt you,' said the woman unconvincingly, tugging on the halter. She had a voice that scratched like a knife on a plate, and a face coated in thick beige foundation a shade darker than her coat. Her eyes were pale blue and she had the preoccupied look of someone who has recently laid aside a book and would like to return to it. 'If you take no notice of her, she'll leave you alone.'

The goat had left a mess of white saliva on the black sleeve of Beech's coat, but Beech still smiled, and nodded, and tried to disappear backwards through the fence, while affecting unconcern.

Beech said, 'I'm so sorry,' and, 'Oh dear, it's all my fault,' and, 'Really, don't worry about me. I'm very fond of goats,' while she wished that they would both go away and leave her alone.

The incident lasted only a minute or two in reality, but it left Beech feeling shaken. She had to stand still for a moment, and concentrate on the sticky buds on the chestnut trees, bowing and swaying in the wind, and the greasy shine on the pavement, and the grey skeleton of the wisteria climbing up the side of a nearby house. The chestnut buds gave a promise that spring would soon arrive, with warmth and soft air and azure blue skies. And she reminded herself that this goat was quite different from the small, bony animal that was pushing its moist black nose up through the dark pool of her memory. And this goat-lady, in her drab tweed coat, bore no resemblance to the dark-eyed, wrinkled woman who shyly pulled the black shawl across her face, securing it with her teeth, before she milked her goat on the kitchen balcony of Beech's childhood apartment. *Arwa. Her name was Arwa.*

Hot sunlight faded, sharp foreign voices receded. Beech tried to conjure up one of the bright, happy images from the past: the walk home from school along the dusty street; the heap of dark green watermelons, one sliced open to show its scarlet flesh and black pips; the laughter of the thin, ragged children playing in a doorway while a radio lamented in a back room; hyacinth skies; turquoise sea. The merry-go-round of her fear slowed and stopped. Woman and goat disappeared from view. She was all right again, everything was under control. She could shelter under her imaginary blue dome, inviting in the cheerful memories. The others, like invading barbarians, could be kept at bay.

The man observes the scene from an upstairs window of the corner house. He has been standing at the window, watching the rain and listening to the moaning of the trees, for some quarter of an hour. He pretends to himself that he has a good reason for standing by his window, but he knows really that he is waiting to see the woman in the green hat. He has observed the incident of the goat, which took up a minute or so, and which seems to have upset her more than it should.

She is walking towards the corner where his house stands. He notices the way her hat hides the left side of her face, while a sweep of brown hair waves down her right cheek to cover her ear. And now he can see that her mouth is smiling, although perhaps there is an expression of wariness in the eyes. It is difficult to be sure. Perhaps she is just screwing up her eyes against the cold and the rain. There is an eagerness in her gait, her shoulders inclined a little forwards, that suggests that she is going to meet her lover. But at nine o'clock in the morning? Perhaps not. Look again. Although she is wearing lipstick, she doesn't appear to have put on any other cosmetics. No eye shadow. No blusher on the colourless cheeks. Just a swipe of an indeterminate brownish-pink lipstick across the lower half of the white oval that is her face. And yet she has put on that green hat, and pulled it down at that rakish angle. A sudden shaft of pale sunlight darts from behind a cloud and strikes her face. From that angle it lights just one side of her features, leaving the other half in shadow. The shadowy side retains the possibility that she might still be a young woman, with that easy stride and the curiosity that she appears to have in everything around her. But the low-angled white light is unkind to the illuminated side of her face, revealing small lines and imperfections and the lack of certainty in the expression. But her head is lifted now, so that he can be sure that she really is smiling, which she certainly wasn't doing a couple of minutes ago. A woman who gives out contradictory signals. He wishes he knew what she felt about him.

This form of detached observation has become a habit with him which he should perhaps break, but will more probably not. What was he hoping for from his fifteen-minute vigil? To catch some expression unawares on her face, that would show him something of her hidden character? To find out why she telephoned him, hurriedly and breathily, early this morning and invited herself over for a mug of instant coffee? He leaves the window and moves back into the room, waiting for the peal of the doorbell. When it comes, he waits for a moment, then walks slowly down the stairs, as though called unwillingly away from some other activity.

'Hello, Beech,' he says. 'Come in by the fire. You must be frozen.'

'Thank you, Fergus,' she replies, smiling.

3

Beatrice Waring and Fergus Burnside had first met three months previously, in Tesco's, in a crowded aisle, in front of the frozen fish cabinet.

'Ouch!' cried Beech.

'I'm so sorry,' said Fergus. 'I've never been much good at steering a supermarket trolley, and I believe this one has a wonky wheel. Was that your ankle?'

'Oh, bother!' said Beech, with commendable self-restraint, and hopped up and down on one foot.

'Have I hurt you?' asked Fergus.

'Yes!' said Beech.

'Oh dear. I see what you mean. You're bleeding, I'm afraid.' Fergus abandoned his trolley, which contained only a 240-gram packet of frozen peas and a small white sliced loaf, and frowned at Beech's ankle. 'Wait here,' he said.

'I can't move! I'm in pain!' said Beech, and she stood, dripping blood, and watched Fergus's long, thin back disappear into the crowd. None of the other shoppers took any notice, but merely reached round her to pick up family packs of frozen cod steaks for their Friday night dinners.

Just when Beech thought that he had disappeared for good, Fergus returned with a selection of bandages from the pharmacy counter.

'Have you paid for these?' she asked doubtfully as he dropped to his knees, ripped open packages and inexpertly stanched the flow of blood.

'Of course I have,' he said, resting her foot on his knee as he placed an antiseptic pad against the cut and wound a yard or two of muslin around it. 'Should I get one of those stretchy ankle supports, do you think?'

'I don't think so. I'm sure this will be enough.'

'And now I should at least buy us a cup of coffee to make up for the damage I've inflicted on you.'

Beech looked at her watch. It was half-past six and she had an hour and a half before Jack would expect his dinner to be on the table.

'I think this deserves at least a small whisky,' she said, examining her lumpy white padded ankle. The size of the bandaging seemed out of all proportion to the injury.

'Whisky? Even better. Have you finished your shopping?' asked Fergus, looking doubtfully at the contents of his re-claimed trolley.

'Yes,' said Beech, who hadn't, but who was feeling unusually irresponsible that evening.

'Will you be able to drive?' asked Fergus solicitously.

'I think so,' said Beech, who had by now realized that she was suffering from nothing more than a slight graze on the back of her heel, but who was unwilling, for the moment, to give up her role as victim.

When they had paid for their few items, they went to their respective cars and Beech followed Fergus out of the car park. She felt reckless, suddenly, as though she had spent too many years doing what was expected of her. She wondered fleetingly whether she could persuade Jack to eat a Chinese takeaway later that evening.

It was a cold, wet night in early December, and she drove close behind Fergus on to the bypass and then a mile or two down a narrow road to a village pub.

Fergus never told her that he had steered his trolley into her ankle on purpose. If she had wanted to know why he had done it he would have been pushed to give her a reason. But there was something about the expression on her face as she chose between one fish and another, the way she bit her lower lip, the gleam of amber and russet in her mid-length hair as it swung across her face; then there was the awful black coat she was wearing that couldn't disguise her slim, gorgeous legs. Somehow they all added up to a woman he wanted to know. So he had made her acquaintance in the only way that occurred to him on the spur of the moment, and welcomed the chance to take her out to a pub.

Once they'd got their drinks – small ones, since they were both driving – they sat at a table by a window.

'Perhaps we should begin by exchanging names,' said Fergus. 'Mine's Fergus Burnside.'

'Beatrice Waring, but I'm called Beech.'

'As in seaside, or like the tree?'

'The tree. I tried to call myself Bice when I was in my teens –' she spelled it for him – 'because I thought it was Italian and romantic. But everyone rhymed it with mice, which was simply embarrassing.'

'Beech,' repeated Fergus. 'It suits you. It goes with your hair.' He wanted to wrap one of the strands around his fingers and caress it with his thumb. He wasn't sure what her reaction would be if he did.

They looked at one another for a few seconds, then Beech lifted her glass. 'Here's to Tesco's,' she said.

'I'll drink to that,' said Fergus. All his small talk had deserted him. If he didn't think of something interesting to say soon, Beech would finish her whisky and leave, and he would never see her again. Around them the pub was starting to fill up and the buzz of conversation and the exhaled smoke surrounded them like a cocoon so that they felt more isolated, more private, than before.

Beech said, 'I'm married. Did you realize?'

'Yes. You're wearing a ring. I noticed.'

'And you?'

'No. I've never married.' He could have added something corny, like, I haven't found the right woman yet, but he found himself asking, 'Are you happy?'

'Happy?'

He thought she was going to ask him what he meant. *What is happiness?* He had no answer to that.

But she said, 'We're not unhappy. He's a perfectly ordinary man and we live a perfectly ordinary life.' She sighed, apparently without noticing that she did so. 'We have a daughter called Alice.' She was biting her lower lip again, the way she had when she couldn't choose between the giant pack of tiger prawns and the breaded cod steaks. 'The trouble is I'm not the same person he married, but he hasn't noticed it yet.'

I'd have noticed, Fergus wanted to say. Instead, he looked sympathetic and asked her where she lived.

'In north Oxford.'

'Really?' He brightened. 'So do I.'

They lived just a few hundred yards apart, they discovered. 'I can't think why we haven't met before,' he said. 'I've lived on the corner of Lewis Road all my life. We must have passed each other hundreds of times. We could have been old friends. We probably cycled to the same school, played in the same park when we were children.' He felt elated as he thought of their shared history.

Beech shook her head. 'I don't think so. I grew up abroad. I came back to England when I was sixteen, but to a girls' boarding school in the depths of Sussex.'

'Whereabouts abroad?' It seemed extraordinary to Fergus, this exotic childhood of Beech's. His own upbringing, in the same house from birth to adulthood, must appear horribly dull to her.

'In the Middle East. My father was an engineer, and we lived in the Levant.' She spoke as though she didn't want to think about the past, as though she had dismissed it.

'Didn't you enjoy it?' he asked.

'Yes, of course. Mostly, anyway. No childhood is perfectly happy all the time, is it?'

'Like marriage,' he said.

'I think in childhood there are greater extremes of emotion.'

He wanted to ask her for details, but they had hardly known one another for an hour yet, and it was too soon. He hoped that they had many more hours ahead of them – long, luxurious hours – in which they could explore all the alleyways of the past.

Beech, who was apparently fascinated by the chipped advertising slogan on a tin ashtray, finished her drink and looked at him enquiringly. 'It's time to leave,' she said.

'I suppose so. But now that we've met, we will see one another again, won't we?' He paused, hoping that he wasn't sounding too desperate, but Beech said nothing. 'Just as friends,' he added. 'For the occasional cup of coffee.'

'Why not?' she said.

She looked at him and smiled, and for the first time Fergus felt as though he was seeing Beech with no defences in place. The smile transformed her into someone young and vulnerable. He took her hand as they walked back to their cars and tucked it under his arm. She didn't pull it away.

On the way home, Beech found that she was grinning foolishly to herself. Her head hummed with the echoes of their conversation. Back in the pub she had felt shy, held back by all her middle-class inhibitions about talking to strangers. But now, alone in the car, she could pull out the images and linger over them for as long as she wanted. She read and reread the messages that had passed wordlessly across the table. I think he likes me, she said to herself.

And I like him. I like the way he isn't really dishy, but tall and skinny and wiry. I bet he has a knobbly spine like a row of scrubbed baby potatoes. And I like the way his hair grows straight up from his forehead, and how defenceless the back of his neck looked when he walked away to search for the bandages. And the pang I felt when I thought – just for a few seconds – that he might never return.

Why couldn't I talk to him properly in the pub? He must have thought I was a complete idiot. I should have told him about my life in the Levant. I should have been witty and informative.

Sunlight so dazzling it hurt your eyes. Virtually no rainfall from June to October, just the implacable heat and humidity. Purple bougainvillaea spilling over mud walls. Scarlet hibiscus in a terracotta pot on the terrace. The scent of jasmine. The honeyed stench of rotting flesh.

She pulled up outside the house and sat for several minutes with her eyes half closed, enjoying the memory of his slate-blue eyes and black eyelashes; quite a big nose, but straight, dominating his face; his mouth, with the full lower lip; the small white scar on his chin which came, he had told her, from falling off his bike at the age of eight. She pictured his dark blue tweed jacket, darker than his eyes, and the green pullover with the lighter green shirt collar visible at the neck.

She could remember it all, she found, including the feel of his hand, tucking hers into his arm so that they could walk close together to where they had parked their cars.

'Can you come round for coffee?' he had asked. 'Tomorrow?'

'Not tomorrow,' she had replied. 'But how about next Tuesday?'

'Four days away,' he had said.

Perhaps it was too soon, perhaps she should have suggested some much later date, but with Christmas fast approaching, she would find herself submerged in family chores.

'Tuesday,' she had repeated.

She opened her eyes, sighed again, climbed slowly out of the car and made her way into the house, her single carrier bag of food in her hand. Jack looked up at her enquiringly from the sofa and for a moment her heart thumped too loudly and she thought he could see her secret revealed in her face.

'What's for supper?' he asked.

'I thought we'd have a Chinese takeaway.'

Why should he suspect her? In their twenty years of marriage she had never before had a drink with a strange man.

As she went through to the kitchen, the phone rang. She put down the carrier and turned back into the hall to answer it, but Jack was just ahead of her.

'I'll get that,' he said quickly. 'You carry on with the supper.' And he scooped the receiver up to his ear, pressed his lips close to the mouthpiece and muttered, 'Jack here. Hello?'

Amused, Beech returned to the kitchen. Jack was acting as though he had a much guiltier secret than she did. Perhaps the fusty old Fyne Museum was really a hotbed of clandestine meetings. She smiled at the thought, but noticed that Jack was still muttering into the telephone as though he didn't wish her to overhear his conversation.

It didn't take Beech long to realize that Fergus was somewhere in his thirties.

'Thirty-four,' he said, when she asked him. He didn't ask her own age, and she didn't mention that she was forty-five, but in daylight he must have seen the small lines around her eyes and mouth and guess that she was no longer a young woman. Luckily he seemed not to care. They didn't meet often, and over Christmas and New Year they didn't meet at all, but still their relationship, such as it was, had inched forward so that now they could at least have a reasonable conversation when

23

they met, usually in his house, usually around eleven in the morning, as though that were the most innocent time of day.

This morning's meeting, with the clock just striking nine, was, therefore, singular.

4

Once you have passed through Fergus Burnside's front door, which is the colour of fresh ox blood, you walk along a red-papered corridor, between a narrow gallery of pictures. The carpet is of some neutral buff colour, and although it always appears to be recently swept and vacuumed, it is worn in places, and has probably been down for twenty years. More pictures line the walls of the stairwell, several rows high, and hung the whole length of the wall. This staircase, mounts to the small half-landing, then turns and takes you to the broad, well-lit front room. Here the carpet is a pale green, and the door and window frames are a soft ivory colour. The walls of this room too are painted that russet colour that our ancestors knew was best for setting off furniture and paintings. The curtains are polished cotton in the dark, smoky colours of a stormy sunset, and the sofa has been covered in the same faded material. The furniture is good, but a little battered. The house has a feeling of continuity about it: perhaps it belonged to Fergus's parents. Perhaps they still live on some distant upper floor, faded and dusty like the curtains. Or perhaps they died in middle age, leaving Fergus with this house and a moderate income. Fergus himself does not give the impression that he kills himself with overwork to maintain his standard of living, and he doesn't need to let off part of his house to help with its upkeep. Certainly he appears to have time to spend on whatever takes his fancy which is, at the moment, Beech and her history.

Fergus's collection of pictures is an eclectic one, Beech has discovered. There is everything here, from delicate watercolours of East Anglian silt and sky, through pastel studies of some unknown child's head. Seascapes, landscapes, many of them grey-green and English, a few of them more exotic, suffused with the honey-coloured light that shines further south. There are portraits, some realistic and sensitive, some made up from slabs of colour that render the sitter unrecognizable. Her eye tangles with that of a nude, and pauses for a moment.

The woman is lying on an unmade bed, leaning back against a heap of pillows so that her breasts are pushed up and outwards. There is a dab of white paint on her lower lip, glistening like saliva. Has the model just licked her lips with her pointed tongue? She has deep-set dark eyes and a knowing expression. She has not shaved under her arms. There is spare fat on her thighs. She is not sucking in her ample stomach. She has probably not shaved her legs. She does not care whether Beech stares at her or not. A bush of black hair nudges out between her open thighs. Thick red lips smile at Beech. Beech looks away.

Finally, she turns towards Fergus and asks, 'Who is she?'

'I've no idea.'

'She reminds me of someone at a party, many years ago.'

'I hope that time she was wearing clothes,' said Fergus.

'It was a very grand, very big party, and it happened on the worst day of my life. It was a picnic, held by a mountain pool – the Rainbow Pool, it was called, but really it was dark, a real cobalt blue, and it was in the hills, miles away from the city. In fact it was only the English who called it the Rainbow Pool. Now I think about it, it was named after Rimbaud.'

'The nineteenth-century poet?'

'The one who gave up writing poetry and took to travel. He must have visited it and admired the place. He probably wrote something about it. I don't know. But anyway, Rainbow was the nearest that English-speakers could get to it.'

'Won't you come upstairs? It's warmer there. I've lit a fire.'

'Thanks.' She followed him up the stairs. 'You're wearing a suit,' she remarked accusingly when they reached the top. Fergus always wore jeans and a sweatshirt in the mornings.

'I have to go up to London to talk to an Australian.'

'Am I holding you up?'

'No. I'll take the train. And Bryan and I are meeting for lunch, so I don't need to leave for a couple of hours yet.'

'How's it going?'

'I'll meet the deadline easily enough.' Fergus was writing a book on world wool production, a subject which, Beech found, generated little small talk. She followed him into the large sitting room on the first floor.

'I'll make the coffee,' he said. This was part of their ritual.

While Fergus was out of the room she wandered around, peering at the dusty objects that crowded the mantelpiece and bookshelves and jostled for position on the tops of cupboards. She liked this room, full of things that had caught Fergus's eye and which he had brought home and stored in here, or which he thought might come in useful some time, or which perhaps had come down to him from his grandparents and which he was so accustomed to seeing that he no longer noticed. She had to admit that this house was more comfortable than her own. There were no spikes of cold air to prod you in the neck or slam an unexpected door behind you. She liked the feeling of continuity that this place gave her, the sense that Fergus and his family had lived here for three generations. She sighed, for she had rarely felt that she belonged anywhere. And even in this room she was still only a visitor.

When Fergus returned with a tray containing a coffee pot, two mugs in the form of elephants and a bottle of milk one-quarter full, she had at least taken off her hat and unbuttoned her coat, and was sitting on his large, comfortable sofa.

'Now, how about telling me what's up?' said Fergus. 'You

don't usually ring me before nine and ask to see me straight away.'

'Oh, it's nothing really,' she said, frowning. 'Just one of those family things that gets to you so that you have to escape from people. I knew the scene so well, I didn't need to hear us all acting out our parts for the umpteenth time.'

Fergus waited in silence for her to explain what she was talking about.

'Every year it's the same thing. Some families dread Christmas because of the rows; with us it's August. My father retires further and further into his own peculiar world and my mother runs away and hides in the nearest expensive shop. As for me, I try to sit quietly on my own and sort out the tangled memories.'

'Are you going to tell me what it's about? I'd like to know.' He was staring at her intently and for a moment or two she held his gaze. It would be wonderful – didn't people call it 'liberating'? – to confide in another person, especially one who was giving her his whole attention and who appeared to be interested in anything that affected her. But the habit of silence and secrecy was ingrained in her, and the words escaped like prisoners from her lips.

'Have I ever mentioned my brother?'

'No. I didn't know you had a brother.' He spoke patiently, as though he knew he must indulge her reluctance.

'We never speak of him. There was an accident and he died. Every time I try to open the subject, my parents slide around it. Henry tells me that I mustn't upset Rita by reminding her of the tragedy. And Rita says that Henry never got over his son's death, and I shouldn't rake over old, sad memories.'

'But you do need to remember.'

'Yes. It's all such a muddle. I don't think I ever really knew what happened that day. And Rita and Henry won't tell me.'

'When did it happen?'

28

'Thirty years ago.'

'Thirty years?' Fergus stood up and patted his pockets. 'He must have been quite young. Just a child. What happened?' He was padding round the room, lifting up smaller objects and looking underneath them, peering inside larger ones.

'There was a swimming accident at a pool. He drowned.'

Fergus returned to the sofa and sat down again. He waited a moment and then, when she remained silent he asked, 'Is that it? Aren't you going to tell me any more?'

'I'm impossible, aren't I? I can see that you're sitting here, radiating sympathy and friendly interest, and all I can manage to get out is two lousy sentences.'

'Quite pathetic,' said Fergus drily. 'Is this reticence due to a surfeit of emotion on your part, or do you really feel that cool about him?'

'Oh no!' She look up, startled. 'He was my brother. I loved him. I was devastated when he died.' She spoke with the nearest approach to passion that he had yet heard from her.

'Well, you never know. Some families hate each other. Some are indifferent. The lucky ones love each other. I wasn't sure which category the Marklands fitted into.'

Beech had lapsed back into silence, and Fergus got up and wandered round the room again. He was opening drawers now, pulling out the contents.

'Bother!'

'What's wrong? What have you lost?'

'I was hoping I had a packet of cigarettes.'

'But you don't smoke.'

'No. But I used to. I've given up.'

'Do you want to start again?'

'I suppose not.' And Fergus sat down, looking glum. 'Now, explain to me why you had to run away from talking about a thirty-year-old tragedy.'

'No one would explain what happened. Nicholas – that's my

brother – was a good swimmer. He shouldn't have drowned. But when I asked questions at the time, I was fobbed off with unsatisfactory answers, and told that I was upsetting my mother, and I should leave it alone. But I could hear them – Henry and Rita, I mean – arguing behind closed doors. I know they were talking about him, but I was shut out.' She picked at the embroidered flowers on the cushion until the faded silk began to fray.

'You think there's some mystery about his death?'

'All I know is that my mind feels like a strong wooden box, banded with metal and closed with a heavy lock.'

Fergus leaned across and kissed her gently on the cheek. 'Sometimes, just sometimes, I catch glimpses of the colourful woman prisoner. I'm still hoping that one day she'll shear off the padlock, leap out of her box, shout for joy and then explode like a firework.'

Beech laughed at the image. 'Really?'

'Really. And I want to be there.'

Beech smoothed down the frayed strands on the cushion. 'I expect I'm just being melodramatic. I don't suppose there's really much of a mystery about his death. Maybe it was just that they thought of me as a child, and death was something you discussed with adults.'

'And this all happened when you were living abroad?'

'Yes. Just before I came back to England to school. There weren't many opportunities after that to bring the subject up.'

'Perhaps this is your chance to find out what happened. It was probably just too sad for them to deal with at the time. But after all these years you can talk to them about it.'

'I suppose you're right,' she said, frowning as though she disagreed with him. 'You sound so sensible. I could give it a try. I'm not sure about Henry, but Rita might be more forthcoming. She's tough, she should be able to face up to what happened.' Beech picked up her mug and finished her coffee. 'I'd better do my shopping. Thanks for letting me talk about it. I do feel better now.' Even as she spoke she was buttoning her coat. She looked around for her hat, found it, put it on, but not at such a rakish angle as when she'd arrived.

'You've only been here fifteen minutes,' said Fergus. 'Must you go?'

'It's more like half an hour. I'm sorry. I don't seem able to settle to anything.'

In the hall she stopped, looking round at the pictures.

'I used to draw when I was young,' she said. 'I'd have liked to study it properly, but my parents weren't keen on the idea. I've still got some of the drawings I did, though. Would you like to see them?' She asked shyly, as though unsure whether anyone would ever be interested in something she had produced.

'Yes, I would,' said Fergus. 'I'd like that very much. Do any of them date from your time abroad?'

'Yes, most of them.'

'Why don't you bring them next time you come?'

'All right,' said Beech, and she paused.

'Tomorrow?' suggested Fergus. 'The end of the week?'

'Thursday,' said Beech. 'Eleven o'clock.'

Beech's house, with its tall, badly proportioned rooms, usually looked as though an army of servants kept it cleaned and polished. Jack and Rita were behaving as though this army would move in and complete their daily tasks as soon as they gave the order, Beech thought crossly when she returned home after some desultory shopping. She had been out for nearly two hours, and now the table was a mess of buttery crumbs and the sink was piled high with dirty crockery. She looked at the wreck of her kitchen and felt as uncomfortable as if spiders were crawling under her clothes and over her skin. She needed to get it back under control.

'Don't bother with all this now.' It was Rita, appearing at the open kitchen door. 'Jack and I are in the sitting room. Now that you're back, you must come and join us.'

Rita's hair – tinted to the purple of damsons – was piled high on her head and she wore a black silk kimono that fluttered and quivered about her as she moved. It was embroidered with gold and scarlet flowers and leaves that clambered up her back and sprouted their tendrils down her sleeves. Colourful birds peered out from among the branches. The scarlet petals and feathers matched the scarlet of Rita's mouth and nails.

Beech closed the door behind her and followed Rita into the sunless sitting room at the front of the house. Jack, although dressed for work, looked comfortably established on one of the sofas.

'Aren't you going in to the museum this morning?' Beech asked him mildly.

'There you go, nagging me back to the pit face again! I do think I might allow myself an hour or two off, just for once.' He smiled to show this was a joke, then pulled his face down into exaggerated lines of martyrdom to show it wasn't. He had the right sort of face for a martyr, thought Beech. Less so now than when they had married over twenty years ago, for he had put on a little weight. But with that aquiline nose and those deep-set eyes with their mournful, downward-turning corners, he could still pose for a Saint Sebastian or a John the Baptist. Yes, he had the full, pouting lips, like two ripe grapes, that might attract a spoiled child like the youthful Salome. Very *fin de siècle*, very Aubrey Beardsley. The young, unspoiled Beech had certainly found his looks seductive.

'I rang my assistant and told him to expect me in after lunch,' said Jack, frowning at the memory. 'He sounded quite unconcerned. I think young Alan might be getting too big for his boots.'

'Never mind about that,' said Rita. 'I want to talk about the anniversary of my son's death.'

There was a short pause after this statement. Beech reflected that never before had her mother been so open about it. The three of them were sitting on separate sofas and chairs, neatly arranged in a triangle of which Rita was the apex. Beech and Jack looked towards her expectantly.

'You don't have to worry about me, Beatrice. I know it's been thirty years, and still it hurts as much as it did then. But I am reconciled to his death, really I am. You don't have to fear that I'll become hysterical or shame you in public.'

'Really, I know that!'

'No, you didn't. I read it in your face.'

'What did you have in mind?' asked Beech cautiously.

'Come over to Rose Cottage and I'll show you what I've found. You can help me to edit them.'

'You're being very mysterious.'

'I've found his letters,' said Rita. 'His notebooks, journals, or whatever you want to call them, from that last summer.'

'Found them? Were they lost?'

'You know how I've been. I couldn't look at anything of his without getting into a terrible state.'

'I'm glad you're feeling better about it at last.'

'It was a terrible blow, but you know how strong I am! I shall manage to get through what is needed.'

Rita's face regained its enamelled finish and Beech found herself losing the sympathy she had been feeling for her mother. Rita curled her legs up on to the sofa and displayed small feet in high-heeled black satin mules. She reminded Beech of one of those unpleasant spidery things that chewed up the male and swallowed him when it had achieved its reproductive objective. As though she knew the analogy that her daughter was drawing, Rita fluttered her arms from time to time, and set the black silk in winglike motion. She turned her large, dark eyes on her daughter. 'We are going to put together a book, privately printed and published, for circulation among the family and our close friends.'

'We?' asked Beech carefully.

'I thought of asking dear Alice to do it,' said Rita. 'She and I have always been such pals. But it really wouldn't do.'

It was a pity that dear Alice hadn't grown up to be more of a credit to her grandmother's devotion, thought Beech. She pushed aside the mental picture of her daughter, Alice, her greasy hair in rats' tails, her clothes dingy, her complexion muddy, her voice whining as she asked her father for yet another advance on her monthly allowance. 'She leads such a busy life,' she lied. 'It would be difficult for her to fit in such a responsible task.'

'Yes, it will just have to be you, Beatrice.'

'I'll do my best,' said Beech drily. 'What is it you have in mind?'

'I thought you could put together a kind of anthology. A compilation,' said Rita. 'Extracts from his journal and from his letters, together with photographs and contributions from those of us who knew him. We still have friends from the old days; I'm sure many of them will have little anecdotes to add if we ask them.'

'So you'd like me to be the editor?' said Beech. 'I think I could manage that.' She wondered whether Fergus wasn't right. Shouldn't they have come to terms with Nicholas's death by now? Was there really any point in going through a schoolboy's diary and correspondence so many years later? The thought that someone in later years would look through her own juvenile writings made her cringe.

'Right,' said Jack. 'That's sorted then. Perhaps I should be getting off to the museum now after all. I can't sit around all day.'

'It isn't quite "sorted", as you so quaintly call it,' said Rita.

'Beatrice needs to look through the material I've found. I think everyone will be quite surprised by what is in it.' She paused for effect.

'Yes?' prompted Beech.

'It's quite a little love story from what I can tell,' said Rita.

'Wasn't he rather young for that?'

'He was seventeen,' said Rita. 'And very mature for his age.'

'I'll be going now,' said Jack. 'I'll leave the two of you to talk about Nicholas.'

Beech rose to her feet and saw her husband to the front door. When she returned to the sitting room she found her mother gathering her spectacles, cigarettes and lighter together.

'I shall go upstairs for a little rest, and then, I think, I shall write back to Valerie Crabbe.'

'Who?'

'A very sweet person whom you will come to know in due course. And then, after lunch – just a little green salad for me, please – I shall be driving back to Rose Cottage.'

'Are you sure you don't want to stay for another day or two?'

'I have so much to do at home,' said Rita. 'But you must come over soon, so that we can go through all the material I have.'

'Yes, of course. How about this weekend?'

'Come to lunch on Sunday. That will give us the whole afternoon together.' And Rita disappeared upstairs in a billow of black silk to lie on her bed with the two slices of cucumber resting on her closed eyelids that she fondly believed would hold at bay the wrinkles and pouches of old age.

At Rose Cottage, meanwhile, Henry Markland gathered up the scraps of his breakfast: the remnants of toast, the peelings of an apple and its core, and placed them in a plastic box. He snapped on the lid, pressing it down firmly all round, then secured the box with a blue nylon strap, tucking the end in neatly when he had pulled it tight. Box in hand, he unbolted the back door and went out into the cold, misty morning.

He made his way towards the brick-built shed at the bottom right-hand corner of the garden, his footprints dark on the dew-soaked grass. He unlocked the door, pushed it open, then shuffled into the dim, sweet-smelling, rustling interior.

5

Valma Beresford always began reading the *Daily Telegraph* at the small ads. It had started years ago, when she was young, as a joke, a game she played with her friend Nadia when Valma was newly arrived in England.

'One day I am going to be rich,' Nadia said. 'One day a wealthy uncle, of whom at this moment I know nothing, will leave me a large sum of money.'

'You've been reading too many romantic novels,' said Valma, who had learned early that life didn't work that way.

'He will have to advertise to find me,' continued Nadia, whose whole family had arrived in England as refugees and lived on dreams of a prosperous future which would arrive one day soon, complete, gift-wrapped and delivered by an unknown benefactor. 'He will advertise in the Personal column of one of your serious newspapers.'

Valma wondered, briefly, what had happened to Nadia in the intervening years. Probably she still rotted in her family's nasty flat with the black mould creeping up the kitchen walls. Perhaps they had been evicted for failing to pay the rent. She could have pointed out to Nadia where her mistake lay: uncles were unnecessary; all you needed was money, and then people would come crowding to your door, claiming kinship. Money was the important thing. Her mother had known it, so had her father. So, if it came to that, had the nuns at her convent school, though they would hardly approve of Valma's methods of acquiring it. It was no good sitting at home, hoping and dreaming; you had to make an effort.

Still, Nadia was right in one respect: it was surprising how much you learned by studying the Personal columns every day. Surprising too how many of the names Valma still recognized from the old days in her father's shop, and from the parties she'd been to in her teens. She had been an observant child, and had kept a diary, aware even then that knowledge could be put to good use one day. She supplemented the information she had gathered from the newspapers by working her way through the magazines at the public library. She took notes. She started a card index system so that she could make cross-references. And after all this collecting and collating, a simple announcement of a forthcoming marriage might mean so much to someone with Valma's index cards and mercenary mind.

Dear Mrs Smith-Jones, I was delighted to see the announcement of your daughter Pamela's engagement to that nice boy, Piers Brown-White. You must be so pleased that she is marrying into such a respectable *family. Do you still see anything of the youngest Masoor son, by the way? I'm afraid that my parents forbade me to speak to him after that rather louche episode on the family yacht. American sailors, wasn't it? I heard Pamela's name associated with the incident, but I'm sure I must have got it wrong.*

Times, unfortunately, were getting harder. The young and careless were getting older and more respectable. It was some months now since Valma had been able to write one of her letters and hope for anything more than a few pounds in return, and now she needed a lot more than that. Five thousand would clear her credit card balances and leave them ready to do their duty in the shops in Knightsbridge and Sloane Street once again, but it wouldn't change the way she was living. I need at least a hundred thousand, she thought. She sighed. Today's *Times* had yielded no useful items yet again. There had been nothing at all, in fact, since the advertisement, ten days ago, in the *Telegraph*, and that was one that would need careful handling if she was to get anything from it. Rita Markland had been no one's fool.

Valma wondered about making herself a third cup of instant coffee, but even when she bought the supermarket's own economy brand she didn't allow herself more than two cups in the morning. Is it worth it? she wondered as she looked around the small, dark, rather musty-smelling room. But the belief that location was paramount when you were in the business of selling – particularly if the only commodity you had to sell was yourself – was ingrained in her brain. This bedsitter was just on the edge of a good address, and Valma knew this was more important than being able to afford a third cup of coffee.

She turned back to the ten-day-old newspaper, read again the few lines in the Personal column.

The friends of Rita and Henry Markland, and of their late, beloved son, Nicholas, are invited to write . . .

If Valma had not been exactly a friend, then at least she was a close acquaintance. That had entitled her to write. She might receive an invitation to stay for a weekend, and that would represent two or three days' free food. She had checked her index cards and had found nothing of interest, but still she knew that somewhere she had a memory tucked away that would bring her in a profit if she could only root it out.

There was a rustling sound by the front door, a soft thud on to the doormat. The post. Late again. She went to collect the letters and take them back to the sofa where the *Telegraph* was still draped over the arm. She flicked through the envelopes. Junk mail and a bill. And one real letter, addressed in a firm, old-fashioned hand on a white envelope.

'Oh yes.' She said it aloud. If she had been able to whistle, that is what she would have done.

The postmark was Oxford: Rita Markland had replied to the tentative, calculatedly modest letter. Valma was about to be accepted as a friend of the Marklands.

Your father was a shopkeeper, whispered an unfriendly voice in her head. *Mr Crabbe the Grocer. Valerie Crabbe the Grocer's Daughter. You might call yourself Valma Beresford now, but they would never have regarded you as a friend in the old days.*

True, she replied, except for that one occasion when I was invited to join them all at the deLyles' picnic. I was clever enough to engineer that invitation for myself. And something happened that day. An accident to the Markland boy. There was something more, too, and it would come to her eventually.

She opened the letter. Mrs Valma Beresford, who had once been Valerie Maria Crabbe, read what Rita had written just a couple of days before.

When she had finished reading, she sat and thought for a few minutes. So long ago, but yes, even if the index cards yielded nothing, there was another possibility. She went to her bed, lifted up the bedspread and pulled out the suitcase that she kept underneath. The top was dusty and she flapped at the dust impatiently before snapping the locks and opening the case. Dog-eared notebooks of all kinds, papers, letters, old envelopes with foreign stamps. She scrabbled through the contents, turning over notebooks, riffling through sheets of paper, pulling out envelopes stuffed with more pages of writing. What a little magpie you were, Valma Crabbe, she chided herself.

There it was. A pale blue notebook, filled with pages of her own careful handwriting, and marked with the year on the cover. Thirty years ago exactly. This should be the one. There were other papers tucked into it. She looked: letters, mostly. Another notebook, this one written in a different hand. 'Nicholas Anthony Markland' in bold capitals across the cover, and underneath his name he too had written the year, the same one as on her own notebook. And where did you acquire all this material? *Light-fingered little slut, that's what you were.*

She took them back to her seat, and started to read. As she

did so, she smiled. There were possibilities here, certainly.

Any memories, any memorabilia would be gratefully received.

She was still smiling as she found writing paper and pen and started to write.

Dear Rita, (if I may), I am so glad that you remembered me! Of course, I would love to contribute to the wonderful book about Nicholas that dear Beatrice is preparing. I remember as though it were yesterday all those hot, sunny days, and the crowd of young people that gathered on the beach and in the mountains during the long summers. And the Rainbow Pool, with Mrs deLyle and all her smart friends! I should love to talk to you – here Valma looked around at her room with its shameful economies on view – *and perhaps I might come up to Oxford for the day and we could share our happy memories over a cup of tea.* The address at the top of the page, printed in tasteful blue on the grey paper, was imposing enough: no need to spoil the impression by confronting Rita with the reality of her cramped studio apartment. *We called it a bedsitter in the old days*, cackled old Mrs deLyle inside her head.

But even Mrs deLyle, grand as she was, powerful as she was, had been persuaded to do what Valma wanted.

'Vignettes,' said Fergus. 'Isn't that what you call these little thumbnail sketches?'

Beech smiled but didn't reply.

'Such detail!' He turned the pages and saw sea and mountains, a foreign city, its narrow streets crowded with people, donkeys, cars, mules. A beggar thrust up the stump of his arm. A skeletal dog rootled among rubbish heaped in the gutter. Another dog lifted a leg against a mud wall. Then followed some interiors: tall ceilings, plain rooms with rugs on the wall, wooden furniture; an elegant, dark-haired woman sat smoking a cigarette, her face turned away from the artist. A small tumbler stood on the table at her elbow.

'Rita?' he asked.

'Yes. She must have been in her early forties in that one.'

'She's enjoying that cigarette, isn't she?'

'For goodness' sake, if you're missing them so much, go out and buy yourself some.'

'No, I've given up. Really. And who's this?'

'That's Henry, my father.'

He saw a tall, powerful man with heavy brows and a brooding expression. By his hand too there was a glass. And he was smoking, his face partially veiled by blue smoke. It was difficult to read his expression, but Fergus felt a vague unease, as though violence lurked beneath the urbane exterior.

Fergus turned to another page. He was looking at an idealized image of a young man.

'That's Nicholas. My brother. What do you think?'

'Very nice,' he said noncommittally. Fair hair, blue eyes, dark eyebrows, regular features, good bone structure. Not much like Beech. And impossible to form any impression of Nicholas's character through the thick haze of sisterly adoration. If Nicholas had suffered from teenage acne, or adolescent sulks, Beech was too loyal to show them in her drawing. And this was a family that had practised to perfection its public face. Beech too, he added to himself.

'Have you learned any more about how he died?'

'It was a swimming accident. He drowned.' Her answer sounded mechanical, as though dictated and then rehearsed.

'That's what you said once before. Have you found out any more details?'

'No. It's difficult to persuade Rita to talk to me about it.'

'It must be hard for all of you.'

There was a brief silence. 'It was a long time ago.' She chewed the corner of her fingernail. He glanced at his watch.

'I must go,' she said. 'You want to get back to your work.'

'I'm afraid I shall have to. But don't worry about all of this. I'm sure that no very dreadful secrets are likely to emerge from the past lives of respectable people like the Marklands.'

'Respectability is such an English ideal,' said Beech, putting on her coat, looking for her gloves.

'Will you leave me your drawings? I'd like to have a proper look at them.'

'Yes. If you like.'

On her way downstairs she looked at the pictures, as usual. She peered closely at the nude again.

'Valma Crabbe,' she said absently, and then moved on. Fergus followed quickly.

'Who is Valma Crabbe?'

'A very good question. I've always meant to ask you, where did you get all your pictures from?'

'They came with the house.' His expression didn't allow her to ask any more. 'Will you come again soon?'

'I hope so.'

He could shake her. Why couldn't the woman show some enthusiasm? Beech was walking down the road without looking behind her, her heels clicking on the wet pavement.

Fergus went back upstairs and searched unsuccessfully once more for a cigarette.

'Shit!' he said aloud. He gave up and leafed again through Beech's drawings. He picked one up and took it to the light. It showed a small, thin goat. After a minute or two he replaced the drawings in the folder. He knew he should return to his own work, but their unsatisfying conversation paced around his mind.

What did you do about a woman like Beatrice Waring? Why was she warm and human at one moment, and at the next retired behind a thick glass screen where he couldn't reach her? She was a bright, intelligent woman. She had a gift for drawing lively sketches. And yet she appeared to spend her days tending her husband and daughter – who could surely do more for themselves – and vaguely doing good on her committees. Oh yes, and any spare time she had she spent worrying about her elderly parents. It didn't seem as though she had any close friends, male or female, apart from himself. She had shut out the outside world and lived entirely inside her small, demanding family.

He should never have approached her in the supermarket that day in December. He didn't believe in love at first sight, if love was what he really felt for her. But still there was *something* about her that had spoken to him across the frozen cod steaks and had forced him into that gauche introduction. Since then, when she had called in to see him around coffee time, he had abandoned his monitor and his statistics and they had sat and gossiped in his sitting room for half an hour or so, before she thanked him politely and left. The whole relationship was quite innocent, unfortunately. He didn't think it was any strict belief in morals that stopped her from climbing into bed with him. He didn't think she found him unattractive. He was nearly sure that her marriage wasn't worth fighting for. He didn't even think she was the sort of woman who stayed in an unsatisfactory marriage through inertia. But somewhere just below the surface there was something that kept Beech in her prison and stopped her from escaping.

He cleared away the coffee cups and went back to his computer, his statistics and his graphs.

In the bedsitter off the Cowley Road she shared with Kevin, Alice Waring hadn't long been out of bed. To tell the truth, she hadn't been feeling too well that morning.

'Kevin.' He was sitting at the table, smoking a fag, drinking instant coffee, reading the football news in the *Sun*. 'Make us a coffee, will you?'

'Lazy cow. Make it yourself.' He spoke without rancour.

Alice hauled herself to the side of the bed and sat up, dangling her feet over the edge. The room swayed once or twice then righted itself. 'I don't feel too good.'

'Shouldn't have drunk so much at The Duke last night,' said Kevin, without looking up.

'Didn't drink nothing 'cept a St Clement's,' said Alice.

'You ill?'

'Don't think so.'

'You pregnant, then?'

'God! I hope not!' Alice, in a moment of stress, reverted to her middle-class accent and Kevin looked up and frowned at her.

'You're bloody careless enough for anything,' he said, folding up his newspaper and pouring the remains of the coffee down the sink. He rinsed out the mug and left it to drain. He was a much neater person than Alice.

'I'm off,' he said, picking up his black leather jacket and opening the door.

'Leave us a couple of cigs,' she called to his departing back.

Kevin didn't bother to reply, but closed the door firmly behind him.

Alice sat for some time on the edge of the bed until her feet stung with cold and she felt in such need of a coffee that she was prepared to boil the kettle for herself. As she sat at the table, still in her nightshirt, she wondered whether she would ever see Kevin again. There had been something final about his 'I'm off' and she didn't think he was too keen on the idea of being a father. What the hell! The bedsit was in her name, the rent paid by the long-suffering Jack. Why should she need Kevin in her life?

She rubbed at the spot that was erupting on her chin and dripped tears into her coffee mug at the general unfairness of life.

6

If you drive twenty miles or so north-west from Oxford, you find yourself among the hills and stone cottages of the Cotswolds. It is on the edge of one of the villages that Rita and Henry Markland live.

After the damp, swampy air of Oxford, this is an exhilarating country. The hills are rounded and green, there are dry-stone walls edging the swooping roads, and the villages are picturesque. The pubs look welcoming and promise home-cooked food and real ales. And yet, somehow, the Marklands have chosen to live in one of the few unappealing villages in the area. Here in Chipping Hampton the clouds always dawdle overhead for longer than elsewhere, the puddles lie thick and soupy in the lanes, and the stunted roses suffer from black spot, rust and mildew. Clematis wilts, wisteria expires. This, at any rate, is the way that Rita Markland looks at it, and is the reason she gives for escaping from the place as often as she can.

Any outside observer would be able to tell her that this cannot be the true reason.

'Rose Cottage!' mutters Rita, when someone mentions the name of the house and adds that it sounds idyllic. 'I'd rather call it The Black Spot!' And people smile, thinking that this is a joke, if rather a mild one. But Rita has little sense of humour, and her pronouncements should always be taken literally.

The cottage, which is really the size of a house, rambles untidily along the country road. It should be charming, rooted in the earth and blooming in golden stone like the other houses in the area. But somehow its separate parts have never coalesced into a satisfying whole. This part of the roof is too high; that single-storey addition too long; the original stone from which its thick walls are built, a soft, honey-coloured local one, has been masked by smooth rendering and painted a brilliant, gleaming white which is inappropriate for its age. Window frames and doors are an uncompromising dark blue, which gives it a naval appearance. It has a narrow strip of garden dividing it from the road, and a much larger sloping expanse of grass at the back. There is a wide gateway to one side of the house, opening on to a gravel drive. This leads to the double garage and a flat expanse of concrete where guests are expected to leave their cars.

Henry Markland has dreams of creating an idyllic cottage garden. He has in mind the sort of design that is seen on the more sentimental kind of calendar, or in the expensive illustrated gardening books designed to be placed on coffee tables in city apartments. He pictures a row of ten-foot tall hollyhocks. The house will crouch behind them, scowling from its small, deep-set windows at the cars which splash their way up the lane to the village of Chipping Hampton. He can see the frilled pink and red flowers quite distinctly in his imagination, just as in the back garden he can smell the lavender that will border the herringbone-brick path that winds its way up to the beech hedge at the far end. To the right will stand a rose arbour where Rita will sit in the afternoons and read her glossy magazines. To the left will rise a row of beanpoles, with scarlet flowers and green tendrils brilliant against the darker green of the honeysuckle that twines through the hedge. He blinks, and the picture dissolves.

Looking at the rough square of meadow grass lying behind the cottage, you might think that this plan of Henry's is of recent conception, but you would be wrong. Henry and Rita have lived in this house for thirteen years, and Henry's schemes are no further forward than they were that first year when they moved in, when Henry retired from his job and he and Rita returned from the Middle East to settle back in England at last.

And yet it isn't quite right to say that Henry has achieved nothing in his garden in all the years since he moved in. The first of the brick-built sheds is devoted to the study and development of the compost heap, for Henry knows that therein lies the secret of a good garden. He has tried different types, aerobic and anaerobic; he has built various structures, New Zealand and English. He has acquired various types of worms and watched them thrive and multiply. He has examined the resulting compost, he has prodded it, run it through his dry old fingers, rubbed it in his palm as though it were the rarest of pipe tobaccos. He has analyzed it, mixed it with topsoil and sharp sand and experimented by filling seed boxes and sowing cabbages and leeks in it, and striking his lavender cuttings. The seedlings and the cuttings eventually wither and die, for there is nowhere yet for Henry to plant them out. The vegetable plot lives only inside his head and in the pages of his notebooks, drawn in meticulous detail on squared paper, with the rows of vegetables dotted in with coloured pens, and the annual rotation of his crops worked out in successive tables. The perennial borders bloom in colourful profusion, but only in his imagination.

In the second shed lives Gunter. Gunter is Henry's dog, a black Labrador whose coat is speckled with grey and whose muzzle is now white with age. This shed smells overpoweringly of Gunter, of his fetid breath, of his unremitting farts, of the damp pools of incontinence that darken the walls and floor. When he comes into the house, which only happens when Rita is away, he leaves this smell like a spoor everywhere he goes. Henry unlocks the door of this shed every morning, and leaves it wide open so that Gunter can blink at the daylight and amble outside and relieve himself against his favourite leylandii. Later, he will make his slow way to the back door, where Henry will feed him. Henry knows that Gunter is now too old to act as an effective guard dog, but he still believes that Gunter would bark at an intruder and alert his master to the presence of a stranger on his property. In fact Gunter's bark is now too feeble for Henry's elderly ears to hear from inside the house. Henry pats the top of Gunter's head and says, 'Good boy. Good boy.' and then he returns to his worm bins.

Henry lifts the wooden lid from one compost bin and looks inside. He sees a faint stirring of red worms and the flick of their tails as they disappear back into the depths of the vegetable waste that is their home. He breathes in their odour, redolent, he always feels, of Christmas and plum puddings. He scrapes the remains of his breakfast into the bin and replaces the square of old carpet on top of the heap. When they have produced enough of their magic compost he will be able to start building his garden, improving its structure, feeding his plants. But until then, he must continue with his bins and his layers of leaves and grass clippings and discarded vegetables from the kitchen.

Some long time later, when he has put the lids back on the bins, and made notes in the current volume of his log book, he thinks about making himself a pot of tea and a sandwich. A cheese sandwich, he thinks, with pickle and a sliced tomato on the side of the plate. Henry finds this food satisfying both to his palate and to the sense of nostalgia that he carries around with him like a well-worn cardigan.

He returns to the house to make his sandwich, spreading the pickle thickly on top of the layer of cheese, firming down the bread so that the pickle oozes out of the sides. Mauve tongue darts from between lavender lips and licks at dripping pickle. He finds a plate for the remainder, and walks through to his own room.

Henry's room is known as his study, although very little of an intellectual nature takes place there. What it is in effect is a refuge from Rita and her sharp, clacking tongue. It contains a desk, covered in papers which have been there, untouched, for at least ten years. There is an old black-and-white television set on which he can watch the programmes that Rita dislikes. (He is very partial to *Neighbours* and *Home and Away*, and has been known to slip in and watch *Prisoner Cell Block H* in the evening, after he has completed the washing-up to Rita's satisfaction.) There are bookcases around the walls. There is a table, a comfortable chair and a sofa that Rita has long since evicted from the more formal part of the house. Every spare surface is covered in photographs in tarnished silver frames.

He forgets to eat the second half of his sandwich. Never mind, the brandling worms will enjoy it.

He is still sitting in front of the television when Rita returns from her visit to her daughter and son-in-law. She seems to be on top form and full of energy.

'You watch your programme,' she says, 'I've got *lots* to do upstairs, so I shan't disturb you. And then I shall make us a delicious little supper. I've brought some of your favourite oak-smoked salmon from the shop in Summertown.'

Later, at her desk, Rita is writing a letter. She has received Valma Crabbe's obsequious reply to her own first approach, and now it is time to move closer to her goal.

Dear Valma (if I may), she writes. *Now that we have made contact again after all these years, I do agree that it would be so lovely if we could meet, in person. My daughter, Beatrice – I'm sure you remember her – would be delighted if you could come and spend a few days in Oxford at her house. Then we could all get together and reminisce about the old days. I could even call them 'the good old days' . . .*

7

Valma Beresford was rereading the letter she had just received from Rita Markland. Should she reply immediately, as she was itching to do, or should she wait a few days to show that she was not desperate to renew the acquaintance? She decided on a compromise.

She fetched a sheet of the grey headed paper – only a few sheets left, she noticed – and sat down at the small table. She rubbed her cold hands together and massaged her fingers. She didn't like to switch on the single-bar electric fire, however cold the weather, before five o'clock, but she wanted to make sure that she could still write a creditable italic hand. She dated the letter at the top right-hand side, picking one that lay a little in the future.

Dear Rita, she wrote. *How very kind of you to invite me to spend a few days at your daughter's house in Oxford. How I am looking forward to seeing dear Beatrice again! I am afraid that my days are very full for the next week or so* – here Valma conveniently forgot the blank pages that stretched throughout her diary – *but I shall be free in a fortnight's time. Would that suit dear Beatrice, do you think?*

When she had finished her letter she placed it in the envelope, addressed it to Rose Cottage in Chipping Hampton and propped it up between an empty flower vase and a copper coffee pot. She would wait three days before she posted it.

This morning when Beech entered Fergus's house she avoided

the bold stare of the nude that she now thought of as Valma Crabbe and looked instead at an abstract painting, a watercolour.

'A seascape?' she queried. And when Fergus said nothing in reply she added, 'Yes, at sunset, I think. Or dawn, perhaps, when the light is translucent like that and sky and clouds start out that oyster-shell grey colour. I like it,' she said.

While she was drinking the coffee he'd made, Fergus picked up the folder she had left behind a few days before. 'Do you want these back?'

'I suppose so.' She had liked the feeling that something of hers remained in Fergus's house when she wasn't there. 'What did you think of them?'

'I liked them very much, especially the busy street scenes. And your goat. You're right, it's nothing like the pampered animal belonging to Mrs Hopkins. This one has the cowed look of poverty about it.'

'It isn't an it, it's a she. She belongs to the goat-woman, Arwa.'

'And are you going to tell me about Arwa?' said Fergus as Beech retreated back into silence.

'I don't think there's anything to tell.'

This morning she was wearing neither her usual jeans nor that awful dress with the white collar, but purplish-red trousers in a wool crêpe, a slate-blue top and a long, knitted silk cardigan in a shade lighter than the trousers.

'And tell me who this is.' Fergus pushed across a drawing of a young man with curling dark hair and a wonderful bone structure.

'That's Arwa's son, Khalil. While she was away – having another baby, I believe – Khalil would bring the goats round to the kitchen balcony and milk them. That's how it was done: if you needed milk, the goat-woman would milk her goat into your jug. Anything she couldn't sell as milk she made into leben. Yoghurt, I suppose you'd call it.'

'And she had a wonderfully good-looking son,' said Fergus. 'Well, either that, or you've flattered him somewhat in your drawing.'

'Both,' said Beech, remembering how her fourteen-year-old self had been entranced by those cheekbones and the dark, curling hair. 'I think he knew his effect on women, even then, when he was about sixteen. I believe he practised his chat-up lines on anyone who came his way.'

She spoke in a light, amused voice, but Fergus wondered just how struck she had been when she was an impressionable fourteen.

'More coffee?' he asked.

She stuffed the drawings back into the folder. 'I really have to go now. I have to get to the post office before it closes. Jack will be very cross if I don't renew our television licence before it expires.'

Fergus looked as though he would like to say 'Sod Jack!' but he merely smiled and accompanied Beech downstairs on her way out of the house.

'I was wondering if you'd like to come to lunch one day.' As Fergus looked surprised, she said, 'I could make something simple. It wouldn't take up too much of your working time.'

'There might be gossip. Would you mind that?'

'What do you want to do, creep round to the back garden and climb over the fence so that no one sees you?'

'No. I'll arrive at the front door. And I'll bring a particularly large bunch of flowers.'

'Tomorrow then, instead of coffee?'

'One o'clock.'

Rita left Henry to his compost bins and his log books and went upstairs to the end bedroom. Nicholas's bedroom.

You could not forget a son, even if he had died thirty years ago. He was still her only son, her first-born. And since she was alone in the room, and no one could read her thoughts, she could admit to herself that he was also her favourite. She had loved him more than Beatrice, certainly, and more even than Henry. Although Henry in those days had not been unlovable. Tall and upright, masterful and amusing, she remembered, and found it difficult to equate that person with the man downstairs, drawing yet another garden plan and talking to that decrepit old dog. Not that he was really off his head or anything, just getting a little old and eccentric.

But Nicholas had been a golden child: tall and fair-haired, with a skin that tanned as easily as her own. And so gifted at everything he did. Athletic, brave. And talented at music; so good at drawing and painting. And such an amusing, charming boy. So popular with all their friends. Everybody had loved him.

Rita wandered round the room, touching a model aeroplane, an ancient teddy bear, a ragged volume of adventure stories. Of course, she knew everything here. She had arranged it herself, putting all his belongings in the places she imagined Nicholas would have done. If it looked like the bedroom of a very old-fashioned seventeen-year-old, and a clean and tidy one at that, it was because the dead never did grow up and grow old. *They shall grow not old, as we that are left grow old.* She had always thought that the tragedy was not that she and Henry grew old and odd, and grey and lined, but that Nicholas never did. He stayed golden-haired, clear of eye and skin. He did not descend into wrinkles and obsessions the way his father did, or go off on secret assignations like Beatrice. What was Beatrice up to?

Rita sighed, perhaps because the wrong child had died. Not that she would ever allow Beatrice to guess at what she was thinking.

She shook her head, as though to clear it of unwanted thoughts. There was work to be done if she was to achieve her aims. She went over to a box, an old cardboard shoe box, in the cupboard to the right of the fireplace. She had of course looked at it, as she had looked through all Nicholas's possessions, soon after his death. But it was only recently that she had taken the time to investigate it properly, and had found the notebooks that she was going to spring on Beatrice at the weekend. She opened the box.

Inside was a sheet of paper, covering the contents. PLEASE DON'T TOUCH. THIS MEANS YOU. KEEP OUT. PRIVATE. And for a moment Rita paused. Then she lifted it out. The notebook was an ordinary one, old-fashioned quarto-sized and with a pale blue cover. The paper inside was plain.

Rita looked at the first page. When she had first opened it, some months ago now, she had felt a genuine pang of loss and regret as she saw that neat italic script, running down the page in line after legible line. Something this personal should be harder to read, she felt.

This is a city of light, *she read*. Of light, of water, and of noise.

The yellow ochre building stands on high ground, overlooking the town, and this is where we live. You walk through an entrance gate, flanked by two small villas, their windows permanently shuttered under their red-tile roofs. Then through the garden, sand-coloured and dusty in the summer, smelling of cats, dotted with tall date palms. To the right is an archway, spilling bougainvillaea red as blood and the machine-gun fire of Arabic from invisible figures beyond.

Inside the house, the stairway is wide, leading to the first and second storeys, and the floor of cool grey marble. It is a long way up to the third floor, since the ceilings are so high, and I don't often go up there, since that is where the servants sleep. I would be greeted politely, but I would not be welcome if I went up there. I can hear the popular music they play, and their voices. They sound as though they are quarrelling, but perhaps Arabic always gives that impression. The front door is straight ahead, painted dark blue, fitted with entry-phone, spyhole and doorbell. To the right, another, smaller, narrower, also dark blue, for the servants. This second one stands ajar and I hear the cook, Munira, shouting at the maid, Amani and Amani's voice, defensive, tearful, raised in reply. I can smell cumin, and coffee, and the goat that the woman milked on the doorstep a short while ago.

'Eh!' exclaims Amani as I put my head round the small, open door. 'You wait there, I come in a minute and let you in.'

While I am waiting, I watch the cockroaches – big as fieldmice – scuttle across the mottled tiles of the kitchen balcony. I would like to step on one and hear the satisfying *crack* as it died, but I do not dare cross the frontier between them and us without an invitation, so I stand outside the door, looking in on the alien world, and wait for the sound of shuffling steps, and the opening door. I go into my side of the house and watch Amani amble off, back to the servants' quarters. I hear a burst of Arabic, a blare of music, as she opens the kitchen door, then the slam as it closes, and I am alone in the silent hallway.

What a sensitive and observant child he was, thought Rita, closing the notebook. How beautifully he wrote! Thank goodness these notebooks weren't thrown away. The world should be allowed to read them, edited and corrected of course, so that they could all know Nicholas, my son, for what he was.

But people will answer my advertisements. They will all help to bring the story of our life to public knowledge. I don't care what people said, we *were* happy. We *were* successful.

* * *

Much later, Rita was still sitting, reading. She had leafed through a number of the notebooks now, many of them filled with details of hobbies long-forgotten, of friendships with other boys she knew nothing of. She reached the bottom layer: a bundle of crisp grey writing paper covered in that same stilted black writing. She had been surprised the first time she had read them, but now they were growing familiar and she had woven a romantic narrative to explain them to herself.

Dear Arrie, she read. *Something happened this afternoon.* She skimmed down to the signature at the end. *All my love, Nico.*

Nico and Arrie. Romeo and Juliet. But who were they? Nico must be a pet name for Nicholas, but who was Arrie? She couldn't remember anyone with a name like that. Was she even English? She could have come from *anywhere*. And why did I know nothing about this? My son, my Nicholas, should have told me about it. Why did he keep me out of his life?

She went downstairs and into Henry's study. He looked up from the television screen. 'Yes, dear?'

'I know this is difficult for you. It's difficult for both of us. But do you think you could think back for me to . . . Nicholas . . . and that last summer in the Levant.'

'Yes, dear.'

She was sure he was pretending to be vaguer than he was in reality.

'Do you remember anyone called Arrie?'

'Arrie? No.'

'It would have been a girl. Young. Pretty. Clever.'

'No, dear. No one of that name.' Henry returned to the old black-and-white film.

'I believe that this girl, this Arrie, must have been at the picnic. If I'm going to write an account of Nicholas's life, I shall have to find out more about her. If she was the one great love of his life, she must have been there, don't you think?'

'I must go and check on my compost bins.'

'*Must* you?'

'And then Gunter must have his walk.'

'That dog is too decrepit to walk!'

'He needs his exercise.'

Henry rose creakily to his feet and shuffled out of the room.

'He does it on purpose!' muttered Rita.

Henry poked his head back round the door. 'Do you think I should add the hedge prunings to my compost bins?'

8

On Sunday morning, Beech duly arrived at her parents' house and, after a short interval for exchanging family news, she retired to the kitchen and began the preparations for lunch. She cooked a leg of lamb, which Henry liked, and an apple crumble with bright yellow custard – also Henry's favourite. She knew that Rita wouldn't get round to talking about Nicholas until after the meal.

'You two can take your coffee in the sitting room,' said Rita. 'I will leave you on your own so that you can have a good chinwag together without silly old me to interrupt. I am going upstairs for half an hour's contemplation and relaxation.' She left the dining room, chopped a couple of slices from the cucumber in the refrigerator, and went upstairs, leaving Beech to clear the dishes and make the coffee.

When Beech took the tray into the sitting room, Henry was already seated by the gas fire, looking into its artificial glow.

'Have I told you about my compost bins?' he asked.

'Just once or twice,' said Beech.

She drank her coffee and watched the counterfeit flames, letting her mind wander. Henry reached out a hand and stroked the sleeve of her jacket. 'Nice,' he said. His dry old skin rasped on the shiny surface. 'I've always liked it.' The jacket was made of a dark green silk brocade, with flowers and exotic birds that shone silver as they caught the light. The sleeves were cuffed in velvet, the lining pistachio green silk.

'It reminds me of the sea,' said Henry after a time.

Beech looked down at the worn pattern of peacocks and pomegranates.

'Why the sea?' she asked.

'Oh, I was just thinking. About the past. About Nicholas.'

It was the first time she had heard him mention that name for years.

'Yes. We'll have to think about him again, won't we?'

'It couldn't be helped. Rita blamed you, though, didn't she?'

'Did she?' said Beech. 'I've forgotten.'

'Henry! Beatrice!' cried Rita, entering the sitting room an hour later, where Henry and Beech were quietly chatting. She stood by the door with her arms raised slightly away from her, palms facing upwards like some all-embracing Madonna, gathering their attention to herself. At first sight this was a young woman, slim and lithe in a misty blue silk kimono and high-heeled sandals. But the hands she raised were networked with veins, and her gesture lacked the oiled smoothness of youth. She lifted her chin a little higher to minimize the tiny pad of fat that had recently made its unwelcome reappearance. Beech found herself wondering whether her mother bought her kimonos by the dozen, in every colour available. Perhaps there was a little woman somewhere in Chipping Hampton who ran them up for her on her sewing machine.

'His letters! Here are his letters!' Rita's voice cut through Henry's drone and he faltered to a halt, raising his vague blue eyes to the figure of his wife.

'Henry!' cried Rita again. 'Beatrice!' And this time they both stirred themselves and smiled at her and responded with nods. 'Didn't you hear me? I've brought you his notebooks and letters to look at.'

Her small face, normally pale as junket, beamed down at them like a raspberry blancmange. A wilful strand of hair was stuck to her forehead.

'What was it you said, dear?' asked Henry. 'What are we talking about?'

'Nicholas!' cried Rita.

'Tell us about the letters, Mother,' said Beatrice. She smiled at her father and patted the back of his hand. 'I'll have to leave soon. I'd like to get home before it's dark.'

'These are old letters, from when he was a boy. And his notebooks. Beatrice is to include them in the album.'

'Ah!' said Henry. 'Well, let's look at these letters, shall we?'

Rita laid out the letters on the low table. 'Here,' she breathed. 'Look.'

Goodness, thought Beech, what neat handwriting we had in those days. All of them, she remembered, when they were about twelve years old, carefully learning the italic alphabet, practising with straight-nibbed pens and black ink on crisp pastel paper, until they had perfected the shapes and produced hands that were indistinguishable one from another. In fact, looking at the page that Rita had opened, she could not be sure that she had not written it herself thirty years previously.

'What does he say?' asked Henry, scrabbling around among the sofa cushions, looking for his bifocals.

'She. It is from someone called Arrie,' said Rita reverently. 'It appears to be a love letter.'

'Oh, surely not!' exclaimed Beech. 'I expect it's just a friendly note.'

'Why, Beatrice? Do you suppose that Nicholas at seventeen had never had a girlfriend?'

'There was that dreadful Caroline person when he was sixteen,' said Beech. 'All uplift bra and swinging blonde hair. And then little Amanda Bell, who had a crush on him and followed us everywhere.'

'This is obviously something quite different,' said Rita. 'A Romeo and Juliet story, I believe. Shakespeare's lovers were seventeen, weren't they?'

'Juliet was only fourteen, but that would land them in court nowadays,' said Beech.

'Don't be disgusting,' said Rita.

Henry leaned across, picked up the top letter and started to read. After a moment's hesitation, Beech took the second and did the same.

Dear Nico, the letter began, written in that same neat, impersonal italic hand.

'Nico and Arrie, a love story,' said Rita.

'What?'

'*Nico and Arrie: a Love Story*. I can see it on the title page, can't you?'

'What title page? I thought this was just going to be a compilation of notes and photographs.'

'But don't you think it would be a wonderful idea?'

'Toe-curling,' said Beech.

'And, of course, we must find out who this Arrie is. She could have become my daughter-in-law, after all.'

'Perhaps she's married with grandchildren by now,' said Beech.

'Don't be so prosaic. Why must you always try to spoil everything? You are being quite ridiculous today, Beatrice. I feel that there's more to this story about Arrie than appears in these few letters and notebooks. Perhaps she was involved in his death. Don't you think that's possible? Wouldn't our dear Nicholas have been likely to lose his life in the vain effort to save another's?'

'You're inventing it, aren't you? I'm sure that Arrie was just a friend, and Nicholas drowned because he had cramp.'

'I do think you're being selfish. Is it because you're jealous of your brother?'

'No, of course not.'

'And didn't you say that you had to get home before dark?'

'Yes. I must go, you're right.'

'Whatever is poor Jack doing on his own for the whole afternoon?'

'I expect he's managed to survive.' Cold sauvignon blanc at the director's house. The company of librarians and academics.

But as she kissed her father's papery cheek and offered her own to Rita's impersonal lips, she said. 'We must talk about Nicholas's letters again, before you do anything with them. It's important that we should only do what he would have wanted, don't you think?'

'And who would know what that is better than his own mother?' said Rita.

It was not far from her parents' house to the one she shared with her husband, and Beech drove slowly so that she could think about what had happened.

She had started the day with such good intentions: she was going to talk, calmly and lucidly, about the events of that day thirty years ago. Her parents would share with her the few facts that they knew, and they would each speak of their sorrow at the waste of the young life. But somehow she and Henry had spent the afternoon discussing compost heaps, and Rita had managed to lead them off into her fairyland of young lovers.

Arrie! Perhaps she should have told Rita who she was. Perhaps Rita wouldn't have believed her.

She was no nearer the truth of the matter, while Henry and Rita seemed to have wandered even further away from it.

The approaching headlights dazzled her tired eyes. She wished it was Fergus that she was going to see, rather than Jack. She could talk, and then they could discuss her day, and she would know that he was listening to what she said. As she neared Oxford she wondered about driving to Lewis Road rather than Enderby Road. But what would he think? Would he be embarrassed if she turned up out of the blue like that? And perhaps he wouldn't be alone. Why should she think that he sat in his house, waiting for her to arrive? Why should he, when she had done nothing to develop their relationship? She found that she had lifted her foot from the accelerator so that the car was slowing down. She took control again and aimed for the Woodstock Road and Jack.

As she sat at red traffic lights, waiting for them to change, she thought how she was glad that her mother was facing up to the fact that Nicholas had died. Rita's son. Her own brother, Nicholas. He would be forty-seven now, probably with greying, receding hair and a paunch. No, not Nicholas. Nicholas would be forever seventeen. Fair-haired, brown-skinned, unmarked yet by life. At seventeen he had been bonily thin. His face was that long English one, made up of straight lines and flat planes, that on a woman looks horsy, on a man, distinguished. He resembled his father, Henry, more than he did Rita, but with something of her positive colouring. He would probably have broadened in the shoulder, put a thicker layer of muscle over the bone, but his was the type that does not alter radically with the years, until in its late seventies it collapses into old age.

The car behind her hooted, and she wondered how long the lights had been green. She was as bad as her parents in her determination to keep his memory unchanging, she thought. Someone hooted again, and she quickly took her foot off the clutch and accelerated away from the lights in a series of kangaroo bounds.

She turned left, and the tree-lined road lay free of traffic before her. Nicholas's room, Rita had called it. But the house where her parents now lived had never been his home. And if he had lived past that distant, sun-soaked summer, thirty years and several thousand miles way, he would never have settled in a village a few miles outside Oxford. Even then, at seventeen, he was ready to move out and on and make his own life. Anyway, he would have hated the house where his parents had lived for the past thirteen years. He would have loathed its low ceilings, gloomy rooms, and mean windows. He would have hated the dull, unfriendly village and the muddy fields. For some reason, Rita, whose taste was usually immaculate, had been in a grey phase when they moved in to Rose Cottage, and the walls had all been painted in colours from dove to storm-cloud. The carpets were silver and pewter, the only relief the coloured embroidered cushions that scattered across the cream linen chairs and sofas. There were few ornaments. It looked as though it was created, whole and complete, in 1985. Nothing remained from the Marklands' previous life in the public part of the house: no elephants' feet doorstops, no pictures of exotic desert Arabs, no photographs of Rita and Henry with visiting royalty. There was no photo of Beech either, although there was rather a nice one, laughing, the sun slanting off his face, of Jack. There was a picture of Alice, aged six, shyly smiling into the camera lens, and a recent one of Henry and Rita, probably at a wedding, for Rita was wearing a hat.

Nicholas would have hated it. Seventeen-year-old Nick would have hated it. But would the forty-seven-year-old man have done so?

What would he have thought of Henry and his 'funny little ways'?

But then, with Nicholas alive, who knows what Henry might not have been.

Beech gave one last look towards Lewis Road, suppressed her desire to see Fergus, and turned into Enderby Road. She reversed into the parking space in the roadway. She glanced up at the windows. The lights were on in every room.

It was time to switch off the headlights and the wipers, which still swung and thumped regularly across the windscreen in front of her. It was time to think about getting Jack a proper evening meal. She slammed the car door behind her, erasing a little of the resentment she felt at always doing what was expected of her, putting her own needs to one side, forgetting that they existed. *You'll never be happy if you think only of yourself.* The gate to the drive was open, and she banged it shut behind her. She was sure that she had closed it on her way out this morning. Jack must have taken his car out. She ran a casual hand along the bonnet. Yes, the engine was still warm. She smiled as she found her front door key and pushed it into the lock.

'Hello, darling!' she called.

Jack was slumped on the sofa, the cushions squashed into cabbage shapes around him. On the television screen muddy men in scarlet and white shirts chased each other around an improbably green field.

'What?' he said, failing to look up.

'Have you had a nice afternoon?'

'I went to the director's place for lunchtime drinks. It was just the usual boring crowd.'

I was right, thought Beech. And I wonder whether the director's nubile daughter was there, or the new tarty assistant librarian.

'Any news of people I might know?'

Jack used the remote control to switch off the television. 'Miranda's hoping to register for an M.A. next year.'

'The director's daughter? She's a bright girl.'

'I'm sure she'd prefer it if you called her a woman,' laughed Jack. 'She's a fiery little thing.'

'Are you hungry? Shall I get you something to eat?'

'That's a happy thought. Shall I pour you a glass of something?'

'White wine,' said Beech. The fiery little thing had left Jack in a good mood, certainly. He hadn't even grumbled when he'd switched off the football.

Beech pushed the door closed and went to the fridge and started getting out ingredients for Jack's evening meal. She wouldn't be able to face much herself after lunch at her parents' house.

She was slicing onions when the phone rang. There was no point in hoping that Jack would heave himself out of the sofa and answer it. She picked up the extension in the hall.

'Hello?'

'Is that Beatrice? Mrs Waring?'

'Yes.'

'Is Jack in?' The voice was female and sounded angry, aggressive, even.

'Yes he is. Do you want me to fetch him?'

'No, don't bother.'

'Who is this?' But Beech found herself addressing the buzz of the dialling tone. She dialled 1471 and listened to the impersonal voice as it gave her the number of her caller. It was not one she recognized. She knew that the prefix meant that the call came from Kidlington, but she knew no one there. She thought about ringing back, but didn't wish to face that cross female voice again.

When she went back into the sitting room she found Jack once more engrossed in the game on the screen.

'That was a very odd phone call.'

'What was it? A heavy breather? Call the operator, tell them what happened.'

'No, it was a woman, asking whether you were in.'

'Well?'

'When I told her you were, she just hung up.'

'Probably a wrong number.'

'Then why did she ask for you, and how did she know my name?'

'How should I know? Probably some nuisance call. I don't know what you're making such a fuss about.' His eyes, all this while, had not left the screen.

'Something odd happened this afternoon too.'

'What was that?' He didn't sound interested. Why should he be interested in her family, especially in a brother who had died thirty years before?

'Rita has been going through Nicholas's things in his room.'

'Well, what was odd about it?'

'She's found some letters, and she's sure that Nicholas was having a passionate love affair with some young girl called Arrie.'

'That's all right, isn't it? Keep the old bat happy for a change.'

'She wants to include them in the memoir.'

'Slot them in as an envoi or something,' said Jack.

'It's embarrassing. Toe-curling. How would you like your seventeen-year-old diaries and letters to be published?'

'Me? You wouldn't catch me writing junk like that when I was seventeen. I was too busy playing rugger and chasing girls. But I'm sure your brother was an articulate and wonderful person.'

'He was no Rupert Brooke, that I do know. And anyway, it's an invasion of his privacy.'

'Have the dead the right to privacy?'

'Yes. They have the right to keep their diaries and letters private from their mothers.'

'I don't suppose there's anything very interesting there. The Swinging Sixties had hardly arrived in your privileged outpost in the Levant, had they?'

'Life was more sophisticated out there. It's different in a hot climate, you see. People grow up faster.'

'Beatrice, is that you?'

'Yes, Mother.'

'I'm ringing to tell you about the wonderful letter that came this morning.'

'Who's it from?'

'Valma Beresford. You'll know her as Valerie Crabbe.'

'The grocer's daughter.'

'Don't be unkind. I'm sure she's married very well. I know she wasn't exactly our sort of person in the old days, so downtrodden and dim I always thought, but she's writing from a very good address.'

'What does she say?'

'She wrote to me originally in response to my advertisement in the *Telegraph* and when I told her about the memoir she wrote back to tell me what exciting memories she has to add to it. Apparently she does remember our dear Nicholas so well.'

'I didn't realize that they knew one another at all.'

'Well, they did. She shared one or two precious memories of him with me, and promised that she would tell me a whole lot more when she saw me.'

'And you believed her?'

'Why are you being so negative? I do think you should go and see your doctor about your hormones.'

'There's nothing wrong with my hormones. Tell me what Valerie – sorry! *Valma* – has to say.'

'She has letters and a journal that she wants to show us. She's coming down to Oxford next week, just so that she can do so. Isn't that sweet of her?'

'I look forward to it. Where are we meeting? I'll put it in the diary.'

'I told her that she could stay with you, darling.'

'Why can't she stay in a b and b? Or go back to London in the evening?'

'Don't be so unsociable. You've got plenty of room, haven't you? And it will save her all the bother of finding her way up to Chipping Hampton. I've arranged with her to be at your place in time for dinner on Wednesday.'

'That was kind of you,' Beatrice said drily. 'I wish you'd consulted me before inviting the Crabbe girl to stay in my house. Is her husband with her?'

'She didn't mention a husband. I imagine he must have died or been divorced or something.'

'There's a double bed in the big spare room, so they can both squeeze in if he turns up.'

'I know you'll manage beautifully,' said Rita, and rang off.

In her bedsitter, Valma Beresford sat at her desk with a pad and pencil and considered which of her outfits she should take with her to Oxford. She didn't want to pack too large a suitcase, since it would look as though she was expecting to stay for a long time. What image did she wish to project? Respectable, of course. But still youthful, reminding them of the young girl she had been when she knew Nicholas. Did Oxford count as town, or country? She would pack her good suit, but should she take sensible walking shoes, or smart ones with heels? Would they expect her to wear tweeds? Ugh! In would go a silk blouse, of course, and her new winter coat. Valma recrossed her legs and smiled at the swishing sound her nylon stockings made (no vulgar tights for her). She wondered what Beatrice's husband was like. She remembered how tall, flat-chested and awkward Beatrice had been as a teenager. Probably not a great catch. But then, the Marklands seemed to have plenty of money, and probably connections, so he might be all right after all. She would put in her new cerise outfit, just in case he was worth impressing. She sucked in her stomach and rotated her right foot, admiring her neat ankle. The black patent shoes with the slender heels. And the black and gold dress that looked just as good as real silk twill. Oh yes, she was still a woman to be reckoned with.

9

Fergus sat far back in his chair, as though trying to disappear into the wallpaper, so that Beech could pretend he wasn't there and concentrate completely on what she was doing.

He had come to her house at one o'clock that day, they had eaten a simple lunch ('There's nothing as quite as good as thick smoked salmon sandwiches,' as Fergus had said), and now Beech was showing him a picture she had painted that morning.

'I had a dream last night,' she had said. 'Or rather a scene that I was watching. I tried to get it down on paper.'

A transparent wash of shimmering blues and greens bled into each other.

'Well?' asked Fergus.

Beech was remembering that there was nothing so boring as another person's dream. 'I could lose myself in that limpid water, dive into it, disappear for ever.'

'And what would you find at the bottom?'

'I forget.' A quick shutter drew across her mind and blocked out the glimpse she had gained of the objects she might find there.

'What are these?' Small red squiggles swam in the turquoise. 'What are they? Something organic?'

'I don't know. I'd better put it away. Or throw it out,' she said. Why had she wasted her time with Fergus on showing him this ridiculous picture?

Fergus knew he should go home. He had work to do, and he would miss his deadline if he spent too much time here in

Beech's kitchen. He looked around him. It was a very ugly room, surely more typical of Jack than of Beech.

'I can't understand why you married him,' he said.

'Have you met Jack?'

'No. But I have a fairly clear idea of what he's like. So why?'

'It seemed a good idea at the time.'

'You can't get away with that.'

'I thought he was wonderfully normal, and solidly English. Marriage to Jack meant the end to the strange, foreign affair with the Middle East that he had never understood, never wished to know about. And I wanted an end to that part of my life. I wanted someone to put a lid on my memories, firmly, like the big metal lid of the dustbin, then snap up the metal clips so that no one could accidentally open it and let the rubbish spill out on to the pavement.'

'It would be simpler if you told me that you married Jack because you loved him. Now *that* I would understand.'

'Oh. Love.' The word dropped on to the floor between them like a grey pebble. They both stared at the spot where it might have landed, avoiding one another's eyes.

'I'll have to go,' said Fergus eventually.

'I suppose so.'

The house in Enderby Road was blissfully empty without Jack and Rita. Beech checked her watch. She found she had a spare hour before she needed to start the preparations for supper. She could go upstairs and read at least some of the notebooks which Rita had handed on to her. She must search too for the notebooks of her own that she was sure she had put by somewhere. It had certainly been the year for writing journals.

She found the box that Rita had given her and opened one of Nicholas's notebooks at random.

Arrie was wearing her new swimsuit today, *she read*. It has vertical stripes in black and silver – wide, waving stripes, so that as she swims and turns in the water, I see her in first one colour then the other, like a shoal of small fishes playing in the turquoise sea. Black and silver. Her hair was silver in the water too, waving like weed, raining silver drops when she surfaced and swung the rope of it round in a sunlit arc. You can never really tell with people, can you? What are they? Silver or black? How you see them depends on the light, or how they are moving, or how you are looking at them just at that precise moment.

Coming to it, knowing nothing of the people involved, what would you think? Maybe this really was a love story. Maybe Rita was right in a way. Her own memories of that year were different. Was she seeing the past through a mist of distortion? How had she written about it at the time? She went to search for her own notebooks. She should have thrown out all her old childhood rubbish, but with a large house like this to store it in, she hadn't bothered.

She had kept them in a box, stowed away in the back of a cupboard in the spare room, together with a pile of hats she would never wear again and a very old, wooden-framed tennis racket. She pulled out the dusty brown cardboard box, still with the childish messages scrawled all over it: 'DON'T TOUCH. PRIVATE. KEEP OUT. THIS MEANS YOU.' Not that the 'Private and Confidential' stickers all over her brother's letters had kept them from Rita's eyes, or stopped her from insisting that they should be transcribed and typed out and produced for all her friends and relations to read. Don't worry, Nick, she thought. I'm doing all that by myself. I'm not having a stranger reading your letters before I do.

She wiped the dust off the box-lid, using her sleeve.

Again, the neat handwriting, hardly possible to tell hers

75

from Nick's. And at this distance of time the world she had lived in seemed unfamiliar, as though it had all happened to someone else.

The light blazes down out of a cloudless sky and reflects in brilliant white off the pavements and the squares, hitting pale European eyes with the force of a missile. I put up a hand to protect my sight, pull down the brim of my hat to stop the light from leaching out the oil from my fair English skin.

'Never go out without a hat,' said my mother, arranging the white linen collar high on the back of my neck. 'And gloves,' she added, and she pulled her own up over pale arms and fastened the pearl buttons on her milk-white wrist.

Inside my kid glove, the sweat rolled down in warm drops, so that I felt the leather as a hot, living thing. More sweat slid down inside the waistband of my skirt, and between my toes in their stiff leather sandals. A child ran past, bright trousers loose on her legs, feet bare and hardened by the stony ground. Dark hair swung and shone in the brilliant light, gold gleamed in her ears and nose, beads rattled on her ankles and clicked against her bony wrists. Knowing black eyes laughed at my stiff brown sandals.

She barely recognized this passage as one of her own. Though she remembered how it felt to be fifteen, and hot, and foreign, in that strange land.

10

On Wednesday afternoon a long red car with a white and blue sign on the roof drew up outside Beech's house in Enderby Road. A woman opened the door and emerged on to the pavement. She issued instructions and the cab driver opened the boot of his car and handed her a bulky suitcase.

'You may carry it for me to the front door,' she ordered. Her accent wasn't quite English.

She followed the driver to the door, paid him, and rang the bell. Beech appeared. For a moment she looked gob-smacked.

'Beatrice! Darling!' There was a trace of a 'k' on the end of the second word.

'Valerie?' ventured Beech, forgetting for a moment.

'Valma. I have not been called Valerie for, oh, far too many years to count.'

'Beech saw a woman of indeterminate age. Not tall, but quite wide. Lots of curling black hair. Green coat with a blue collar. Very high-heeled black patent-leather shoes. She was standing next to a purple suitcase.

'Well now, aren't you going to ask me in?'

What a loud, vulgar voice! It cut through the refined north Oxford air as easily as wire through overripe cheese. Valma added a laugh that started somewhere below her navel and bubbled up through her wide red lips, and threw wide her emerald green arms as though to enfold Beech in an extravagant embrace. Beech stepped cautiously forward and bestowed two pecks a centimetre away from each of the scarlet cheeks.

'Please. Do come in,' said Beech.

The two women entered the house, taking the purple suitcase with them.

It had taken Beech a short, shocked moment to recognize her visitor. She had expected her to arrive later that day, and she had also been expecting someone quieter and more modest. Where the young Valerie Crabbe had known her place as the grocer's daughter, this loud, bright creature looked as though she could outsparkle Beech and even Rita Markland.

But when Beech got closer, she saw that behind the emerald-green coat and the layer of pancake make-up she was still Valerie Crabbe. It was the knowing black eyes that gave her away. She had always doubted the demure exterior and the downcast eyes when they were children, but she had accepted it as the normal way of surviving when your parents expected too much from you. She smiled at Valma, a tentatively welcoming smile. Was that suitcase not a little on the large side for an overnight visit? Valma smiled back, a calculating expression on her round, powdered face. Well, thought Beech resignedly, at least she no longer looks as though she's concealing a mother-of-pearl rosary in that black patent handbag of hers, and I doubt whether she ever wears a high lace collar on her dark dresses.

'Valma,' she said, 'how lovely to see you after all this time. Come in. I must introduce you to my husband.'

'And to your dear daughter!' cried Valma. 'I must meet your child, Beatrice dear!'

'Alice doesn't live here any more,' said Beech, trying not to sound like the title of a sixties pop song. She didn't add a comment to the effect that Valma should be glad of Alice's absence. Few people took to dear Alice on first meeting, or even on successive ones. Valma was letting loose light peals of laughter that bounced around the high-ceilinged hall, so Beech kept quiet about Alice.

'Valma, this is my husband. Jack, do meet my very old friend Valma . . .' She stopped as she realized that she had forgotten Valma's married name, remembering only that it was something unlikely.

'Beresford,' supplied Valma.

'I'll just take your case upstairs,' she said. 'Jack will look after you for a few minutes.'

Jack rose to his feet and took Valma's coat. 'Do sit down,' he said.

'Aren't you well?' she heard Valma enquire sympathetically.

'Me? Oh yes, I'm fine,' replied Jack. 'I've just taken the afternoon off to work on an article.'

Beech closed the sitting-room door and went upstairs. The suitcase was surprisingly heavy for its size, and she was out of breath by the time she got to the top. She left the case in the spare bedroom and hurried to find clean towels for her visitor. Then she ran a damp cloth around the surfaces in the bedroom and checked that everything was respectably clean in the bathroom.

Downstairs again she made more welcoming noises in Valma's direction and offered to show her up to her room.

'How frightfully kind of you to put me up like this!' cried Valma with her oddly correct diction.

'It's lovely to have you here,' said Beech politely.

'You always were a sweet-natured little thing,' said Valma.

'I was?' Beech remembered herself as being tall, rather gawky, and far too wrapped up in herself to be kind to others. 'You must be tired after the journey.'

'Such a wonderful coach from Notting Hill to dear Oxford and so much more convenient than the train,' said Valma. 'Really, one hardly misses a car of one's own. And the fare from the station wasn't too extravagant. But of course I would like to freshen up a little now.'

'Do you think you could rustle up some food?' said Jack,

when they were alone. 'I don't think the poor thing has managed to get herself any lunch.'

Beech went out to the kitchen and peered into the fridge. She assembled salad, cold meat and a few left-over boiled potatoes, then returned to the sitting room.

Apparently it took Valma some time to freshen up, and she reappeared in a shining ultramarine trouser suit and newly painted, matching eyes.

'Do help yourself to some lunch,' said Beech, and she ran upstairs again to look at the other bedroom. This one had once been Alice's and still contained many of her discarded possessions. She hastily bundled those that were on view into a cupboard and tried to make the room look respectable enough for Rita's taste. Rita, losing no time, was expected shortly. Then she went downstairs. Did Valma expect a pudding? Beech took in the fruit bowl and hoped its contents would satisfy her.

'Tell me,' said Beech, catching the ambient verbal style, 'how are your dear parents? Do they still live in Essex?'

'Oh, Daddy never recovered from the shock,' said Valma.

'What shock?' asked Beech.

'Aren't you being insensitive?' hissed Jack. 'Perhaps she doesn't want to talk about it?'

'Doesn't want to talk about what?' asked Beech.

'I don't know, do I?'

'No, of course dear Beatrice must hear all about it,' said Valma. 'I feel so close to you all that I would hate to hide anything from you.'

'I'm glad you're feeling at home,' said Beech, while Jack made faces at her behind Valma's shoulder.

'My father went on running his grocery shop, as people liked to call it, until he entered his seventies. He decided then that it was time to retire and looked around for a buyer for the business. He found one quite quickly, and was offered a very handsome sum, for the business and for the continued use of his name. He and my mother packed up all their furniture and possessions and came back to England, settling, as you so rightly say, in Essex. The very best part of Essex.'

'Of course,' said Jack hastily. 'It would be the very best part.'

'But my mother did not like England. She hated the climate and the dull colours. She hated too the immorality and the laxity in matters of religion that she observed in the people around her.'

'I've heard that Essex can be a wicked, godless place,' said Beech.

'Unfortunately for my father, she received an offer to return to the Middle East, and she took it.'

'But the offer didn't cover the continued use of your father's name?' enquired Beech delicately.

'Exactly.'

'Have you seen her since?'

'No. I do not know where she is now.'

'What happened to your father?' asked Beech.

'When my mother left she took with her the largest part of the money that my father had received for his business. He had made the mistake of having all his assets in their joint names, and she simply removed everything and took it away with her.'

'Everything?'

'Just about. He still had the house, of course, but he had to sell it and move into a small flat so that he had a little capital to live on.'

'And then?'

'He died. Just faded away,' said Valma, dabbing at her jewel-painted eye with a serviceable-looking cotton handkerchief. 'All the fight just drained out of him.'

'How sad. And what about you?' What about Mr Beresford, if there ever was such a person? she wanted to ask.

'I had married quite young,' said Valma, then reconsidered.

'Very young. Almost straight from school. One was so foolish at that age, didn't you find?'

An unfortunate marriage. A major mistake. That's what she's working up to.

'Personally, I can make mistakes at any age,' admitted Beech.

'But you are fortunate enough to have dear Jack at your side,' said Valma.

'True enough,' said Beech, and commented no further.

'And I had already, even at so youthful an age, lost the one true love of my life.'

'You had?'

'Of course. Nicholas. Dear, dear Nicholas.'

'So you married Mr Beresford on the rebound.' Beech hardly bothered to hide her disbelief, but the long, deadly habit of good manners stopped her from an argument.

'I would not put it quite like that. As any young girl of my class would, I obeyed my parents. I believed that they were wiser in such things than I.'

'And were they?'

'We were all sadly deceived.' Another dab with the hand-kerchief punctuated this statement and indicated that the subject was now closed.

Later that afternoon, Rita arrived, and Beech showed her to Alice's old room.

'Here we are!' she said, knowing that Rita would not be pleased. But since she was the one who had invited Valma to stay, she could just lump it. Rita peered out of the window at the view of the garage roof, and sniffed.

'The furnishings look as though they've been put in here because they have no other home: too good for the tip, not valuable enough for a dealer, too ugly for any other room in the house,' she said.

'This room was Alice's. I'm afraid that she didn't have any strong ideas on decoration.'

The wardrobe door stood ajar. Rita opened it wide and revealed a drunken row of wire coat hangers and a smell of very old face powder. She pushed the door closed, but it drifted open again.

'And there's plenty of drawer space,' said Beech. She didn't offer to open any of the drawers, but she knew that all would stick and when Rita persuaded one of them to open, it would doubtless contain a rusty paper clip and a toothless comb.

'How lovely!' said Rita without enthusiasm. 'Don't worry about me, dear. I shall soon make myself at home. Does this room run to the luxury of a bathroom?'

It did, but the shower, basin and lavatory were all a virulent pink.

'How delicious. It reminds me of strawberry ice cream,' said Rita.

'Come down and meet Valma. I'm sure we're going to have a wonderful evening,' said Beech desperately.

'What do you mean, you're going out?' hissed Beech.

'Well, you don't want a man around, do you? You can have a proper hen party if I'm not here.'

'Where are you going?' she found herself asking.

'I'll pop down to the pub, see who's in, get myself a meal there. No need to worry about me.'

Odd how her mother and husband both urged her not to worry about them when that was exactly what they wished her to do. 'Very well. Enjoy yourself!'

'I shall,' said Jack, sliding out through the front door and into his red BMW.

'Why are you taking the car if you're going to the pub?' called Beech. But Jack had already swung its nose out of the drive and up the street towards Lewis Road. I suppose he'll turn left in the Banbury Road, thought Beech, but that's not the way I'd go if I were driving to the pub. She wondered whether she should confront him on his return about his new habit of deception, but put it to one side, just as she was putting so much else at this time. Soon, she promised herself; I'll deal with it quite soon.

My goodness, I've been in this kitchen a lot today, thought Beech as she washed lettuce and grated carrots. ('They have been organically grown, haven't they?' asked Rita. 'Of course,' said Beech, who really did buy organic vegetables when they were available but was not certain of the origin of these particular carrots.) She removed the skin from the chicken she had cooked earlier. She jointed the chicken, boned it, and arranged it on an oval dish, then washed watercress, shook it dry and draped it artistically around the chicken. Mayonnaise with a little added cream and a dash of mustard for herself and, probably, Valma. Raspberry vinaigrette for Rita. Small potatoes, boiled in their skins, decorated with a sprig of fresh parsley. She took a bottle of white wine out of the fridge, opened it and poured herself a glass. Yes, really rather good. She might enjoy the evening after all. For a short moment she wished that Fergus was with her. It would all be so much more amusing if she had a like-minded companion to share it with. She allowed herself to imagine lying in bed with Fergus, in a friendly sort of way, talking over the people and the conversations of the evening. Why couldn't she do that when she was with Jack? Because, she reminded herself, Jack would be bored within thirty seconds, would roll over, fall asleep and start to snore. She wondered whether Fergus snored. Of course he didn't.

'Supper's ready!' she called, and started to ferry dishes on to the dining-room table.

'Yes, Rita, it is a free-range chicken. Corn fed,' she said, as her mother opened her mouth to ask.

She finished her first glass of wine and offered the pinot blanc to the other two. Wasn't it supposed to be a bad sign when you started to pour yourself an extra glass of alcohol? Oh well, anyone would develop a drink problem if they had a family like hers.

'Thank you so much,' said Valma, starting to eat.

'Potatoes, Valma?'

'Do remove the skins before you eat them,' said Rita. 'The skins are poison, you know.'

Beech drank more wine and cheered up. The other two had started to eat, discarding potato skin, refusing mayonnaise, approving of the watercress.

'So full of wonderful minerals,' said Rita, masticating a couple of leaves.

'Salad?' offered Beech. 'Free range,' she added absent-mindedly, but neither of her guests noticed her slip.

'Now that we're all so comfortable together, there is just one little thing I'd like to ask you, Valerie dear,' said Rita.

'Please call me Valma.' A certain crispness had entered her voice.

'Valma. Of course. Well, Valma, there is a question that has been taxing my brain ever since I read dear Nicholas's diaries and letters.'

'Yes?' Valma's voice had risen a little higher. 'What is it?'

'Who was Arrie?'

'Arrie?'

'Yes, in the dear, dear days that we all spent together in the Levant. Arrie. Did you know her?' said Rita.

'Yes, Valma. Do you remember her?' asked Beech, who was watching Rita's tense face.

'Arrie? But of course I do!'

'So tell us, do,' said Rita. 'Who was she?'

'Don't any of you know? I should have thought you would.'

'Shall I bring in the pudding?' asked Beech. 'I've made an

apple pie.' The trees in the garden had cropped surprisingly well last season and her freezer was still stocked with containers of pie filling.

'Oh no! Pastry is poison to my system,' snapped Rita.

'Coffee, then? It is decaffeinated.'

'Bring it in quickly and stop interrupting dear Valma!' said Rita. 'What is wrong with you, Beatrice? Aren't you interested in the past?'

'Of course. After all, I've never managed to escape from it.'

'I'd love a slice of pie,' said Valma.

Beech went to fetch pudding for the two of them and set the kettle to boil. The conversation turned to the apple trees and the garden while they ate.

'And I'll pour us all a brandy, shall I?' she said, when they had eaten apple pie and she had prepared and brought in the coffee. Rita lit a cigarette for herself. 'Would you like one?' she asked Valma.

'I should have thought they really were poison,' said Beech.

'They're menthol, my dear. They do you no harm whatsoever. They hardly count as cigarettes. Valma?' Valma shook her head. Beech went to find her only ashtray. 'Thank you, Beatrice.' Rita drew on her cigarette with a hissing noise and blew out a thin, grey jet of smoke. 'Now, hurry up with the brandy, then we can all relax and listen to Valma's revelations.'

'I will go and fetch the things I've brought to show you,' said Valma. 'They will convince you of the truth of what I have to say.' She left the room.

'Here,' she said, when she returned. 'Look at these.'

Letters written on familiar grey paper tucked into grey envelopes. Equally familiar italic handwriting.

'Open them,' said Valma. 'Please, read them.'

Beech and Rita took a letter each, opened it, read the neat, legible script.

Dear Arrie . . . read Beech. She skimmed down to the bottom . . . *With all my love, Nico.* She looked over her mother's shoulder. Hers was similar. News from England, jokes, *wish you were here.* Beech looked at one of the envelopes. It was addressed to Miss Valerie Crabbe at Crabbe's Provisions.

'So, *you're* Arrie,' said Rita faintly. Beech watched as she turned the idea over. She looked at Valma and back at the letter, as though trying to bring the two ideas together in her mind. 'Well!'

'Your parents didn't mind your receiving them, from a boy?' asked Beech.

'Why should they? Your brother was a very respectable young man.'

'Of course he was! Why on earth should they object?' cried Rita.

'It's just that you said your parents were so strict,' said Beech. 'And you weren't very old, were you? Fifteen?'

'Girls from the convent would leave to marry at fourteen,' said Valma. 'It was the custom in the country.'

'Disgusting!' said Rita. 'How could their parents allow such a thing?'

'When a man married a girl straight from the convent like that, it was a guarantee of her virginity,' said Valma. 'That was essential and the nuns were known to look after such things.'

'Oh!' Rita gave a little cough to show how shocked she was at the idea. 'But then, Nicholas was hardly in a position to speak of marriage at the time, was he? He was still a schoolboy.'

'But a very mature one,' said Valma firmly.

'Are you telling us that Nicholas wished to marry you?' asked Beech.

'If he hadn't died that summer, who knows what we would have been to one another. What we *all* would have been to each other.'

87

One of the problems with Valma, Beech was discovering, was that when she spoke about those years, her English sounded as though she was speaking a foreign language, as if she was thinking in French or Arabic and then translating rapidly, if unidiomatically, before speaking.

'We were in love,' said Valma, and she managed to roll her eyes, a thing which Beech had never seen anyone do before.

Rita had been silent for a minute or two and Beech could hear the wheels turning as she decided how to play this new game. She rose to her feet, dominating the little group. She motioned to Valma to rise, as though she were a priestess in some arcane rite. Beech was left as the only spectator.

'Welcome to the family, Valma *dear*,' Rita said at last, and threw her batwing sleeves wide in a yellow silken embrace.

'How kind! How kind!' came Valma's muffled voice from the vicinity of Rita's bosom.

'At last I have found my true family!' exclaimed Valma, emerging damp-eyed from the folds of Rita's kimono. She smiled at Beech and clutched her hand. Beech felt the warm, damp fingers clinging to hers. They reminded her of the five-year-old Alice, her hands sticky with the remnants of an ice cream, dragging her towards some distant prospect of roller-coaster or candy floss. Alice, at least, had been more direct in her demands, and if thwarted would merely throw a noisy tantrum. She felt that Valma would attempt to get her own way – whatever that might be – in a quieter, but more effective, manner. Well, I don't care what you do, there'll be no candy floss for you, Valma dear, she resolved, steadily refusing to return Valma's sisterly smile.

11

Jack returned home after Beech, having done the washing-up single-handed, had retired to bed. He didn't bother to hide the fact that he had been drinking. How different from their early times together, she thought. She remembered – perhaps it had even started on the awful night of their wedding – when he had disappeared into the bathroom and she had heard vigorous brushing sounds, followed by gargling and spitting. He would emerge and approach the bed, preceded by the strong smell of peppermint toothpaste, in the vain hope that she wouldn't notice how much he had had to drink. When he had started to kiss her the taste of mint was overwhelming.

But these days he no longer cared whether she noticed his drinking or not, and tonight she could smell no toothpaste, only the whisky he must have had with his friends at the pub. She opened her eyes and checked the time on the glowing digits of the bedside clock. Well after midnight. Ten to one, in fact. Surely even Jack couldn't believe she was taken in by his story about being at the pub. She sniffed discreetly. Single malt, she thought. Glenmorangie probably, since that was his favourite. Someone was doing him proud. She feigned sleep and he climbed in beside her. Within minutes he was snoring. Now thoroughly awake, Beech sidled out of bed and crept downstairs to the sitting room. She pulled the curtains back so that she could sit in the dark and look out on the moon-bathed garden. She loved coming in here in the early hours of the morning, just to stand and watch the smoky orange dawn creep across the sky. It was the feeling that she was alone in the world, that nothing could touch her, anything was possible, that attracted her.

The white mist hugs the valley floor and grey shadows of trees stand up against its whiteness. Spiders' webs, made visible by the white dew that clings to their strands, hang everywhere, swaying in the slight breeze. Come on, Arrie, come and look.

No, that was another time, another place. There was no valley visible outside this window, only a suburban garden. And this wasn't dawn, but a moonlit night in early spring. What had she been thinking of?

The cold of the night was winning the battle against the residual heat from the fire, and she thought of Jack lying in their warm double bed upstairs, alone. The cold was starting to make her feel sleepy again, and she yawned and stood up, drew the curtains and then returned upstairs and slipped under the duvet. *She had been lying to herself again: Jack hadn't been drinking late at the pub, he had been with a woman.* Oh no, it couldn't possibly be so. Not Jack.

'Your feet are cold,' he murmured, but he didn't wake up.

Suppose it were Fergus lying there? she wondered, but fell asleep herself before she could pursue the thought to its conclusion.

She dreamed she was standing in a desolate landscape. Her arms were bound to her sides by her restrictive clothes. She seemed to be wearing a garment that resembled a sari, or a baby's swaddling clothes. Or maybe it was a shroud. Her feet were free but she could only move in slow, jerky steps across the uneven ground. There were crowds of people in the distance, laughing and singing. She wanted to join in, but was waiting for a signal. When the conductor lowered his baton, or the director called 'Action!', she could take her part in the drama. Then someone would walk on to the stage and cut her bindings so that she would at last be free.

The next day was warm and damp, with a soft westerly wind bringing in unseasonably warm weather. Beech went out into the garden and wandered through the straggly grass and brown leaves which remained from the previous autumn. The damp air and faint drizzle raised fruity, puddingy smells from the drenched earth. Secateurs in hand, she wandered from bush to bush, snipping at dead stalks and twigs bearing dried-up berries. She pictured the drifts of columbines and stocks that would bloom in the coming months as she ambled from shrub to shrub.

Ah well! Now it was time to go indoors and prepare breakfast for four people. She hoped that she could persuade Jack to go to work in his office today. She was tired of having him hanging round her feet all day. He bores me, she thought. And why should I feel guilty at such a thought, since it is the truth.

To her relief, Jack came down to breakfast wearing a suit and tie and talking of a meeting he had to attend.

After breakfast, she, Valma and Rita retired to the sitting room to get back to the interesting subject of life in the Levant, thirty years ago.

'Here, do please take a look at this, if you'd like to,' said Valma.

'This' was a pale blue exercise book, just like the ones that Rita had found belonging to Nicholas, and identical too to the diaries that Beech had kept all those years ago.

'We must have bought them at your father's shop,' said Beech.

'He didn't keep a very large range of stationery, I'm afraid,' said Valma. 'The writing paper was always grey and the notebooks were always blue. Not much choice!'

'Of course not!' said Rita impatiently. 'Crabbe was a grocer, a superior purveyor of provisions. And such excellent bacon. One simply can't find smoked back like it any more, and always cut so thinly.'

Beech, meanwhile, had picked up the familiar exercise book and opened it. It was only when she examined it carefully that she saw that the writing in this notebook was very slightly different from her own and Nicholas's. She read a few paragraphs.

You think you know so much, you and the others from the privileged life. But you know nothing of the world outside your clubs and your big houses with the servants and the chauffeurs. Your mothers spend their days at coffee mornings and the dressmaker's, or in long hours at the beauty parlour, getting their legs waxed and their cellulite firmed. Cellulite! Try working in the shop and the storeroom for a week or two. You'd have no more problems with your cellulite.

But while you sit on a terrace, underneath a green-striped umbrella, sipping your drinks from frosted glasses, I spend long hours in the shop, with its dim light and the great paddles of the fan that swing slowly overhead and move the spice-rich air around that claustrophobic space. There's no lazing about in our household. My mother wouldn't know where the beauty parlour is, and she despises women who have never had to work for their living. We all work: Father, Mother, the servants and I.

All the long days of the school holidays I spend in that shop, or in the storerooms behind, unpacking, labelling, checking. But can you imagine getting passionate about groceries? Perhaps when you are middle-aged or old, yes. But at fifteen? It is the most humiliating thing. It wouldn't be so bad if the English customers pretended that I was just an anonymous shop assistant with no identity of my own, if they hid behind their panama hats and linen suits and pretended not to recognize me. But no. They have to creep around being polite to me, and saying, 'Good morning, Valerie, and how are you today? What a good girl you are, helping your mother like this.'

I hadn't realized how bitter she was, thought Beech. And who am I to criticize, anyway? I'm one of the people who made her feel like that.

'Which part are you reading?' asked Valma sharply.

Beech leafed through another couple of pages and found a bland passage about going to church with her mother and father, followed by a brief résumé of the sermon.

'What a well-behaved child you were!' she said.

'There was no choice in my family,' said Valma. 'My parents were very strict.'

'You didn't go to the English school with Beatrice and the others, did you?' asked Rita. 'I don't seem to remember seeing you or your parents at any of the concerts or at prize-giving.'

'My mother was a Catholic. I attended one of the many convents in the city. It was a very suitable education for a young girl,' said Valma primly, though her angry dark eyes and the brilliance of her eye shadow belied her words.

'I'm sure it was a better school than the dim little place that the Misses Hapsted ran,' said Beech. 'I was horribly behind when I came back to England.'

'That was because you were lazy,' said Rita. 'We couldn't get you to concentrate properly on your studies. But then, you weren't really interested in academic work, were you?'

'I was bored by the Misses Hapsted.'

'There was nothing wrong with the school your father and I chose for you and it's very wrong of you to suggest such a thing.'

'When are we going to meet your lovely daughter?' put in Valma quickly.

'I'm not sure,' said Beech, not liking this subject any better than the previous one.

'Beatrice and Alice don't always see eye to eye,' explained Rita. 'Beatrice was always so hard on her, I felt. But then, my granddaughter and I have a very special relationship.'

'I suppose it can be easier with a gap of a generation,' said Valma. 'The very young and the very old seem to have a sympathy for each other.'

'That has nothing to do with it! Alice and I have always been *pals*. We do not notice the difference at all in our ages when we're together.'

Both of them are selfish, irresponsible and impossible, thought Beech. Also vain.

'I'll give her a ring and see if she'll come to lunch one day this week,' she said.

When was it she had last seen Alice?

Beech thought guiltily how she hadn't spoken to her daughter at all this month. Had she been over to the Cowley Road *last* month? She had a nasty feeling that she put it off so often that her last confrontation with her daughter had possibly been at Christmas or the New Year. She had been such a dear little child. When had it all gone wrong? Somehow, Alice never seemed to surface from the depths of adolescence. Was it perhaps her, Beech's, fault?

She would ring Alice now. She would arrange to go over there *today*. She would make friendly noises and invite Alice to meet Valma. Alice, unfortunately, would undoubtedly hate Valma and would make her dislike quite plain. She would have to soften Alice up. She would take her a present: some flowers, some food, some article of necessary clothing. Her heart sank. Whatever she did, whatever she took, she knew she would get it wrong.

She phoned. A mechanical BT voice told her that the number

was no longer available. Unavailable? That probably meant that Alice had forgotten to pay her quarterly bill and was now cut off.

'Just popping out to the shops,' she called to Valma and Rita.

She left them happily reminiscing in the sitting room. In Summertown she bought a bunch of flowers, a large loaf of Greek bread, half a pound of cheese, some apples and two cream doughnuts, and set off for Alice's bedsit. She wondered about picking up a six-pack of imported lager. Alice's boyfriend, whoever he currently was, would appreciate it. To hell with it! Beech knew that Alice received a more than generous allowance from Jack that encouraged her to laze around all day and indulge her messy life-style. Alice wrote her parents off as being greedy and materialistic, but that was easy enough when you didn't have to bother about earning your own money, thought Beech.

When she arrived at the much-occupied building off the Cowley Road, the first thing she noticed was that there was something different about the front door. Someone had washed the paintwork and cleaned the chrome fittings. Surely not Alice? Alice dismissed housework as bourgeois time-wasting, something that wouldn't exist if Beech would only stop going on about it. Beech rang the bell. After a short time, the door was opened and a strange figure stood in front of her.

'Yes?'

That solved the problem. Alice had moved away from her room without telling her parents that she was doing so. The bedsit now had a new tenant. Simple.

'Yes?' The woman was large and intimidating.

'I was looking for Alice Waring,' said Beech.

'And who might you be?'

'Her mother.'

'*Alice!*' the woman turned and shouted. Her voice was powerful.

'I'm Francesca,' she said. 'Hi.'

'Oh? Hello.'

'I expect you've heard about me.'

'Not really.'

'What does that mean?'

Before Beech could answer, heavy footsteps approached, and Alice's head appeared over Francesca's shoulder. 'Hello, Mum,' she said.

Francesca stood to one side and Beech took a good look at her daughter. She looked surprisingly clean, and her clothes were quite neat, if rather tight. Her hair was washed and brushed and had even acquired an unwilling shine. Beech noted too that Alice appeared to be about four months pregnant.

'Can I come in?' she asked. Perhaps Alice was merely getting fat. She had always been a plump child. She looked again. No, the girl was definitely pregnant.

'I've brought a few little things for you,' said Beech, handing over the plastic carrier bag, and glad now that she hadn't wasted her money on beer. Alice could probably use all the money she could lay her hands on, in cash. And what had happened to the boyfriend? Did he know about the baby? Had he done a runner?

'Yeah. All right,' said Alice. Beech translated this as 'Thank you,' but she might have been mistaken.

'So,' said Beech, when she was seated on the plastic-covered sofa, having not been offered anything to eat or drink. 'You and Francesca are sharing this place?'

'Yeah.'

She wondered how to ask about the father of the child, which had not yet been referred to by either Alice or her friend.

'That's nice for you,' said Beech. '*Especially at a time like this.*'

'God!' exclaimed Alice. 'If you want to say you've noticed I'm in the club, you might spit it out, instead of hinting at it like that!'

'Pregnant,' said Beech. 'If you want to stop using euphemisms you can say you're pregnant. What are you going to do about it?'

'You want me to have an abortion! Honestly! You are unreal!'

'No. I'm simply enquiring what your plans are.'

'Well, I'm not getting rid of it. Me and Francesca's doing all right. You don't have to worry.'

'I'm glad to hear it. Is Francesca staying for a while?'

'We're together,' said Alice. 'I know you don't understand about stuff like this, and you and Dad can't help being homophobic, but you better get used to it.'

'We'll try,' said Beech mildly. 'We'll try to get used to the fact that you are now a lesbian, and that you're expecting a child. I used to think the two were mutually exclusive, but I was wrong. When will you tell your father about the baby?'

'You can do that,' said Alice.

'Thanks.' It was no good arguing. Alice would never do anything difficult if she thought she could force someone else – usually Beech – to do it for her. 'And what about your grandmother? She's very fond of you and she'll have to know what's happening.'

'Yeah. Gran's all right. No need to tell her yet, though. It'll keep.'

'As long as she doesn't find out about it from someone else.' The pregnancy was surely as obvious to other people as it was to her, thought Beech.

'She won't hear about it. Not unless you tell her,' said Alice.

'I'll keep your secret. But you may find that Rita is very helpful and supportive. I'm sure she'll love the idea of being a great-grandmother.'

'Thass cool. I like Gran. She's much nicer to me than you ever was. She understands me. I wish you could be like that.'

Two selfish people on a single wavelength. 'I'm sorry about

that, Alice, but you'll just have to make do with me as a mother.'

'I got Chess now,' said Alice. 'We're cool.'

'Are you sure you have everything you need for the moment?' asked Beech. 'I noticed that your phone's been disconnected. Do you want me to have it put back for you?'

'Don't need it. Got the mobile.' This sentence contained so many glottal stops that it took Beech a second or so to work out what her daughter was saying.

'Then perhaps you'd give me the number.'

Alice did so. 'Don't worry, Mum. I'm fine now.'

'Mothers do worry. It's in their nature. Oh, and when's the baby due?'

'Some time in August. Not sure exactly when.'

'You are going for your checkups?' asked Beech.

'Course I am. Chess makes sure I get there on time.'

'Well, do let me know if you need anything,' she added lamely. It seemed as though her maternal duties had been taken over, and quite competently, by the imposing Francesca.

'Can I get you anything? Coffee? Tea?' asked Alice belatedly.

'Thanks. I'd better be getting back now,' said Beech. 'Keep in touch.' She knew that Alice would do just that when she next needed something. When should she tell Jack about Alice's pregnancy and about her new relationship? About her new orientation, if it came to that. Not yet, anyway.

Alice's double bombshell had left her dazed. In one way she was used to her daughter's disagreeable behaviour. Perhaps it had been her own fault. Perhaps she had never made enough of an effort to understand Alice when she was small. But it had seemed to her that Alice must have dropped in from another planet. She and Beech had nothing in common. Alice, from an early age, had rejected her parents' values and beliefs and had gone her own rocky way.

So, Alice, at least for the present, was gay. And Alice was

pregnant. Beech was sure that if there were bills to be picked up, they would be picked up by Jack. And if there were difficulties ahead, it was Beech who was expected to deal with them.

She would, eventually, come to terms with it all.

It was only when she was on her way back to Enderby Road that she realized she had forgotten to tell Alice about Valma. Would she now have to invite Francesca to lunch as well as Alice? And what would Valma think if she did? Perhaps it would be better to invite them both after Alice had broken the news of her pregnancy, and Francesca, to her grandmother.

When she was nearly home, the car turned left as though of its own volition and drew up outside Fergus's house.

She rang the bell. This was an unscheduled visit and he might not be pleased to see her. He might be busy. He might have another friend with him. What the hell was she doing here?

Fergus arrived at the door looking exactly as usual: blue sweatshirt, grey slacks, wavy brown hair that needed cutting.

'Come in,' he said. She entered and started walking through the hall before he had closed the door.

'You're looking very cross today,' said Fergus.

Beech was stalking past the watercolour seascape, ignoring the Valmaesque nude, stamping upstairs and into the sitting room overlooking the road towards her own house.

Fergus looked at his watch and Beech said hurriedly, 'If you're busy or have another appointment, I can go away again.'

'I was just checking to see whether it was coffee time or whether it was near enough to lunch to be able to offer you a drink.'

'And which is it?'

'Late enough. Would you like some wine? I have a shiraz open, or otherwise we could look through my inadequate collection and see if there's something you'd like better.'

'I've got a house guest. A time-consuming and emotionally demanding house guest. So yes, I'd love a glass of your shiraz.'

Fergus's goblets were satisfactorily large. Beech took two big mouthfuls and closed her eyes. 'Mmm. I don't often drink more than a single glass of wine, so it has a wonderful, instantly intoxicating effect on me,' she said hazily.

'Really? I must try offering you wine more often. Now, tell me what's up.'

'The house guest. Invited into my house by Rita to stay for ever, it seems to me.'

'I believe I've heard about her.'

'You have? Where?'

'There was some lurid gossip being exchanged in the post office while I waited for my new road fund licence. Some old biddy with a mouth like a rat-trap was telling of an exotic foreign visitor with a purple Lurex suitcase and wearing a short, tight lime-green costume. "Costume" was the word she used, by the way. I haven't heard it since my father's Aunt Elspeth died. She was bartering this information for fascinating tales of adultery among the staff of the local junior school. I'm afraid that my tax disc was prepared much too quickly and I had no excuse to stay to hear the end of the story.'

'The suitcase wasn't Lurex, just purple,' said Beech. 'And the costume was emerald rather than lime.'

'And the voice was loud, vulgar and foreign, apparently, and she engaged in much laughter and *kissing*.'

'Everybody kisses these days,' said Beech. 'There's nothing odd about that. And she's only half-foreign, though I have to admit it is quite a noticeable half.'

'So you have an ordinary, dull visitor. What's all the fuss about? Who is this woman who's come to stay?'

'Valma Crabbe.'

'The knowing nude.'

'The very one. She has invited herself into my house – no, that's not quite fair, it was Rita who invited her into *my* house – and there she is staying. She has announced that she was my brother's lover (in the nicest and purest possible way) and that if things hadn't turned out so tragically, she would now be my sister-in-law.'

'And what does your mother say to that?'

'She is welcoming her into the bosom of the family as her long-lost daughter.'

'She already has one daughter.'

'Huh! My nose is severely out of joint.'

'Has this Valma been introduced to Henry yet?'

'That is a pleasure still in the future. She hasn't left my house since she first set foot in it. I have only just managed to escape her insistent questioning this morning.'

'Is there any evidence, as it were, that what she's saying is true?'

'She's turned up with letters, supposedly from my brother to her, and a single volume of her diary.'

'Have you looked at them?'

'Briefly. At first glance they seem genuine.'

'Maybe she's telling the truth.'

'No. I know parts of what she says aren't true, and the rest – I just don't believe it.'

'Why not?'

'Nicholas had better taste than that!'

'Never overestimate the taste of a seventeen-year-old. You've finished your wine, I see. Would you like another glass?'

'I'm quite drunk enough, thank you. I shall go and pick a fight with my mother now.'

'Have a glass of water first. Alcohol really does get to you, doesn't it?'

'Yes. Good, isn't it? I must do it more often.'

She left ten minutes later. Fergus, encouraged by her remark about the prevalence of kissing, said goodbye with a less-than-brotherly embrace.

12

'What on earth is wrong with you?' asked Rita, greeting Beech in the hall. 'If I didn't know you better, Beatrice, I would say that you were drunk.'

'Me? Good Lord, no!' said Beech, taking great care with her enunciation. 'You know how dreary I am over alcohol. Head like a dandelion, as Jack always says. Now, how have you been getting on while I was out?'

'And that's another thing. Where have you been? Obviously further than the shops. You didn't tell me before you left.'

'No, I didn't. That's because I'm an adult, this is my house, and I'm not answerable to you for where I go and what I do.'

'You must have been drinking to speak to me in such a way!'

'I'm sorry if you're offended, but it's true. Now, I'll just have a wash, and then I'll get the lunch,' said Beech, and disappeared upstairs to splash cold water over her face. Fergus was right. Water was wonderful. Effective both inside and out. She drank another glass of the stuff and then went downstairs to face Rita and Valma. She found Rita in the sitting room.

'Where's Valma?'

'She's gone into Oxford for a little sightseeing, or so she says. What sights are there? I asked her. Just a few dreary old colleges and a couple of museums, not a decent shop left, but she insisted on going, goodness knows why. I'm just going to meet her at that new French place for lunch. Then I suppose we'll take a look at a dress shop or two – if there are still such things. You have the afternoon to yourself in which to recover from your overindulgence.'

The water gurgled from innumerable fountains in invisible courtyards behind high stucco walls. There must be water, for the green leaves grew huge as elephants' ears in the warm, moist air, and the faint plashing noises drifted over walls hung with scarlet bougainvillaea. But the water was invisible, hidden behind high walls, splashing into stone fountains behind wrought-iron gates. Birds sang.

And on three sides of the town the sea stretched in turquoise and cobalt, flickering with silver, hissing against the rocks of the harbour, drumming against the sand of the bay, leaving its petrified ripples in the wet sand of low tide.

Did I really write this? mused Beech, leafing through one of her old notebooks. I don't think I'll include it in the anniversary book, not without simplifying it a little, anyway. Didn't I ever write about more personal things? She flipped through a few more pages.

The thought of reading through old diaries had been an enticing one to begin with. And there was the hope that she would find out whatever the secret was that lay in her past, but the reality was less interesting. She must have kept them all these years with the thought that one day she would read them. Surely any diary was written in part at least for posterity? Always, she felt, there had been someone leaning over her shoulder and nodding with approval as she found the right word. Too many of the right words, she felt now, but that was adolescence for you.

She wondered what Fergus was doing. With this unexpectedly free afternoon, she could steal an hour or two away to see him. Twice in one day? Perhaps he wouldn't wish to see her so often. But then, there had been the unaccustomed warmth in their leave-taking. She went to make herself a bowl of salad instead.

Valma and Rita arrived home half an hour after the shops closed, and laden with carrier bags.

'I see you managed to find Oxford's cultural sites,' said Beech.

'What?'

'Nothing. Shall I make tea? Or pour you both a long, cold drink?'

'Cranberry juice!' said Rita. 'It is so very reviving both to the mind and the body.'

'Cranberry juice?' queried Valma.

'So full of vitamins and minerals,' said Rita. 'I would add a little liquidized carrot to it for the beta carotene, if I were you. You must let me work out a regimen for you, dear. What exercise routine do you follow?'

A look of unease passed across Valma's face.

'Pour us out the juice, Beatrice,' said Rita.

'For you as well, Valma?'

'Lovely,' said Valma faintly, so that Beech wondered whether she wouldn't like a large slug of gin in hers. 'I'll just go upstairs and hang up my purchases. I wouldn't want them to get creased.' Perhaps she kept a bottle handy in her bedside drawer.

'I should do the same,' said Rita, picking up black and gold carriers.

Beech went to find ice, wrapped it in a clean tea towel and bashed it with a hammer. She placed the crushed ice in tall glasses and poured on the cranberry juice that she always kept ready for her mother's visits. The meat for their dinner was marinating in the fridge and she had already prepared the vegetables. She could relax – with a glass of white wine, perhaps? – in the sitting room for the next half-hour.

'Drinking again, Beatrice?' asked Rita, taking her glass of cranberry juice and sipping delicately.

'Yes, that's right. You should try it some time.'

'Here I am!' trilled Valma, re-entering the room, breathing gin fumes over Beech, and taking her glass of juice with a happy smile.

I was right, thought Beech, she has a secret gin supply in her room. And who can blame her? She knows she's not really Arrie, and she must know that I do, too. But why on earth is Rita taken in by her?

Next morning after breakfast, Beech was glad to find her mother alone. She had had enough for the moment of Valma's cloying sister act.

'Why?' she demanded. 'Why are you doing this?'

'Doing what, dear?'

'You know perfectly well what. Valma Crabbe used to be the grocer's daughter. You invited her into our house under sufferance. You wouldn't dream of entertaining her parents. And now, suddenly, she's one of the family.'

'You are being very unkind, Beatrice. Valma has had a sad, sad life, without any of your advantages. And yet, if Nicholas had lived, she would have been one of us.'

'I don't believe it. And I can't believe that you do either.'

'You're being quite unreasonable, and I refuse to discuss it any further. Perhaps we could get on with the memoir. It will never be finished the way you've been going on. Now, I have some letters here.'

'What letters?' asked Beech.

'The ones that came in response to my advertisements. Please concentrate, Beatrice – if, of course, you don't object to my suggesting such a thing.'

'I'm concentrating,' said Beech, acidly. 'Now, please tell me about the letters.'

'They're from all sorts of people. Friends of ours, of mine and Henry's. Probably people you didn't know.'

'Try me.'

'I don't understand what's got into you, Beatrice. You never used to be like this. And it's no good glaring at me like a sulky five-year-old.'

Years of training in respect for her parents battled with a feeling that her mother was turning into a monster. 'I'm sorry if I was rude,' she said with an effort. 'I apologize for that. But I am not a child any more and you must allow me to have my own feelings and my own opinions.'

Rita looked outraged, but Beech ignored her. 'Now, may I see the letters?' she asked.

Rita gave a long-suffering sigh. 'There's this one from Mena deLyle. Such lovely thick writing paper, and an address in Knightsbridge. Old Mrs deLyle died in the eighties, of course, and Conrad inherited the family business. Or all of them, I should say. They had interests all over the world. Very well connected.'

'Conrad? The name seems familiar.'

'Mrs deLyle's son. Her husband – Vincent I believe he was called – left her in charge when he knew he was dying and she bullied poor Conrad and his wife when she took over. Well, this letter is from Mena, and Mena is Conrad's wife, though how she managed to stay married to him through the years with her mother-in-law, and then all the talk about his, well, mistresses, I just don't know.'

Vaguely, Beech saw a tall, well-built man in very careful casual clothes. His wife – Mena, presumably – a beautiful woman in expensive French dresses. They treated everyone politely and formally, but she remembered little else.

'What does she say?'

'I have them here for you. You can read them and make extracts to include in the memoir. Mena's is all about the annual picnic that Mrs deLyle presided over. Do you remember? Up at the Rainbow Pool. Everyone scrambled for invitations. It was the social event of the summer. Of course, *we* were always invited.'

'And Valma?'

'I'm afraid that Mrs deLyle was a snob. Valma's father's grocery business was not at all like the great trading empire of the deLyles. She was invited just the once, and without her parents, naturally. No one could invite that mother of hers. Of course, once they knew about Nicholas and Valma, I'm sure the girl would have been acceptable anywhere. Here, take the letter.'

'Thank you. What was wrong with Valma's mother?'

'Nobody knew where she came from. There were stories that he picked her up in a brothel in Alexandria.'

'Really? She always looked so strait-laced to me.'

'Well, she'd have to be, wouldn't she, with a background like that. And I've heard from the Barrs,' continued Rita. 'They've retired to somewhere in South Africa – how odd, but I suppose it's because of the servant problem – but Simon, that rather plain son of theirs, is living in England and is sure to have some memories of Nicholas.'

'Simon? How awful.'

'Didn't you like him?'

'Just an irrational adolescent hatred, I expect. I remember him as having quite horrific acne and large, hot hands.'

'Do try to be more mature, Beatrice dear. Now, there's a letter here from the Cottinghams. Birdie encloses some old photographs. She wants them back, so you will be careful with them, won't you? Oh, look at the strange hat she's wearing. What on earth is that budgerigar doing perched on the brim? And here's one of Henry, looking distinguished.'

Looking like a stuffed shirt, thought Beech. I don't believe he was often as dull as that. And what large pink gins they're all holding. Everybody smoking, of course, some with cigarette holders. That dates them.

As though prompted by the photograph, Rita took out a packet of her menthol cigarettes and lit one.

'And here, there's rather a muddled letter from someone called Bérénice. Why on earth does she need all those accents on her name?'

'I think she's French.'

'Not *real* French. Not for a couple of generations, anyway. And a dreadful chichi accent. But she's married to some man called Serge, and she says she remembers the last picnic up at the Rainbow Pool. Serge is in the diplomatic service, and is stationed in London. I wonder which diplomatic service that would be? Not ours, certainly, though it is full of all sorts of riffraff these days from what one can tell. Still, diplomatic is usually all right. You must write back to her, Beatrice.'

'What did you say their name was again?'

'Something impossible. Baalbecki, is it? Copy it down from the letter. Do try to keep up, Beatrice.'

'And what about our aunts and uncles? Surely some of them ought to remember Nicholas. They might even have photographs of him.'

'We can't rely on any of them. And they're all old and gaga by now.'

Beech persevered. 'Aunt Laura and Cousin Catherine.'

'Are they still alive? I doubt it.'

'Yes. We exchange Christmas cards. They were very kind to me when I came to school in England. Don't you remember? They had me to stay for the holidays.' *Whenever you couldn't be bothered to have me at home.*

'Very dull people as I remember. But contact them if you must.'

'I wonder, Rita,' Beech said slowly, wondering how to get

through to what her mother really thought. 'Are you absolutely sure about Valma and Nicholas? Do you really think she's the girl he would have chosen?'

'What are you suggesting? That she's lying about their friendship? I'm sure if the nuns taught Valerie Crabbe one thing it was how to tell the truth.'

'As long as you're happy about it,' said Beech.

' "Nico and Arrie", ' said a voice behind her. 'We were in love, and you would have been my sister, Beatrice, if things had been different.'

'If you say so, Valma,' said Beech. Dear Valma had always been on the make, even as a child. She gathered up the heap of letters. 'I'll find a folder for these. We don't want to lose any of them.' And she left the room.

A few minutes later she returned, wearing her coat. 'I'm going out now,' she said.

'Why? Where are you going? We haven't nearly finished here.'

'Why don't you ask Valma to give you a hand? I'm sure she'd love to be involved.'

'But I want to know where you're going.'

'Just out. I have a few chores to do.'

'I don't believe you. I believe you have a man friend. How could you, Beatrice?'

'Goodbye, Rita.'

'Come back here, Beatrice! I want to know what you think you're doing!'

'I'll be back in time to make everyone's dinner.'

'Is this our coffee break?' asked Fergus as she pushed open the door of his sitting room and plumped herself down in a chair.

'Yes.' Then after a few seconds, 'Please.'

'The one good thing about the arrival of Valma Crabbe in your life is that I'm seeing a lot more of you,' said Fergus, when he brought in the coffee. 'Though I miss the lunches at your house. My visits must have electrified the curtain-twitchers.' He set the mugs down on the table, making a new set of milky rings.

'Cabbages,' said Beech, picking up her mug.

'This one is a cauliflower,' said Fergus. 'And I have spinach, carrots and radishes in the kitchen cabinet.'

'Do you collect strange pottery?'

'My mother did.'

'Is she still alive?' Beech felt oddly shy at asking a personal question.

'No, she died five or six years ago.'

'I'm sorry. She can't have been very old.'

'Probably not. But I hadn't seen her since I was about seventeen. I don't think she was very interested in children.'

'I'm sorry,' Beech repeated, feeling it was inadequate but unable to think of anything better.

'Now, let's get back to tales of your past life.'

'The diaries. And Valma.'

'Does her diary look like the others?'

'Yes. An ordinary quarto exercise book with a pale blue cover. It was the year for writing diaries. We thought it was romantic, and that our adolescent feelings would prove fascinating to future generations. Valma's is full of her most glutinous thoughts.'

'My goodness! You really don't like this woman.' Fergus buried his face in his cauliflower mug. Beech hoped that he wasn't using it to hide his amusement.

'She is quite poisonous.'

'Now, is there any reason for your dislike – distrust? – of Valma Crabbe, or is it a simple case of jealousy?'

Beech finished drinking her coffee and then said, 'It's more than just jealousy, I think. It's that I don't trust the woman. She was a calculating little bitch when she was a child, and such a

111

meek, demure little thing, and I don't believe she's changed for the better.'

'Are you trying to say that the letters are a forgery?'

'They're addressed to someone called Arrie, and signed "Nico". Valma is saying that these were the names they called one another. She has given no explanation for why she was known as Arrie, but children do give each other funny names, after all. The letters look genuine, from what I remember of my brother's writing. But I know *she* wasn't Arrie, and I believe that she's . . . fabricated the envelopes.'

'How do you know she wasn't Arrie?' asked Fergus.

'I know who Arrie was, and it wasn't Valma. If he'd been serious about her, I'd have known. He told me things like that.'

'Maybe this time it was too serious to tell.'

'Perhaps. But I don't believe it. *I would have known*. And anyway, if you'd seen Valerie Crabbe you'd know that no normal boy would have been serious about her when she was fifteen.'

'So she's making things up. But is it important? If it's giving pleasure to your mother and Valma, does it really matter?'

'It's smothering the past with yet another layer of falsehood. I want to know what really happened, and the truth is slipping further away.'

'You're very insistent about that. You always talk as though people have been hiding the truth from you on purpose.'

Beech stood up and paced around the room, peering at pictures, picking up small objects and putting them down again absentmindedly.

'That one's rather nice, rather valuable actually,' said Fergus mildly, as Beech picked up a plain green bowl and looked as though she was about to toss it on to the floor. 'Sit down again and I'll tell you what I think you can do.'

Beech obeyed. 'It's a bugger, isn't it? What do you suggest?'

'You have the notebooks that your mother found, the ones that belonged to Nicholas. You have your own notebooks, you told me. Now you have this notebook of Valma's. You have the letters that Rita found in Nicholas's room, and the ones that Valma claims he sent to her. Well, read them all. Start another notebook, writing down everything you can remember about that time. Make notes. Put them together. Compare and contrast. See what emerges.'

'Not a bad idea,' said Beech. 'I've really been putting off reading through all the material too carefully. And if I do it in a spirit of research, I could actually enjoy it. Thank you, Fergus.' She crossed the room, took his face in both hands, and kissed him on the mouth. He responded in a most satisfactory way.

'Do you really have to go now?' he asked, as she disengaged herself, plucked her jacket from the arm of the chair and strode towards the door.

'Oh yes. I do think I should get straight on with it.'

'I thought you'd like to stay for a little longer.'

'What about your work schedule and your deadline?'

'Perhaps I'd better return to my computer screen.'

They smiled at one another without either of them finding the courage to say what was on both their minds.

'Goodbye then,' said Fergus.

'Goodbye.' She hesitated, and then she said, 'I think Jack really is having an affair. Do you think I should be more upset than this?'

'I think you should break free and enjoy yourself.'

'Have an affair myself, do you think?'

'If that's what you want to do.'

'Mm. I'll think about it. You don't think I've left it too late?'

'Definitely not.'

'Good.'

And instead of walking home, Beech took the bus into Oxford and bought herself a large quantity of new underwear, some of it silk, all of it expensive.

* * *

This was a good idea, thought Beech, unpacking her shopping, folding unfamiliar, strange-shaped garments and slipping them underneath the pile of her usual white cotton Marks and Spencer bras and pants.

When she had finished, she thought, Fergus is right. I'll look through all the notebooks in detail, compare them with everything I remember and then I bet *I'll find that Valma's lying*.

I'll start with my own diaries, just to remind myself what I was doing and thinking that summer.

13

We live in an old part of the town, up on a hill with views of the sea on three sides and the mountains on the fourth. Our house is ancient compared with the white concrete blocks that are going up in the newer, smarter parts of town, and was probably built some time in the last century. It is square, with a flat roof, and painted an earthy, ochre yellow. Our balcony overlooks a courtyard belonging to the house next door, full of lush, large-leaved plants. Perhaps I have seen some of them before, in Europe, but here they have grown to gigantic proportions and are unrecognizable. Out of this vegetation sprouts a tall palm, its bark marked like a pineapple and its head shaped like a feather duster. My bedroom looks down into this courtyard, and I can hear the constant sound of water from the fountain which plays, invisibly, at its heart.

'Bloody noise!' my father shouts when he is in a bad mood, which seems to happen quite often, especially in the mornings. 'Why can't they shut the bloody thing off? Can't hear myself think with that bloody noise going on all the time.'

My mother has impressed on him that he must not use bad language in front of his daughter, but he has settled for this one swearword, 'bloody', which he uses whenever I am at home. Sometimes, in the evening, when he returns from some party or other, and the whisky he has drunk makes him forget, he uses these other words, loudly, until my mother shushes him for fear of what the neighbours will think. I suppose they have forgotten that I am there, listening from my room above the balcony, and they do not know that these words, aggressive and abusive, even when spoken in such educated accents, upset me.

'Bloody girl!' my father would bellow if he knew. 'What sort of world is she living in? Time she found out what life's all about.'

And after the late night and the heavy drinking, next morning he would be in one of his bad moods.

But the fountain continues to play its soothing tune, and in the background, on the other side of the mud walls that protect both the garden and our house from the world beyond, I can hear the constant blaring of car horns and the shouts of people in the street, the tinny sound of music competing from a dozen open doorways. Odd, that: the only contribution by the West to the music of our background is the car horn. No Beethoven nor Wagner, no Beach Boys nor Beatles, just this monotonous, cacophonous, intermittent noise. There it goes again. There must be a traffic jam down at the cross-roads by the Greek church and the melon stall. Traffic jams in this part of the town are usually due to a couple of bad-tempered donkeys and a taxi full of shouting passengers. The taxi-drivers rely on their car horns and the swinging statuette of the Virgin dangling from the driving mirror to get them out of the impasse. The donkeys care for neither klaxons nor religious images and make for the watermelons.

But I was describing our house. It is three storeys high, as I said, with a balcony round three sides of the ground floor and the top floor smaller than the other two, sitting up like a square pillbox. The living room runs almost from the front of the building to the back, with just a small entrance lobby where you will be met by one of the servants. On the ground floor too there is my father's study, and my mother's sitting room – or workroom, or writing room, or whatever she is calling it this week – and the dining room, and the room where the cases of whisky and gin are kept, and various rooms at the back where I have never ventured, but which belong to the servants.

On the floor above are our bedrooms: mine, Nicholas's, my parents', the two guest bedrooms, and all their attendant bathrooms. On the second floor are the servants' bedrooms.

The balcony below my room looks out to the sea. It is down there that we spend most of our time during the summer, Nicholas and I. We swim, we take out our boat. The water is our element. Halfway across the bay, where the shadow from the hills falls on the water, the sea changes abruptly from a clear turquoise, so transparent that you can see the creatures that play on its bed, the weed that sways in its currents, the warm sea that I swim in and sail over, suddenly, as I say, abruptly, it changes to a dark cobalt, so that the seabed is shadowed, and the water feels cold against my trailing hand. The line is both sudden and visible, as though at that point we pass over a boundary separating one country from another, or one state of being from another. From happiness to tragedy. From content to fear. A state of grace to a state of sin. Who knows? But as we sail over that boundary a shadow marks my skin, a breath of cold breeze flickers down my back. Then the sail fills, the breeze tugs at the main sheet, and the sea hisses against the hull as it thuds through the miniature ripples of our peaceful bay.

'Put about,' calls Nick. 'Let's get back into the sun.'

Nick. My brother, Nicholas.

He is home from England for the summer holidays. In September he will return to England and leave my world a little colder, a little less sunny.

In the brilliant sun, you can't see the details of our faces. The light flattens out features, leaves only the arch of eyebrows, the gleam of teeth in a smile, the outline of an ear. Only when we pass into the hill's shadow can you see any detail. Then you see that Nick's eyes are English blue, his hair mixed strands of silver and yellow. Our skins have darkened to honey colour.

That summer I saw the sheen of hair on his upper lip for the first time. It was odd, that. I had thought of Nick just as my brother, forever a child like me, but now I saw that he was moving into that other world where men and women were separate, different, impenetrably difficult to understand. Already Nick was assuming that he had the right to boss me around, that I would automatically obey what he said, since he was boy, near-man, and I was only a child, a girl. Nick was crossing over a boundary as defined as the one painted on the floor of sea. But was he passing from the sunlight into the shadow or the other way round? And where did that leave me?

I wish we had taken more photographs. There should have been more. There were photographs taken by real photographers, of course, and a few taken by our parents. But these had the carefully arranged faces that children put on for approval by adults and were nothing like Nick's face that I remembered when we were out on our own. That was the summer I first had a camera of my own. Something simple, where you just pointed the lens at the object and pushed a red button. But still, with the motion of the boat, and my own overeagerness to catch the magic of the moment, the pictures were blurred, or partial, and I could never recapture the clarity of my memories.

Mostly I left sailing the boat to Nick. I liked to dangle my hand in the water, feel its tug against my fingers. I would bend down low and stare into the water. When we reached the dark line I liked to imagine all the life that swarmed under the surface. In the sunlight you could see everything, there was no room for imagination, but in the dark, you could people the water with unimaginable animals. They could have horns and teeth; they could have long, sinuous bodies, or a dozen waving limbs with suckers for feet. They could be blind, or they could sing me loud siren songs. Sometimes I went home and drew patterns of their scales on sheets of paper. I wished that I could have gold and silver paint so that I could reproduce properly the pictures in my head, but in those days I had only the coloured crayons that I had been given for Christmas, and they produced only dim reflections of the brilliance that lived behind my eyes and in my imagination.

'Your trouble is that you have too much imagination,' Nick would say.

'And what's wrong with that?'

'You'll never be satisfied with what you can have. And that means you'll never be happy.'

'That's not fair!' I cried, for I knew even then that he was right.

'Never mind! We're crossing the frontier again,' he cried, as we sailed over the line on the seabed. 'On the other side we can be whatever we want. You can keep all your fantasies here. We can choose. It's up to us.'

And I believed him.

The adult Beech thought, Yes, that's just how it was. I remember it now. She turned to another page.

This afternoon I drew pictures of Henry. I can call him that here in this notebook. I don't want to call him Father or Daddy, because that isn't what he is, not really. Not like fathers in the books I read.

I have drawn him the way he would want to be seen, not the way he seems to me when I look at him. In my pictures he is sitting in a chair, reading a book, dressed in old, soft tweed. An old-fashioned English country gentleman. But that isn't the way he really is. That isn't the way I have him fixed in my memory. I will draw him again, as he actually is, but only when I am sure that no one will see the drawing. Then I will destroy it, so that no one ever knows.

The first drawings are there in the diary, smiling at her in a lazy, friendly way. Did she ever complete the others? If she did, there is nothing of them left.

She remembered hot nights, sweaty afternoons, the sun that lay in red-hot bars across the bed, and the cruel sound of Henry's laughter from the balcony below.

'I don't know how you ever produced a daughter like that, Rita! Do you think she'll ever improve?'

'All she wants to do is bury her nose in some book. Or else she's wasting her time with her drawings. She'll ruin her eyesight. And her looks. Have you seen the awful round shoulders she's getting?'

'Maybe they'll disguise her height!'

'She claims she's serious about the drawing.'

'I've seen some of them. Quite clever, in a superficial kind of way. Of course she hasn't got real talent and I've told her, without a real talent there's no point in going into Art.'

'A nice secretarial course, perhaps one of those cookery schools, and then we can pray for a suitable man.'

'She's much too tall, of course, but she could *try*.'

Too tall for what? Beech wanted to shout. And what should I try to do? Or be? What's so wrong with being *me*? I would try hard to be small and pretty, but I don't think I'd succeed.

'I expect we'll find some dim Third Secretary for her, or maybe one of those dull little men from the Levant Bank.' They both laughed. 'We'll be landed with her for life, otherwise!'

Why don't they lower their voices, or move to a different

part of the house? Don't they know that I'm lying in bed,
listening to every word. Or don't they care? She pulled the
sheet up to her ears and thought about closing her window. But
then she would suffocate in the hot, humid night air. And they
might hear her, and she would feel ashamed to think that they
had found her out in eavesdropping.

Through the sheet, she heard the two people on the balcony
laughing again. At least they were in a good mood. She didn't
have to feel afraid tonight.

This afternoon I heard him come home. We had already
finished our lunch and the servants had cleared away the
dishes. He must have been down at the club, or maybe
meeting his friends in the English bar, swallowing down the
gin and tonic as though it were lemonade. 'You have to keep
drinking in this climate,' they would tell each other. 'You get
dehydrated otherwise.'

As soon as I heard his key in the lock, that faint scrabbling
sound that meant he was having trouble fitting it in properly,
I knew it would be a bad afternoon. The bell rang,
impatiently, He shouted, swearing at the servants because
they didn't respond fast enough. I heard Munira shuffling
unwillingly through the hall towards the front door, and then
the click of the bolt as it opened. His anger preceded him
into the house like a wild animal. It stalked ahead of him,
looking for its prey.

The words in the notebook ended there, but Beech could
remember what happened next, or if not that precise occasion,
then one of the many.

'You can go!' he shouted at Munira. 'Get back to the kitchen
and make sure that lazy woman gets my lunch.'

Munira's backless sandals slip-slopped back towards the
servants' quarters, moving much faster now, as though she was

afraid she would be caught and mauled by the wild beast of his anger.

'Not straight away, mind. Give me ten minutes.' The ten minutes was so that he could pour himself another drink, Beech knew, and she held her breath so that he wouldn't hear her.

Henry's footsteps, heavy and slightly irregular, moved towards the drawing room and the drinks cabinet. Beech heard the gurgle of whisky into a glass, the clink of ice. He added no water or soda. She was sitting at a table on the balcony, at the shaded end, next to a pot of flowering hibiscus. She had been drawing, and now she turned the paper face down, and tried to hide it with her arm. If she stayed very still and very quiet, she might escape his notice.

He came out on to the balcony, walked over to the shaded part, which at least gave the impression of being cool. He cleared his throat, the sound reminding her again of an animal, and lit a cigarette. As he sat down and swallowed half the tumbler of whisky, he noticed that she was sitting there.

'What the hell are you doing, lurking there like a thief? Can't you even say "Hello"? Hasn't that school of yours taught you any manners?'

Where was Rita? Why wasn't she here? No, she was out, playing cards with her women friends, drinking down the gin and gossip at someone else's house, or in the St Maroun Hotel. No need to worry about dear Beatrice. The servants would keep an eye on her. And it was time the girl learned to be more self-reliant, anyway. She couldn't expect her mother to be fussing round her all the time, mollycoddling her.

'Well? What have you got to say for yourself, skulking around the house, mumbling to yourself? Why don't you ever have a little fun?'

The big predatory cat had padded across the black and white tiles of the hall. It had stalked through the rooms of the house until it chose its prey, and now it was ready to pounce.

'Such a solemn little thing it is!'

She was never sure whether it was better to stay silent or to try to speak. She knew that rational conversation was impossible, but perhaps she could assert herself just a little.

'I *was* enjoying myself. I was drawing.'

'Don't try to be clever with me. I don't like children who answer back.'

Beech closed her lips so that no more words would escape, and stared down at the table.

'Well, and what have you been drawing? Why can't I see this great work of art?'

'It's private.'

But Henry had seen the drawing block underneath her arm, and he pinched her elbow painfully between his thumb and index finger until she released it and he could drag it out and open it.

'Let's have a look.' His words were slurred now, his eyes bloodshot. She saw the effort he was making to focus on her drawing.

'Well now, this isn't so bad.'

It was the picture she had drawn of Henry, looking the way he saw himself. The perfect English gentleman, with reserved expression, fair hair brushed back from his high forehead, dark eyebrows lifted as though laughing at himself, dark eyes looking straight at the observer.

'So this is how my little girl sees me, is it?' His voice had taken on a sentimental note.

No, it isn't! It's the way you see yourself.

'Quite a clever little thing, really, aren't you? Though not so little, unfortunately. Maybe they'll have you in the police force if you go on growing like that.' A heavy arm dropped across her shoulders, like a bar across a door, preventing her from leaving. 'And you'll have to stop showing off just how clever you are. Nobody likes that.' Whisky breath was in her nose and mouth. His face was so close it was out of focus, red and blurred, with the full lips parted, and a fleck of spittle gleaming on the lower one.

Let me go!

His hand was clamped on her upper arm, his voice murmuring into her ear. She felt hot and suffocated and involuntarily she struggled to free herself. His arm tightened. She was pressed close to his damp shirt. His teeth bit playfully into the bare skin of her neck. She wanted to scream, but she knew that if she did so, something unimaginable and horrible would happen.

'Your lunch is ready in the dining room, sir.' It was the quiet voice of Amani. She stood three or four feet behind Henry's chair, as though staying out of his hitting distance. He turned round to snarl at her, then thought better of it.

'I suppose you've eaten ridiculously early as usual?' he asked Beech. It was now ten to three.

'Yes.'

'Then I'd better have mine. I have a meeting at four.' He turned back to Amani, who was still standing passively behind his chair. 'Hurry up, woman! I haven't got all day!'

A few seconds later, Beech was left on her own again. She pulled the drawing of Henry out of her book and tore it across and across until the pieces were smaller than postage stamps.

'I'll clear that up,' said Amani. She could walk as quietly as a cat in her sandals when she wanted to. 'You want come with us this afternoon? We going down to souk, buy food for dinner party tonight.'

'Yes, please,' said Beech.

She knew the servants felt sorry for her, and asked her to share their extended family life on the kitchen balcony and down in the market to try to make up to her for her own lack.

They didn't understand the way she was treated by her parents, for their own small children were spoiled rotten and never allowed to cry. She envied them, runny noses, fly-ridden eyes, poverty and all.

What had happened to change Henry from that loud, over-bearing man to the shadow who worried about his compost bins? And what had happened to the girl who wanted to learn to draw and paint? Surely *that* Beech wouldn't have settled for marriage to Jack, and a life hiding in an ugly north Oxford house?

They were all gone now: that Henry, Nicholas, Beech. Only Rita seemed to have remained much as she was.

Beech read on.

And then in October the water fell out of the sky, suddenly, violently in thick glassy rods, stabbing at my skin, drenching my hair, bouncing off the ground to splash knee-high. And to disappear as quickly, leaving the sky washed bright blue and the town smelling clean, free of the smells of dead dogs and sewage that had grown so familiar that I no longer noticed their existence, only their absence.

And the noise. The sound of music that issued from every open door – and as I walked down the street to school, every door stood open, framing a chair with a seated figure, and a child or two playing in the dust. The voice of Fayrūz singing of unhappy love, of doomed passion, wailed over the top of taxi klaxons, the shouts, the drumbeats of the street dancers, the loud voices, the call of the muezzin.

I'm going to paint a picture of what I saw today.

She had the picture still: the clouds, massed on the horizon in angry coils of grey, lean down on the pewter sea. The mountains and the narrow coastal strip are blocked in navy blue, the buildings picked out in silver. On the sea, a third of the way up from the base, and to the right of the picture, she had placed a small sailing boat, its hull white, its sail a red teardrop against the metallic sea. Even now, when she looked at it, she could feel the oppressive heat reflecting down from the clouds, the hot, dusty wind blowing grit into her eyes. Blowing the boat, like a grain of sand, on to the rocks in the right-hand bottom corner. She painted the picture all those years ago, when the memory was still fresh in her mind, when she could look out of the window and see that view, those waves, that mountain, like the grey pelt of a sleeping animal, lying just beyond the coast road.

She kept the pictures in a drawer in her bedroom. The early ones were faded, dog-eared, with pieces of dark-coloured Sellotape attached to the corners. Then, as the years went by, her pictures gained colour, and assurance and technique. But none of them outdid the early efforts in passion.

14

'I'm not sure I'm enjoying my visits to the past,' said Beech. 'I'd forgotten just how uncomfortable the place was.'

'It's where the source is to be found.'

'Oh come off it, Fergus!'

'No, I mean it. You have to look at the roots of your emotions, your feelings. And that's where they are: back in your childhood.'

'That's ridiculous! And so trite.'

'Did you know that when you try to tell a lie that your cheeks go pink. There's a round spot of scarlet just here,' he touched her cheekbone so that it flared red again, 'and so I know that you are not speaking the truth. Perhaps you have never practised enough, like the rest of us, to let the lies slip past your lips and fall unregarded on the air.'

'Perhaps it is just that you are embarrassing me,' she said.

'Perhaps it is that there is something you have managed to forget and that you do not wish to speak about.'

'I prefer to live in the present.'

'Do you? I haven't seen you doing much living since I've known you. When did you last do anything that wasn't prompted by Rita, or Henry, or Jack?'

'Or Valma,' added Beech. 'It's just that I'm very busy at present. And I can't live a completely selfish life, can I?'

Fergus still looked unconvinced. 'I don't see why not. They all do, don't they?'

'But I don't see that this digging about in childhood is doing any good.'

'Why don't you paint any more? Why did you give up?'

'Perhaps I once had talent, and now it has gone.'

'Talent doesn't come and go like that.'

'The enthusiasm, the belief in the future, all those can die and leave you cold and dead.'

What had made her say that? She really hadn't intended giving so much of herself away. Fergus was looking at her, waiting for her to continue.

'You know I'm right, don't you?' he said eventually. 'I'm not asking you to tell me all your secrets, but why don't you go home and read some more of those notebooks? I'm sorry if they make you feel uncomfortable, but perhaps that's necessary.'

'If it doesn't hurt, it isn't doing you good?'

'If it hurts, you're probably in the right area.'

There was no escaping from the past. How often had she heard that said and thought what a cliché it was. But now she could see that it was one of those aphorisms that held more than a small gobbet of truth. She would have to travel back and look again, and let her mind argue with the stories that Henry and Rita had invented for themselves. Here was an opportunity to get beyond the invention and find the truth at last.

'Do you know yet when Valma will be leaving?'

'No one's mentioned a day. I don't know what's wrong with them. You'd think she had some hold over Rita.'

'Perhaps she has.'

There was a small room beyond Beech's kitchen, probably once a scullery, used now to store tins of tomatoes and bottles of spring water. Beech had piled up the boxes more neatly, moved the spring water to the kitchen cupboard, and swept out the cobwebs from the corners. It wasn't much more than a cubbyhole, but there was room for a small table (discarded years before by Alice), and an upright kitchen chair. Beech pushed a new light bulb into the wall-fitting, found a lampshade that was better than the naked bulb, and persuaded the window to open a few inches.

'My office,' she said aloud.

She brought the materials for Nicholas's book into her new office in a red plastic box and placed them next to the table. She wished that the door had a lock with a key that she could remove, but at least there was a bolt, which should deter people from walking in and removing things.

She thought for a moment of sticking a notice on the door: 'PRIVATE, KEEP OUT, THIS MEANS YOU, DANGER DE MORT!' But why draw attention to herself?

In here, when she had escaped from her family and Valma, she spread drawings and notebooks out and looked through them, from time to time making notes in a new, black, spiral-bound book that looked nothing like the blue ones from Crabbe's Provisions.

She had started with a rough chronology, putting the books in order, so that they made some sort of sense when she read them.

'How good you are, Beatrice dear,' said a soft voice from the open doorway. Valma had picked up a faint Essex whine in her years in that county, noticed Beech. It persisted in spite of the careful enunciation and formal nature of her usual speech. 'Working away at these diaries every day. Wouldn't you like me to help you?'

'Really, no,' said Beech. 'They're private. Family things, you see.'

'But I am part of your family now,' said Valma.

Beech turned round so that she could see her properly. 'Only by invitation. Not by right,' she said.

Valma lifted a plump hand and patted her carefully combed hair. 'When you have read through these,' and she gestured at the papers in the red plastic box, 'I think you will find that there is something missing. You will be seeking an explanation, I believe. Then, you must come and see me. I will tell you where to find the rest of the story.'

'You mean that you have diaries of your own?'

'I have. And the things that I saw that I still remember.'

'How odd that you've kept them all these years, in spite of your travels.'

'When you leave the place of your childhood, you need to hold on to things, like diaries, which will bring it back to you in every detail.'

'Your diaries must be better written than mine!'

'The nuns were very particular about our written style. We were encouraged to write well.'

'In English or in French?' asked Beech.

Valma hesitated for a moment.

'Or perhaps you wrote in Arabic?'

Valma laughed. 'I was never very good at that language. No, I wrote in French at school, for my mother, you might say, and in English at home, for my father.'

'So your diaries are in English?'

'Why are you so sceptical? Don't you believe me?'

'Frankly, no.'

'You were such an innocent little thing. I believe there were many things which you saw but did not understand. This is true of all children, of course, but most of us look at these events, later, and reinterpret what we saw. Did you do that?'

'No,' said Beech. 'I didn't need to.'

Valma smiled at her, as one might smile at a sulky child, and then she left, her heels clicking on the tiled kitchen floor as she disappeared from view.

Beech turned back to her work. She would put the unspeakable Valma out of her mind. She picked up another blue notebook. Black marks marching down the white pages of the notebook. The ink had faded to a very dark brown. Like dried blood, she thought. Perhaps everything reverted to that dark brown colour in the end. This is one that I wrote, she thought, picking it up. And this other one was written by Nick.

I am crossing the boundary. There is a boundary that one crosses when travelling from west to east, from England to the Levant. I am not sure precisely where it is, but it separates the cold grey countries from the hot bright ones. It divides those who speak in measured tones, using their words like sharp-bladed knives, from those who hurl them around like rocks. It separates white bodies encased in stiff, buttoned clothes, from warm golden ones which are open to the sun and air.

Over there, everything is defined and predestined. Over here, everything is open, everything is possible.

How odd, she thought. I saw everything quite the other way round. She picked up one of her own notebooks and looked for a half-remembered passage.

The balcony faced west. I stood leaning against the railings, watching the sun go down. They say that just at the moment when the last sliver of sun dips into the sea, there should be a green flash. I have watched, but I've never seen it. That evening the sun was enormous and scarlet, wavering like a strawberry jelly sitting on a pewter plate. The sky was amethyst with purple streaks of cloud, the sea growing darker as the light left the sky, but still glowing with a scarlet, flickering pathway leading from the sun towards me, standing on my balcony.

I went back into the drawing room, my head still full of the magic of the sunset. The smell of frangipani followed me indoors and Rita looked up from her magazine. She twitched her upper lip, stared at me for a moment and frowned.

'You need to wear a bra,' she said.

Why do I feel in the wrong? I really don't understand it. Is it my fault that I'm growing?

'And why are you wearing that awful blouse? Why is it so small?'

I know there are these lumps appearing on my chest, I can feel my blouse is tight under the armholes. I've left the top two buttons undone to reduce some of the strain. It's an Aertex blouse, old now, once yellow but bleached and faded to a greyish cream colour. It's hard and scratchy with many washings, but I'm used to it, and anyway I have nothing else clean in my cupboard.

'We'll go out and get you one tomorrow morning,' said Rita crossly.

The way she says it, it sounds as though she is going to buy a new set of bars for my prison window, a new set of manacles for my wrists.

I remember the shopping expedition next morning, thought Beech.

They left the flat at ten o'clock. Rita was already in a bad temper.

'Why can't I have the car?' Beech heard her ask on the telephone. 'What do you mean, he's busy? Isn't it his job to drive us around when we need it?' There was a short, sharp reply from the other end of the line and Rita drew the receiver away from her ear, as if scorched, scowled at it and placed it back on its rest with a loud bang.

'Haven't you got anything else to wear?'

'Not really.'

'I don't know what you do with your clothes!'

Beech wasn't sure what she did wrong: she wore her clothes,

she put them out for the maid to wash when they were dirty, and then every year she grew a little. It seemed to her that other children did the same, but somehow they were entitled to, while she wasn't.

Rita was dressed in cream linen, and her hair was newly set. She stopped in the hall and smiled at herself in front of the mirror. She pushed a curl into place, pulled out a tube of dark red lipstick and reapplied a gelid layer to her lips. She had pencilled in her eyebrows with a dark brown pencil so that her expression appeared stern and permanently surprised, like a prison officer who has just been told that one of the inmates has escaped over the wall.

The mirror was tall and narrow and consequently flattering. Rita appeared even slimmer than she really was, and her rather ordinary nose acquired a patrician thin beakiness. Her hair was newly tinted to a rosy-gold colour and she pushed her scarlet-tipped fingers with their flashing diamond rings up into its luxuriant folds. She took out a tortoiseshell comb, drew it through the side of her hair and pushed it back in at a more flattering angle. She picked up her neat little Swiss straw hat and set it carefully atop the golden tresses. Then she turned her face sideways, pursed her lips and looked upwards so that her eyelashes once more curled up on to her eyelids. She frowned.

'Don't do that!'

'What's wrong? What mustn't I do?'

'Come up behind me like that,' said Rita. 'My nerves are all on edge. You know how I suffer from my nerves, Beatrice.'

'So why mustn't I stand behind you? Surely it's better than pushing myself in front?'

'Stop being clever with me!'

What she meant was that she didn't want to see Beatrice's face and hair, unexpectedly, like that in the mirror, just behind her own. Beech's hair darkened later to a hazel brown, but at that age she had golden blonde hair, slightly wavy and nearly to her shoulders. It caught the light from the window and framed her face in an aureole of spun silver. The effect was heightened by the string of looking-glass beads that she wore round her neck, reflecting the light back a hundred times more brightly than did the diamond rings that Rita wore.

I forget what we bought, thought Beech. I know the blouse and skirt would be uncomfortable and unflattering, and the bra felt like a medieval torture, stifling and restraining me so that I no longer had the freedom to be what I wanted. She wriggled her shoulders. As a matter of fact, she still preferred to go braless. It was much more comfortable. And even today, if she did, Rita would be horrified.

15

This evening Henry came home early. I heard his ring at the bell, Amani's footsteps, his voice, his shoes on the tiled floor as he came through into the long sitting room. I sat very still until I could be sure what sort of mood he was in. He saw me sitting at the table by the doors on to the balcony.

'Where's Rita?' he asked.

'I don't think she expected you home this early,' I answered.

'I'd still like to know where she is.' His voice, which until now had been quite normal, almost pleasant, was acquiring a serrated edge.

'She went down to the St Maroun Hotel. She was meeting one of her friends, I think.'

'Who?'

'Birdie Cottingham,' I improvised.

'Who?'

'Mrs Cottingham. Birdie.'

'The woman with the greying hair and a face like an anaemic mule?'

'Mrs Cottingham,' I repeated idiotically.

'I can't believe Rita would want to meet her. What are they doing?'

'Playing bridge,' I invented wildly.

'Really?' He wandered past me and stood on the balcony looking down through the town and towards the sea. He lit a cigarette and smoked it in silence for a few minutes, then he turned suddenly, as though he had made up his mind about something, and came back and stared at me.

'Have you something better to wear?'

'My blue Swiss cotton with the white dots,' I said.

'Put it on. And hurry, please, Beatrice.'

I went upstairs and changed into the blue dress. It was very light, with a matching pale blue slip. I wore white sandals, cleaned that morning by Amani, and bare legs. I combed my hair and went back downstairs. Henry had changed his shirt, but wore the same linen suit as before.

'I suppose you'll do,' he said, looking me over in a way that made me feel self-conscious and hotter than ever. He fussed with my collar, made me turn around, pulled the belt a little tighter. 'Come on.'

'Where are we going?'

'The St Maroun Hotel, of course.'

Of course.

Henry had a way of entering a room that was unobtrusive to the point of invisibility. This was odd when Beech thought of his usual habit of filling their house with his presence and controlling everyone just by being there. On this occasion he made Beech walk behind him, shielded by his tall, broad form, so that she too was unnoticed by the people in the hotel bar.

They went into the opulent, air-conditioned room that was the meeting place for a certain set in the town. Tourists, even if they dared to enter and were rich enough to pay its prices, would be seated on the terrace, in the sun, where they would contend with sunburn and insolent waiters who told them that there were no seats available indoors. They would eventually give up and try somewhere livelier. Journalists used the noisier, less classy Cricketers, which tried hard to be an English pub, situated further round the bay. The young went to the Poseidon

Beach where they could show off their oiled brown bodies and designer shorts to the accompaniment of the latest French pop music. But the Manet Room at the St Maroun was the place where one would expect to find Rita Markland. (There were in fact at least two genuine Manets hanging on the walls there, along with a Braque and a couple of early O'Keeffe abstracts, bought by an art-loving proprietor when prices of such things were still affordable.)

'There she is,' said Henry. 'But I don't see the Cottingham woman.'

The light in the Manet Room was filtered through grey-blue blinds, a welcome dimness after the brilliance outside. Tables were placed in alcoves, two or three comfortable chairs at each. The room was cool enough for the chairs to be upholstered, and for there to be cushions, and rugs on the blue and green tiled floor.

There were one or two groups of half a dozen or so people, but most of the places were taken by low-murmuring couples. With the discreet arrangement of tables and alcoves, it wasn't easy to see both members of the pair, and now Beech could pick out Rita, but she couldn't identify her companion. Henry was right: whoever it was, was male.

Beech wanted to leave. She felt out of place in the dim, cool, sophisticated air of the lounge. Her starched blue cotton skirt and childish sandals were incongruous among the linen suits and silk dresses. The last thing she wanted to do was follow Henry across the wide expanse of Persian rugs to confront her mother.

'Come on!' ordered Henry, and she found herself compelled to trail after him.

Rita had just removed her gold compact from her handbag and was dabbing at her face with the pink powder puff, all her attention on her reflection in the oval mirror. For a moment she didn't notice that Henry and Beech had joined her.

'Hello, Rita. I didn't expect to find you here.' You'd hardly think he was lying.

'Whyever not? Everyone knows that I come here on Wednesday afternoons.' She finished working with the powder puff and put the compact back in her bag.

'Are you going to introduce us?'

'If you like. This is Billy Echevin. Billy, this is my husband, Henry.' Then she saw Beech, still hovering behind her father, not knowing where to put herself. 'Oh! What on earth is that child doing here?'

'I thought it time that she was introduced to more adult company and ways of behaving. She won't be a child much longer.'

A waiter appeared with two more chairs. Beech and Henry were seated and their order for drinks taken.

'Olive?' Billy pushed the bowl across to Beech.

'I'm sure that Beatrice will be as bored with the conversation here as she is at home,' said Rita. 'She would much prefer to have her nose buried in a book.'

'What are you reading at the moment?' asked Billy kindly. The other two seemed perfectly capable of carrying on their fight – for that was what it was, Beech recognized – without the help of outsiders.

'*Les Liaisons Dangereuses*,' said Beech, who was working her way through her parents' bookshelves without any guidance from them as to what she might enjoy.

'An excellent choice,' said Henry. 'It will be most useful to you when you try to make sense of what you are seeing here in the Manet Room.'

'Stop trying to be so clever,' said Rita, then recollected that she was being observed by someone outside the family. She opened her handbag again and took out her cigarettes.

She should get out the mirror as well, thought Beech. She always watches herself, whatever she is doing. She knows exactly what she is doing now. First, she removes the flat silver case from her handbag, flips it open with one finger, extracts a cigarette, fails to offer one to either of the men, closes the case in one snapping movement, taps the cigarette on the case, applies it to her lips, where it is in danger of drowning in the thick ruby lipstick. She pauses and looks first at Billy and then at Henry. Henry ignores her, but Billy quickly brings out a gold lighter and flicks it under her cigarette. Rita sneers at Henry. Henry still ignores her. Rita draws in breath in three short puffs, then inhales deeply as though the smoke contains life-giving oxygen.

Rita was then able to lower her lids and gaze at Billy through her eyelashes. Billy could only look uncomfortable, put his lighter away and try to think of something else to say to Beech. Rita leaned back in her chair, crossed one leg over the other with a sensuous, swishing noise, and blew the smoke out at the ceiling.

Disgusting, thought Beech. I shall never do that when I'm old. By 'old' she meant twenty. By 'that' she meant the whole bundle: the lipstick, the slim silk skirt, the lace-edged petticoat, the styled hair, the layer of make-up, the cigarette and the way her mother seemed designed to be a mantrap, and nothing more. What, wondered Beech, did she possibly want to do with the men when she caught them in her trap? They all looked unbearably middle-aged and boring to her. They never read books – Billy had never even heard of Laclos – or went to interesting films at the cinema or had anything original to say.

'Isn't it hot?' said Billy, mopping his pink face with a blue-bordered handkerchief.

'Yes. Wonderful,' said my mother. 'I just *love* the heat. I don't feel it one little bit.'

'I don't think it's hot in here. It's the air-conditioning that keeps it cool,' said Beech, realizing too late that no one was interested in what she had to say.

Rita was smiling at the besotted Billy. He lumbered to his feet and went to order her a fresh gin and tonic. Rita, meanwhile, stretched out her slim ankles and admired the line of her new soft kid shoes.

'Thank you, sweetie,' she said, when he returned. 'And after this little drinkie I suppose we'd better go home, don't you think, or we'll be late for dinner.'

They did leave, as a family, just ten or fifteen minutes later. To Rita's irritation, she was made to sit in front with the driver, while Beech and Henry sat in awkward intimacy on the back seat. As they proceeded in silence all the way home, Beech wondered why she had been dragged along. When the driver drew up in front of the house, her father leaned across to open the door. She felt his breath, lightly scented with whisky, and sensed that he was smiling at her.

'Good girl,' said Henry, patting her knee.

I was there as a witness, she decided later. She was supposed to see what her mother was up to, and take her father's side. And then again, they had been play-acting for the audience in the Manet Room. The whole thing was a performance. Mrs Markland, having drinks with a friend, was joined by her husband and daughter. No fight, no row, no scandal.

Just the usual lies.

It was funny how you looked at something that happened so long ago and saw it in a different way. Beech hated to agree with Valma, but maybe it was true. Were there many other scenes that she could look at now and understand differently? Did she see more clearly things that had been hidden then?

Beech felt again the uncomfortable heat of the car, and smelled Henry's whisky breath. She closed the notebook and pushed it back into the red box.

* * *

140

'I'm not even sure they are memories,' she said to Fergus later. 'Perhaps it's my imagination. Perhaps I'm inventing it. An excuse to explain why I haven't made anything of my life, why I seem to be trapped in my meaningless existence.'

'Is it?'

'What?'

'Meaningless.'

'Most of it is. All of it, except the time I spend here.'

Fergus didn't say anything for a minute or two. Then he said, 'You were going to read the other notebooks. Compare and contrast, remember?'

'And how can I be sure that they tell the truth, any more than my own?'

'You can't. But I think you will recognize the truth when you see it.'

'Maybe. Maybe I was brought up to recognize nothing but lies.'

'Have a glass of wine.'

'No, thanks. I'll stick to coffee. I need a clear mind.'

'Where have you been?'

'Out.'

Rita's kimono was a dramatic emerald green today, with ultramarine embroidery, matching her eye shadow.

'I don't like the way you speak to me, Beatrice. I don't know where you've learned such manners.'

'What have you and Valma been doing today?'

'Valma has been back to London to collect a few more of her things. She went by train this time.'

Beech raised her eyebrows.

'Yes, well, I gave her the train fare. I gather that it really is very uncomfortable on the coach and not at all what she is used to.'

'And what have you been doing?'

Rita sighed. 'Nothing very much.'

'You sound bored.'

'Well, I can't imagine where on earth you've been. We could have had a lovely morning together, just the two of us, if you hadn't disappeared off like that.'

'Sorry, Mother.'

'Oh, and there was a phone call for you from Alice.'

'What did she want?' Please, please, don't let her come to visit while these two are staying.

'Just to tell you that she's all right. She says she's sharing a place with someone called Francesca. I'm so glad that she appears to have given up those awful boyfriends of hers. This Francesca sounds a delightful person. I'm so glad that Alice has found a nice friend at last. Is she Italian, do you think? Do we know her?'

Francesca had looked and sounded Oxfordshire to Beech. 'I suppose she might be Italian,' she said. 'And we don't know her, not in the way you mean.' Rita meant that she and Beech should know Francesca's people. 'Is that all she said?'

'I told her about Valma coming to stay and how we were getting on with the book about Nicholas. She was very interested, very positive about all my ideas. Much more so than you, I have to say, Beatrice.'

'I'm glad you and she get on so well.'

She thought about telling Rita about the baby and the precise nature of Alice's relationship with Francesca, but she couldn't think how to begin. Evidently Alice hadn't either. And watching Rita's animated face, Beech didn't want to disillusion her.

16

Beech knew it was unfair of her to believe that Valma's thirty-year-old diary would be dull. Why should it be any more boring than her own or Nicholas's? She picked it out of the box and opened it. She might as well start at the beginning.

I love going to the Greek Catholic church. It is a low, white-washed building, with rounded, Byzantine towers, humpy arches and a dark interior, thick with the smell of incense and the gleam of gold on the walls. I know it is the same Mass that I am accustomed to, but in an older language than our medieval Latin, and some of it secret, hidden from the view of the participants. And the priest, with his thick black whiskers, sprouting from all over his face, even from his nostrils, so that only the gleam of his white teeth is visible and his pursed scarlet lips, blessing us, talking to us and to God in the gloom that smells of garlic, of olive oil and of sweat. His long black robes whisper expensively as he moves, as though under the plain black stuff are layers of hidden silk or taffeta. Perhaps they are coloured gold or scarlet, or patterned with exotic birds and flowers. Anything is possible in that mysterious building.

It did give a different perspective on Valerie Crabbe. She had always seemed such a goody-goody child, completely under her mother's thumb. She wore the convent uniform, with its navy dress and white lace collar in winter, the cream tunic and white blouse in the summer. On Sundays she was to be seen in her white frock, white socks and sandals, white leather gloves, the left one worn, the right one carried, and her cream straw hat: the perfect young girl walking to church. In her hand a black leather missal. Beech had imagined that she spent the next hour and a half on her knees, praying, mother-of-pearl rosary gripped in her plump fingers. And all the time she had been wondering what the priest wore underneath his cassock!

But then, she hadn't known Valerie very well. It was only that final summer that she seemed to come into their circle at all. She just appeared one afternoon for tea, invited by Rita.

'Why?' she asked Fergus, as they sat on his sofa later that morning.

'Didn't your mother often invite friends over for you?'

'No. And she only invited people at all if she was sure that Henry wouldn't be there. He could be unpredictable. You never knew when he might take against someone.'

'It's hard to square that view of Henry with your descriptions of him now.'

'He has changed. Completely, it seems sometimes. At others, it all seems to fit in.'

'Is there any hint in the diary of why Rita invited her?'

'No. And you don't realize how unusual it was. We talk glibly of our class-ridden society now, but it's nothing to the way we thought and lived back then, in that place. Valerie used to help in the shop in the holidays, wearing an overall, slicing imported English cheese. It wouldn't have occurred to Rita to invite her to our house. She wouldn't invite her out of the goodness of her heart. She would hardly be aware of her existence.'

'So someone or something must have forced her to do it. Could Mr Crabbe the grocer have blackmailed her into it?'

'She had things in her life she would prefer not to have broadcast, certainly. But one hint that Crabbe was a blackmailer would have emptied his shop of customers.'

'So it must have been down to Henry.'

'Why should Henry want to invite Valerie to tea?'

'Was he there that afternoon?'

'As a matter of fact, he was. That's odd too.'

She remembered that it was early in the summer, before the English schools broke up and sent their exiled children back into the sun for the holidays. Certainly it was before Nicholas came home that last time.

'Why don't you ring Henry and ask him? The poor old boy's been on his own for long enough, hasn't he?'

'I should ring him. You're right.'

'Do it from here.'

Beech followed Fergus into the kitchen, where apparently he kept his only phone. She looked around her: this was the first time she had been in his kitchen.

'Here you are,' said Fergus. 'Do you want me to leave you on your own?'

'No. Please stay.'

'I'll make us some more coffee. Are you hungry? Would you like something to eat?'

'No, really. Coffee would be lovely.' She dialled.

'Henry Markland,' said the voice on the other end of the line.

'It's Beatrice,' said Beech.

'Beech. How nice to hear from you. Are you all well?'

Beech went through the polite exchanges about the health of all the family, and then said: 'I've been reading through old diaries, Henry.' She didn't bother to explain that not all the diaries were hers. 'And there's one odd thing I hoped you could explain.'

'If I can. If I can remember. My memory's not what it was.'

'Valerie Crabbe, the grocer's daughter.'

'Cunning little minx,' said Henry.

'We agree over that. But can you remember why Rita invited her to tea at the house? We'd never said more than "Good morning. I'll have a pound of the best Cheddar," before that. It seems such an odd thing for her to do.'

There was a silence at the other end of the line.

'Are you still there?'

'Yes. I remember the occasion, certainly. Rita was at her most charming and the Crabbe girl was on her best behaviour. But I can't help you over the reason.'

After another series of polite enquiries, Beech hung up.

'No joy?' asked Fergus, handing her a mug of coffee. (Mugs in the shape of red pillar-boxes today, Beech noted.)

'No. But I think he *did* remember it quite well. He just didn't want to tell me about it.'

In Rose Cottage, Henry Markland replaced the telephone receiver and went back to his seat in his office. When he re-entered the room the smell hit him anew. He had grown accustomed to it over the hours he had been working there.

Gunter. The poor old thing couldn't help it, but the smell was quite disgusting. Was it time to have the old dog put down? Gunter looked up at him and thumped his tail on the floor, dislodging dust and hairs to float in the air and bring on an attack of wheezing in Henry. No, Gunter had some good months left in him. The dog must go on living, at least for the present.

Henry returned to his log book. He hadn't been keeping it up to date for the past month or two and now he was trying to catch up. His mind had been in a bit of a muddle, as though his thoughts were trying to reach him through a heavy cloud of static. He'd been allowing old memories and old concerns to fill his head. Like the Crabbe girl. Why had Beatrice asked about her? It was long ago and best forgotten. Bury it. Feed it to the brandling worms. Turn it into crumbly brown soil that could be used to raise a new generation of plants.

Henry started to write.

This morning I went to visit the compost bins and in the corner furthest from the door I found a spider. This wasn't an ordinary spider, but the largest I have ever seen, with a body the size of a ping pong ball, but yellowish-brown. Filemot. She – for I'm sure it was a female – looked big enough to trap and suck out the goodness not just from a fly or a moth, but from a fieldmouse or a shrew.

The Crabbe girl. What was her name? Something incongruous for such an ordinary family. Valerie Maria. That was it. I should never have introduced her into my family, I can see that now. But she came in useful. And I thought at the time it was the best way.

'Dear Beech,' said Valma, coming into her office, hitching one round buttock on the corner of the table, 'I do hope you aren't finding my presence a nuisance.'

'Do you mean your presence in this room, or your continuing stay in my house?'

'Why are you being so sharp for such a generally kind person?'

'I just wished for information.'

'I think we both know that I shall stay for as long as it pleases me to do so.'

'Do we? Why?'

'Because we both know who Arrie is.'

'I know, certainly. But do you?'

'Oh yes. And we know too that she wasn't the love of Nico's short life.'

'How can you be so sure?'

'Because I know who was, and so do you.'

And Beech had to look away, because she wasn't sure that she could follow her memories that far.

'You've all lived a life of pretence, haven't you? Rita believes in it, Henry has escaped from it, but you're left in confusion in the middle, wondering what is true and what isn't.'

'And you believe that you know the truth.'

'Oh yes. But as long as no one upsets me, I won't tell.'

Beech stared at her. 'And what would be so terrible if the truth were revealed?'

'Poor dear Henry,' sighed Valma. 'I remember him as such a strong, *virile* man. But now, with his mind in so precarious a state, it would be terrible, would it not, if he were pushed over the edge? If he were made to emerge from his potting shed, or wherever it is he spends his days, and confront the realities of the past.'

'I'm sure he would be able to deal with it,' said Beech, not entirely sure that she believed what she was saying.

'And if he couldn't? What then? Can you see dear Rita giving up her lovely social life to look after a man whose mind had turned to potato soup?'

'Don't talk about them like that!'

'But you are the one who wished to expose the truth, not I.'

'It wouldn't be like that,' said Beech.

'But are you willing to take such a risk?'

Valma's dark eyes sparkled with malice. She reminded Beech of one of the crows she had seen on the roof. Valma's head tilted to one side, her beaklike nose jutting in profile. No, thought Beech. Not a crow, but a vulture.

This is a good day, thought Henry. I should write down as much as possible, before the clouds start massing on the horizon once more and the hills are hidden behind the mist and rain.

I'll start at the beginning, with the meeting in the pub.

He began to describe how, thirty years ago, he had left his

office and walked down through the city, but then his attention wandered to thoughts of his brandling worms, and he left his desk to search for vegetable leaves to take to them.

17

Henry left his office at half-past eleven and strolled out into the oven heat of the morning. He did not want to take a car or a driver. He would, in any case have to leave the vehicle far enough from his destination to make a five-minute walk necessary. And the sight of his driver, sitting idly smoking in the front seat while he conducted his own business would draw attention to his presence in the vicinity. He preferred to go unnoticed, an unremarkable man going about his dull affairs.

So Henry went on foot, a tall, broad, patrician figure in a silver-grey linen suit, his pale hair clinging damply to his scalp. His skin had the yellowish tinge of someone who has lived long in hot climates, who does not go out to seek the sun, but who has acquired this slight, permanent tan. The air moved against his hands and face like warm oil. He moved slowly, but even so within a few minutes the sweat had started to trickle down his back and his shirt felt damp and uncomfortable under the waistband of his trousers. When he got back to the office he would shower in his private bathroom and change into the spare set of clothes that he kept hanging in the cupboard there. He kept clean underwear in his small fridge, along with boiled water and a couple of bottles of vodka. His skin ached for cool, dry poplin.

He paused at the corner of the square and looked around him. He was wearing sunglasses, not for disguise or affectation, but because the sunlight bouncing off the white concrete was bright enough to hurt his eyes. Not a figure of speech, this, but a real, sharp pain as the metallic rays entered his pupils. A small child with matchstick limbs tugged at his jacket and demanded alms. Someone tried to sell him a lottery ticket. These were such usual sights that he hardly noticed as he shook his head and brushed them away.

Henry stepped off the kerb and crossed to the other corner without varying his pace. Grey dust coated his lightweight black shoes and dulled their mirror shine. He continued at the same leisurely tempo down a narrow side street, making towards the sea. Along the broad street overlooking the bay were fashionable cafés and expensive restaurants, but Henry stopped before he got there and turned under a white arch, through a dark wooden door, and entered the building. The sign hanging above the arch read Cricketers Bar.

'A small whisky, please, Joss,' said Henry.

Joss raised his eyebrows. 'Small? That's not like you.' His accent might have been Australian originally, or even South London, but Joss had been behind the bar of the Cricketers for as long as anyone could remember.

'Small,' repeated Henry, who had no intention of dulling his mind this early in the day. One whisky would sharpen his wits, get rid of the liverish feeling that dogged him these days. He took a seat at a table where he had a view of the door.

'Here you are, Henry,' said the barman. 'Shall I put it on your tab?'

'Yes. Thank you, Joss,' said Henry.

'How's the construction business?' asked Joss.

'Buoyant.'

'I hear the government is planning to expand the university buildings again.'

'Really?' But Henry did not encourage the other to linger for conversation. He picked a newspaper from the table in the centre of the room and sat in his shadowy seat, reading last Tuesday's *Times*.

There were already four or five people sitting on the high stools, and drinking the first of their lunchtime gins and tonic, or whisky. Journalists most of them, thought Henry, noting the pink faces, puffy eyes and damp, creased shirts. There were always journalists at the bar, whatever time you came in. This town was a collecting point, a crossroads, where gossip was exchanged. The professional gossips met here in the Cricketers and swapped stories. Some of these stories would be elaborated on, written up and sent off to weighty daily newspapers back in London, and the gossip would be called news. Others would be written up and sent back to government departments, and then they would be called intelligence. Gossip, all of it, thought Henry.

The Cricketers was air conditioned to a temperature that was slightly lower than comfort would require. Henry's damp shirt was suddenly clammy under his jacket, and as the sweat cooled on his skin, he shivered slightly. Bloody air conditioning! The chances were that he would catch a chill when he came out of this place.

There was a movement by the door, a burst of loud voices, and a group of four or five men came in. Oil company, thought Henry. Ignorant louts. And he returned his attention to his *Times*.

The temperature, the lack of windows, and the low level of lighting combined to produce the atmosphere of an English pub. All it needed, thought Henry, was a blazing log fire in the corner. If the crackpot idea occurred to Joss or Nan Denney, they would probably install one immediately, he thought sourly. *And* a jukebox against the wall. Their whole lives seemed dedicated to creating an English corner in this city, to keeping out all evidence that they might be more than a dozen miles from some Kentish village green.

He glanced up casually from his newspaper and looked around at the customers. No, he hadn't missed anyone interesting.

The pub – Joss and Nan described it as a tavern – was large and had been divided into three sections by wooden screens, stained dark and varnished to resemble oak. The bar too was of some dark polished wood, and all around the walls were hung cricketing memorabilia: bats, stumps and bails, many of them autographed by long-forgotten county cricketers. Shelves held old, dog-eared copies of Wisden. Glass cases were packed with scuffed red leather balls, with letters from famous people inviting others, less famous, to play for some team of literary men or long-forgotten political figures. Pottery figurines stood on every flat surface, all of them dressed in flannels and wearing county or national caps. Framed prints hung on the walls, commemorating past glorious matches.

Behind the bar, Joss Denney stood and drank a large whisky of his own. Even at this early hour his face was starting to acquire the red glow that showed that he was getting drunk. The next stage of his intoxication, unfortunately, was to get quarrelsome and start picking fights with the customers. The fights were usually verbal, but had been known to degenerate into the physical. One or two of the drinkers at the bar were starting to drift back to the tables where they studiously read the newspapers provided by the Denneys and pretended not to notice Joss's bulbous eyes and lowered head. In another quarter of an hour or so Nan Denney would appear, probably wearing a scarlet satin blouse, and chalk up the day's specials on the blackboard, and all the drinkers could pretend that they had come in for their lunch.

The odd thing was, thought Henry, as the tables started to fill, that the place was not patronized exclusively, or even mainly, by the British. There were a couple of French pipeline workers in one corner. A South American diplomat, who looked as though he had never sweated into his pristine white shirt in his life, sat at another table, drinking something long and cold. The only thing the drinkers had in common was the fact that

they were middle-aged. The young would be showing themselves off in one of the cafés on the front, or flexing golden
muscles in one of the clubs on the beach.

'Here!' growled Joss, tired of trying to catch the eye of one
of the journalists and start an argument. '*You*'re not one of
those pinkoes, are you, Henry?'

'I'm sorry,' said Henry, who had heard quite well what Joss
was saying. 'What was that you said?'

'Pinkoes,' said Joss. 'The country's full of the traitors.'

Henry might have provoked Joss by asking him politely
which country he was talking about, but at this moment Nan
appeared from the door behind the bar, resplendent in glossy
scarlet, and smiled all round at the customers. There was an
audible sigh, as people rustled their newspapers and acknowl-
edged that they were, after all, present. The English were not
the only ones to pretend that nasty things weren't really
happening, thought Henry, watching them. Then, as Nan turned
to write up the day's menu on the blackboard, he saw that
someone was entering the pub through the door opposite.

The man was, necessarily, at a disadvantage as he entered
from the brilliant sunlight outside into the cool, dim interior of
the pub, and Henry had a chance to assess him before making
his own presence known. It was Irving Watts, a bore, but
still worth having as a companion and a shield against Joss
Denney. Henry raised his folded newspaper and caught Irving's
attention.

'Hello, Henry. This isn't your usual watering-place, is it?'

'I like to come down here occasionally,' said Henry. 'Nan
cooks a decent lunch, don't you think?'

'And Joss serves a decent whisky,' said Irving, raising a
hand to Joss, who presumably knew what Irving wanted to
drink.

Irving was a man who appeared simultaneously dried-up on
the inside and damp on the outside. His hair was mouse-

coloured, his skin pink from the sun, never deepening to a tan. He wore a floppy-brimmed white cotton sunhat in a style normally associated with four-year-olds, and did not remove it indoors. His mouth resembled a smallish prune, turned down at the corners.

'Well, Irving, how are things?' asked Henry.

'Things are going very well. Business is good, and then I do enjoy it when the young people arrive for the summer. Livens things up, don't you think?'

Henry agreed that it did, and then lifted his *Times* to indicate that the conversation was at an end. Irving took no notice.

'You and yours will be going to the picnic, I suppose,' he said.

'Yes.'

'Rita and those two fine children of yours. Beatrice, isn't it? Lovely girl, though a bit tall for my taste.'

Henry frowned and tried to concentrate on an article on interest rates. Irving leaned forward so that his face was near to Henry's. Henry was forced to look at the open pores on his nose, the spot on his chin, the patch of stubble which he had missed when he shaved that morning. Irving smiled at him.

'And then there's your son. Dear Nicholas.' He paused and waited for Henry to say something. Henry pretended that he was still reading.

'Must be a bit of a worry for you,' said Irving. 'But I suppose it will all come out all right in the end. I must say I'm glad I'm not a married man myself.'

Henry was about to ask what the hell he was talking about when the two were interrupted by someone who had just come into the pub.

The man was about forty, Henry supposed, of medium height and somewhat overweight. He had probably been strong and muscular in his youth, but he had softened over the years, and his face had the slightly baggy look of someone who drank too much beer. His hair was dark and thick, but rather long and badly cut, as though his wife, perhaps, took her dressmaking scissors to it and trimmed it back from his florid face. His eyebrows stretched in a straight line, hardly pausing at the indentation above his nose, so that his deep-set eyes were shadowed and his expression difficult to read. He neither greeted Irving nor smiled at him. Irving made an excuse and moved to a table on the other side of the room.

'Hello, Jaroslav,' said Henry.

'Hello, Henry,' said the other. He spoke fluent English, but with quite a heavy accent.

'Care to join me?' asked Henry. 'What are you drinking? The usual?'

He ordered a beer for Jaroslav and they sat and exchanged desultory chat for a few minutes, at a volume that could be heard by the other people in their section of the room. Once he was sure that no one was bothering to listen to their rather dull conversation, Henry said, 'Has anything come up over that business we were talking about the other day?'

'Yes,' said Jaroslav, shortly. 'Your people could be in luck.'

'Not really my people. I don't want to get involved. I'm just the messenger boy. Doing someone a favour, you might say.'

'I know that. But they'll have to be careful. He's being watched.'

'I suppose they all are,' said Henry.

'They must communicate through his daughter,' said Jaroslav. 'And I believe you can help them over that.'

'How?'

'She's at school with the Crabbe girl. It's time you ordered some more bacon.'

'So how's the newspaper business?' asked Henry in a marginally louder voice. 'Found any good scandals to flog to the tabloids recently?'

Jaroslav laughed. 'I leave that to you British. We Levantines

157

concentrate on finance and trade.' Jaroslav did indeed have a Levantine passport, but it was not the one he was using when he made his way out of Czechoslovakia some ten years previously. He was a good journalist though. A few minutes later he left Henry's table to join the pipeline employees on the other side of the room.

Henry ordered a chicken salad, and spoke to a few of the other men lunching at the Cricketers. He ate his meal, paid his bill and left the pub. It was no good going straight to Crabbe's shop: it would be closed for the next couple of hours, until the worst heat of the day was past. Perhaps he would wait until four thirty or so, when Valerie Crabbe would arrive home from school. Jaroslav hadn't mentioned the name of the man Henry was interested in. It hadn't been necessary and it might have caused one or two sets of ears to tune in to their conversation. But Henry knew who they were talking about. The subject had come up a couple of weeks previously, when Henry had been approached by a grey-haired man from the British Embassy at a reception at the Brazilian Embassy. Of course Henry helped out when he could. He was old-fashioned enough to believe it was his duty to his country.

18

'I was wondering whether you had a new shipment of bacon in?'

It was well known that Henry Markland was particularly fond of bacon. It was the one thing that he missed from England. He liked to inspect the whole side when it came in, and choose the best section. Then he would make sure that the bacon slicer was set just right: it needed to be cut thick enough to get a good flavour, but fine enough to fry into the crispy rashers that Henry preferred. He had trained the cook, as he had trained all their cooks in the past, in the correct method of frying bacon for his breakfast.

Stanley Crabbe himself, wearing his brown overall and white panama hat, came out to serve him.

'Would you like to come out to the cold room, sir?'

The cold room lay behind the dark-varnished, brass-handled door at the back of the shop. Mrs Crabbe's bright eyes followed them as they passed in front of the dais where she sat behind the till, but she didn't say anything. Was it really true that she had once been an exotic dancer? Hard to credit it now.

The first thing that struck Henry when they moved out of the shop was the heat. The shop was air conditioned. The corridor behind it was not. He tried not to think of food being carried through this moist heat, the bacteria multiplying as they travelled the distance from cold room to display shelves. He could see that the corridor ran into the family's own part of the building. He hadn't thought before of what Stanley Crabbe's family life might be like. He had seen Maria, his wife, of course, and heard the rumours of her origins. But he had never heard her speak more than the few words necessary to take his money for the goods he had bought. And then there was young Valerie. He had thought of her as the grocer's daughter, no more.

There was a burst of loud laughter and a high-pitched conversation from a room at the end of the corridor. He could hear a radio playing local music, that quarter-toned, wailing stuff that he could never understand.

'A nice child, your Valerie,' he said to Stanley Crabbe.

Stanley raised his eyebrows but said nothing. Henry had never shown any interest in him or his daughter before, so why should he do so now? Watch it, thought Henry, you don't want him to start wondering why. Perhaps he shouldn't have stopped off at the St Maroun after lunch at the Cricketers for a couple of large whiskies. In this heat it could dull a man's brain.

'My Beatrice is about the same age,' he said, as they stopped before the padded door of the cold room. 'It would be nice for the two of them if they became friends, don't you think?'

Stanley Crabbe didn't answer, but, opening the door, he said, 'I have had this brought over from Ireland. I think you'll find it rather special, Mr Markland.'

'Oh, very good,' he said, breathing in the smoky scent of it. The room was a cavern of gourmet delights that he would love to explore. The smoked salmon looked worth investigating, and weren't those poussins flown in from France?

'Look at the breadth of its back,' said Stanley Crabbe. 'That's what a bacon pig should look like, don't you think?'

'Absolutely,' said Henry. 'You can cut me off that section there,' and he indicated with a long index finger just which piece he wanted.

'Very good,' said Stanley Crabbe. 'And trust me to oversee the slicing of it in the machine. I shall do it myself.'

'Of course,' said Henry. 'And put me in a pound of that smoked salmon, will you?' He had probably doubled the week's grocery bill, he thought. Surely he had done enough to ensure that the grocer's girl would come to tea with his dull little Beatrice. 'Oh, and if you could put in another case of the Black Label at the same time . . .'

'It will all be delivered to your house tomorrow morning,' said Stanley Crabbe.

'And young Valerie will come to tea on Thursday, will she?' added Henry, as though ordering a pound of Crabbe's best sausages.

'If Mrs Markland would care to telephone Mrs Crabbe this evening, I'm sure that it can be arranged,' said Stanley Crabbe.

'Better include a case of Gordon's as well then,' said Henry without a smile.

'Thank you, sir,' said Stanley.

And there was not way of knowing what the bugger was really thinking, if indeed you cared to know what your grocer thought. Maybe he should pick up some flowers or something else, for Rita, before he went home, get her in the right mood to phone the Crabbe woman. And he'd have to have a word with young Beatrice too. She must be pleasant to Valerie, get her to feel welcome, whatever her true feelings in the matter might be.

'What do you mean, ask the Crabbe girl to tea?' asked Rita, her plucked eyebrows rising to greet her hairline. 'I don't believe that she's a friend of Beatrice's, is she?'

'I thought it might be nice for the two girls to get to know one another,' said Henry, searching for a better reason for Valerie Crabbe to come to his house.

'The grocer's daughter? I don't think so. I can't see what advantage there would be for Beatrice, do you?'

'Probably none,' agreed Henry. There was a pause, while he

poured whisky an inch deep into a tumbler and followed it with a brief spurt of soda. 'Drink for you, Rita?'

'Gin, please. With tonic. And get the girl to bring in some fresh ice.'

Henry rang the bell, gave the maid the instruction and then turned back to Rita. 'I am asking you to do this for me, Rita, as a favour. Please don't ask for details and reasons, and please, too, do your best to convince Beatrice that she should be friendly towards the Crabbe girl. I'm sure you can think of an excuse. You know the sort of thing that will appeal to Beatrice.'

They were interrupted at this point, as Henry knew they would be, by the maid returning with a Thermos bowl full of ice cubes. Henry added two of them to Rita's gin and tonic and handed her the glass. Rita swallowed fast, draining half the glassful, and her expression relaxed a little.

'Very well,' she said, but the tone of her voice told Henry that this favour would cost him dear next time he flew on a trip to Europe or America. 'Which afternoon would suit you?'

'Make it Thursday,' said Henry. 'I believe that the convent gives them Thursday afternoons off, and I'm sure Valerie would like a break from her studies.'

Rita walked across to the telephone, then paused. 'Have you the Crabbes' number? I certainly don't keep it in my book.'

Henry checked his pocket notebook and gave her the number. If he behaved in a meek and grateful manner he knew that Rita would come through for him. She might forget herself occasionally during the tea party and go off into her *grande dame* act, but then she would set herself to be utterly charming to the Crabbe girl, and would have her believing that she was quite wonderful. Rita's need to be loved and admired by everyone, including even the grocer's daughter, had come in useful to Henry on many occasions. As long as she never realized that she was being used in this way – and her vanity would normally prevent that – she would continue to entertain and charm all the people that Henry set before her.

'You are marvellous, darling,' he said warmly. 'Would you like us to try the new Provençal restaurant that's opened across the bay? How about this Saturday?'

'It's the Barrs' party,' she said regretfully. 'We really couldn't cut it, could we?'

He had seen the yellow silk dress, completed only yesterday by her dressmaker, hanging in her wardrobe. It was just right for those rather vulgar Barrs, but it would be too dressy for the new restaurant, with its gingham tablecloths. Rita smiled winsomely at him, tilting her head to one side.

'Yes, I wish we could give them a miss too. But no, we mustn't,' said Henry, noticing the effect she was aiming for, but ignoring it. 'But we'll go another time. Keep it in mind. You deserve a night out.'

She pouted, and since he didn't want her to lose her previous good humour, he added quickly, 'Perhaps you could pop down into town and look for some material for a new dress. You know I like you in black. Something with a high neck but cut down at the back. Leave enough room around the waist to allow for a generous meal.'

She smiled, and he knew she was imagining a new gold necklace against the crêpe silk. 'I'll ring the Crabbe woman now,' she said. 'What's her first name?'

'Maria.'

'Of course. I knew it was something foreign,' said Rita, and picked up the telephone, first composing her face into a mask of good humour and welcome.

Henry made a note in his diary to come back to the apartment at four thirty on Thursday afternoon. He would think of a reason for doing so before then. Women were easy enough to fool if you used a little imagination and played on their vanity.

'All fixed,' said Rita a few minutes later.

'Thanks, darling.'

'Are you eating out tomorrow evening?' she asked.

'I hadn't intended to. Why?'

'It's just that I'm meeting a couple of friends at the St Maroun in the afternoon and I wasn't sure what time I'd be getting back to the house.'

'I'll pop into the Cricketers for a bite to eat,' said Henry.

'Or I can get Munira to put something out for you. She'll have to serve a meal for Beatrice. Do you want to eat with her?'

'That will be at some ridiculously early hour,' said Henry. 'Don't worry. I'll give Hannes from the German consortium a ring and meet him for a meal. It's time the two of us got together.'

'Thank you so much, darling,' said Rita.

Henry knew now the price he was paying for the Crabbe girl's visit: Billy Echevin, or some other of Rita's hangers-on, would be able to spend an uninterrupted afternoon and evening with his wife. Well, the man had probably already spent many happy afternoons with Rita already, so where was the difference?

cerned that everything should be perfect for

ver let you down?' Rita was affronted. 'And
:s? Are they so very important?'
are,' he said. 'There's talk of a new university
ad would have a say in that. I wonder whether
with Munira whether the smoked salmon has
oussins. There should have been a delivery
e, but please do make sure.'
id Rita, who knew better than to question
nterest in the dinner arrangements, especially
ry well that her cook was at this very moment
young lamb in its marinade.
uld not allow such interference in her sphere
Valerie.
ly, Rita and I see eye to eye on such things,'
rice, my dear, I wonder whether you would
ar for me. I appear to have left my briefcase
lriver to find it for me. It is probably in the
on the back seat. Thank you so much.'
eft the room and walked through the hall
door, he heard Rita's staccato high heels, and
ould intercept their daughter and delay her
ng room for some minutes. Rita needed no
n it came to that sort of thing. She could pick
no trouble. It was one of the reasons they had
l marriage, in spite of the occasional Billy
He turned back to Valerie Crabbe.
e so many interesting pupils in a local school

mean by interesting?' She had left half her tea
t really that bad?
all different nationalities, of course. So many
ounds. So many cultures and religions.'

19

On Thursday afternoon Henry brought a cherry flan home with him. He had stopped in at the French *pâtisserie* in the avenue Blondel and chosen it himself: a cartwheel of a flan, with a thick layer of melting almond custard topped with glazed black cherries, and enclosed in a crisp, buttery pastry.

'Hello, Rita darling!' he cried as he came in through the door. 'Beatrice! Look what I've brought for you!' And then, as though only just remembering the tea party which he had arranged himself, he said, 'And Valerie! How nice to see you here.' He smiled, and then wondering if the effect weren't too wolfish, he toned it down a little.

He bent to kiss Rita's cheek, and then Beatrice's, aware that he had drunk only one small whisky at lunch. He shook Valerie's hand, noticing her dark, watchful eyes. Calculating, he thought. She's adding up the bill, just as she does in her father's shop. Probably always gets her sums right, that girl.

Valerie sat with her back straight and her ankles crossed. She wore a dress of dark green tartan, smocked across the chest, sashed at the waist, and with a lace-bordered white collar. Her hair was brushed and shining, her white socks were clean, her black lace-up shoes were polished. She looked like a nicely brought-up English child – except for her olive skin and dark eyes, and the mature shape under the little girl's dress.

It didn't look as though his entrance had interrupted anything. Indeed, they looked quite grateful for his appearance – and not only for his gift of a cherry flan. Rita had the fixed smile that meant that she had been trying for some time to make herself agreeable to someone in whom she had no interest whatsoever. And Beatrice looked both puzzled and sulky, as though she wondered why this other girl had been foisted on her for the afternoon. She was wearing a faded red-and-white checked dress, her hair was greasy and needed cutting, and she had a small crop of spots across her chin. Next to Valerie she looked a mess, and he found the sight of her irritated him. Why couldn't she make more of an effort? Rita, as usual, was coiffed and immaculately made up, and was wearing a smart navy coat and skirt with a white blouse. He heard the whisper of her nylon stockings as she uncrossed her legs and turned towards him. That was a sound that he always found exciting. When would Beatrice stop wearing socks, like a little girl, and start wearing nylons?

Beatrice looked up, startled, as Henry came into the apartment. You'd have thought he was never in a cheerful mood, never brought them home some little treat. He realized that the lines of his face had hardened and his jaw was pushing forward. Beatrice turned away from him and asked Valerie some inane question. He made an effort to smile again in an avuncular way.

The three were seated in the rather uncomfortable wicker armchairs around the small circular table and he drew up a fourth chair to join them. Of course upholstery was too hot and sticky in this climate, but a cushion or two would have been an improvement. But Rita had been unwilling to spend her afternoons embroidering or sewing. 'So suburban,' she had said. 'You'll be asking me to put up net curtains next!'

'I'll ring for tea,' said Rita, and went over to the bell.

When the servant had brought in the silver tray, and tea had been poured, and slices of flan passed round, Henry saw that Valerie lifted her cup to her lips and sipped with a knowing look on her face. Of course, she had probably been invited to

taste tea on many oc
would pass the Crab
Crabbe's Provisions
purchased the most
could see from her e
which of Crabbe's m

Henry worked har
going when it show
home feeling that s
welcome in this hous

'And do you do al

'Yes.'

'My goodness, how
speak Arabic as well.

'Of course. It is t
market.'

'And Turkish?'

'Yes.'

'I suppose your m
languages.'

'My mother is Malt
home.' Behind Valerie
two peaks of the dis
Valerie's hair was very

'Yes, of course she
isn't he? And do you

'Not really.'

'No, I suppose scho
Conversation pause
another subject. He tri
her face resolutely tur

'It is lovely to see y
Rita. 'But was there ar

'I'm sure you have

love, but I was co
this evening.'

'When have I
the Conrad deLy

'I believe they
contract, and Co
you would check
arrived. And the
by air from Fran

'Of course,'
Henry's unusual
since she knew
turning a joint o

'My mother w
of influence,' sa

'Really? Luc
said Henry. 'Be
pop down to th
behind. Ask th
boot, or perhap

As Beatrice
towards the fro
knew that she
return to the s
explanations w
up his hints wi
such a success
Echevin episod

'There must
in a city like t

'What do yo
in the cup. Wa

'Well, girls
different back

'We have all sorts. Some Europeans, even.'

He wasn't sure whether she was laughing at him. Those dark eyes of hers were impossible to read, and she guarded the expression around her mouth, and kept her hands politely folded in her lap. That was the sort of thing a girl learned at a convent, he supposed.

'Isn't the Bronek girl at your school?'

'She's in my class, yes.'

Again, he wasn't sure whether she understood the different meanings of the word 'class'. It was easiest if he took Miss Crabbe at face value.

'I've forgotten the girl's name,' he said apologetically.

She raised her eyebrows as though wondering that he should ever have known what it was. 'It's Jarmila,' she said.

'Of course,' said Henry heartily.

Outside in the hall he could hear voices. It sounded like Beatrice and Rita arguing. He didn't think that Beatrice was eager to return to this tea party, but he couldn't rely on her absence for much longer. He said quickly, 'I wonder whether you could deliver a note for me?'

Valerie Crabbe looked at him without replying.

'A note for my dear friend Bronek's daughter.'

'I could.'

'It would have to be our little secret,' he said.

'I imagine so,' said Valerie. 'After all, Jarmila's father is an attaché at an Eastern European embassy, and I imagine you, an ordinary English citizen, would not want it to be known that the two of you had been in contact.'

'It's nothing very serious,' said Henry. 'Just a social thing, you know.'

'Of course. Well, you had better give it to me before Mrs Markland and Beatrice come back into the room,' said Valerie.

And Henry handed over an ordinary-looking white envelope, although quite thick, as though stuffed with sheets of paper.

'There is no name on it,' she said.

'No,' said Henry. 'But you understand to whom you are to give it?'

'Oh yes,' said Valerie. 'I understand.'

Henry read on the girl's face as clearly as if words were spoken, *And what's in it for me?* But before he could answer this important question, there was the sound of approaching footsteps, and they both looked towards the door as Rita and Beatrice came into the room.

'More tea, anyone?' asked Henry.

He would have to put his mind to the question of payment for Valerie, he could tell. Nothing too obvious, but he would find something that the girl really wanted, and then buy it for her.

'By the way,' said Valerie quite clearly, when they had all been provided with fresh tea and second slices of cherry flan, 'I have decided to change my name.'

Rita's cup rattled against its saucer. 'Aren't you a little young to marry?'

'In this country girls marry at fourteen,' said Valerie, 'but that is not what I meant. My name is Valerie Maria. Valerie, so English, is the name my father chose for me. I was named Maria after my mother. Both names are rather common.' She paused, apparently wondering whether she had said exactly what she meant. The other three were still silent, listening to her. 'I mean they are both very popular. One meets them frequently. If I put them together – Valerie Maria – they would make a name that is too long, too much of a mouthful, as you say. So I will put them together and contract them. You must call me Valma.'

'Valma,' repeated Rita experimentally. 'Very well, Valerie, we shall all call you Valma from now on.' Her tone implied that she would find this easy since she had no intention of seeing Valma Crabbe again.

'It's quite exotic,' said Beatrice. 'But then, so are you, aren't you?'

Valma turned her basilisk eyes on her and she stammered to a stop.

'I tried to shorten my name,' went on Beatrice, bravely. 'I found out that in Italy it's pronounced Bayatreechay –' her Italian accent was quite awful – 'and that it was shortened to Beechay, which was spelled Bice. I thought it was rather romantic, until everyone rhymed it with "mice". So now I'm called Beech, and I spell it the same as the tree, so people can't get it wrong.'

'Ridiculous,' said Rita. 'Your name is Beatrice, and that is what we shall continue to call you.'

'I shall call you Beech,' said Valma. She caught and held Henry's eyes. 'As long as you call me Valma.'

She is her father's daughter, thought Henry. She strikes a fair bargain. And he dismissed from his mind pictures of gold bracelets, and wondered again what bargain he would strike with Valma Crabbe.

'Are you going to the deLyles' picnic?' Valma asked suddenly.

'Oh, I expect so,' said Rita. 'We always do, don't we, Henry? Such a bore for us, but the children expect it.'

'Are you going?' asked Beech.

'We're not usually invited,' said Valma. 'But I should like to go one year, just to see what it's like.'

Your ingenuous remarks do not fool me, thought Henry, catching Valma's cold eye once more.

'Perhaps this will be the year when you get your invitation,' he said.

Rita frowned at him. 'It's hardly a thing one can ask for,' she said. 'It comes as a gift from the deLyles, not as a right.' She rang the bell for the maid to clear the tea table. 'You mustn't expect such a thing, Valma dear.' The maid entered the room and removed their cups and saucers and the remains of the cherry flan. 'And I expect the girls would like to go to Beech's room for some girl talk. Wouldn't you?'

Beech cast a hopeless plea for help at her father then said, 'Would you like to see my stamp collection, Valma?'

'I think not,' said Valma. 'I have no interest in such things. I believe it is time for me to return home. Thank you so much, Mrs Markland, for a very enjoyable afternoon.'

'My driver will take you,' said Henry. 'I'll come down with you and tell him where to go.'

'I'm sure he knows where Crabbe's Provisions may be found,' said Valma. 'But thank you. And goodbye, Beech. I hope we shall meet again soon.'

As he accompanied her down the stairs and out to the ageing black Humber, it occurred to Henry that if Crabbe had sent his car for his daughter, it would have been a newer, flashier one than his own.

'I hope I did everything that you needed from me,' said Rita later, when she and Henry were alone. 'May I ask what it was all about? I can't believe that a grocer's daughter can have any importance to you or your work.'

'Better not to ask,' said Henry. 'I was just doing a favour for a friend.'

'Of course,' said Rita. 'I am glad to hear it. I would not wish to entertain the vulgar little daughter of a grocer for no good reason. And now we must get ready for this dinner party. The deLyles expect everything to be done in style, and I shall have to oversee Munira and Amani every step of the way.'

'You're so good at it,' said Henry automatically. 'What are we having, apart from the smoked salmon, that is?'

'Poussins, don't you remember? Isn't that what you told Valerie Crabbe?' Rita rarely made a joke and Henry looked at her blankly for a moment before smiling at it. 'Though in fact

I believe we are serving lamb. And I have six different young vegetables and the first of the strawberries. Amani will make some of her hot snacks with pine kernels and minced lamb to serve while we have our cocktails.'

'Sounds wonderful.'

'Yes. Are you going back to the office for an hour or two?'

Henry could take a hint. 'I expect my driver is back by now. I'll see you at seven then.'

20

The morning was cloudy, although there was no forecast of rain. Beech was wearing an old pair of Levi's and a white T-shirt, and blue-and-white trainers on her feet. She pulled on a dark green sweatshirt and left the house. She had evaded Valma and no one had questioned where she was off to.

Fergus let her into his house as soon as she arrived on his doorstep. He had given up pretending that he didn't watch out for her approach.

They sat down with their coffee in his sitting room with the ease of old friends and picked up their conversation at the point where they had left off as though no time had passed between.

'But you don't really notice the smell of a place until you're away from it,' said Beech. 'I remember the first time I came back to England after a long stretch away in the Middle East. I travelled across France by train and so my first sight of England was the the white cliffs of Dover. Such a disappointment! Lower than I had imagined them, and greyer. And as I disembarked, I noticed the smell, compounded of diesel oil and rotting seaweed. That's what defined England for me.'

And the sea, so different from her own Mediterranean that it might have been an animal of a separate species. She saw it as an animal – sullen with its wrinkled grey-brown pelt, growling and snarling and flinging itself in impotent rage against the concrete of the quay.

'There's probably a point from which you should view the

cliffs, and then they'll appear tall and imposing. But that gangplank wasn't it,' she said.

'And perhaps there is, too, a point in time from which you should view the past. A moment when the complexities and contradictions would fall into place and you could see it clearly. You would see all the players going about their business, their clothes in sharp focus, and the story of your life would have meaning at last.'

'Maybe you're right and that moment is now,' mused Beech. 'I feel as though I could look down – no, look *back* – and see them all, tiny figures at the bottom of a long tunnel: Jack, Nicholas, Rita, Henry, Valma, Mrs deLyle.'

Beech was watching them in her mind's eye, dancing in the light, turning, twisting, coming towards her and then retreating in a stately dance. Dolls, mannequins, puppets. She could reach out and pick them up, look at each of them in turn. Examine them. And then decide what they all meant.

'Well,' said Fergus. 'So how *did* you meet Jack, and fall in love and agree to marry?'

'Blame the bloody cat,' she said.

'I didn't know you were a cat lover.'

'It wasn't even mine.'

The cat had brought a fieldmouse into the house: through the cat flap, across the kitchen floor and down the hallway into the sitting room. Beech really shouldn't have left the door open, but there was the mouse on her pale green carpet, and there was the cat, Monty, playing with it as though it were made out of fabric and stuffing. The stuffing, Beech saw, was ruining the carpet. She shouted at Monty then grabbed him round the middle and lifted him up, gathering him under his solid rump. In return, Monty sank his sharp teeth into her arm and brought up his back legs to kick his way free. His front claws raked down the back of her hand. She let him go.

Beech's arm was running blood, and there were long scratches along the back of her hand. One of the scratches was deeper and more painful than the others. Even after washing it, she couldn't make it stop bleeding. When she went downstairs, still dripping blood, she found her mother in the sitting room.

'It needs a stitch,' said her mother, dropping ash on to the carpet next to the remnants of mouse. The house was rented by Rita while she spent three months in England, and all depredations would have to be paid for. But since Monty came with the house, as part of the fixtures and fittings as it were, when it came to the reckoning, Rita put all damage down to him and refused to pay for anything.

'I hate hospitals,' said Beech.

'Well, have a stiff gin instead,' said her mother, pouring herself one and gesturing with the bottle at Beech.

'No thanks,' said Beech, and wrapped a clean table napkin round her hand. She found her car keys and went out to her Mini.

'And that is how I met Jack,' she told Fergus.

Jack was sitting in Casualty, looking too large and generally healthy to fit in one of their grey plastic chairs. He had a white bandage around his shapely head and his long fair hair was artistically arranged over it.

'Rugger match,' he said to Beech, as she sat in the only free chair, which happened to be next to his. On Jack's other side sat another young man, six inches shorter than Jack, and with sandy red hair which already, at the age of twenty-three, was growing thin and receding.

'Actually,' his friend said, 'it wasn't during the match at all. It was afterwards. He got himself pissed as—'

'Shut up, Edward,' said Jack, without even turning round. 'My name's Jack,' he said to Beech, and gave her his full, charming smile.

'Beatrice. But they call me Beech.'

Beech wished that she had paper and crayons with her. She wanted to put down the exact shape of his eyes, the line of nose, the way the lock of his hair flopped forward and lay over the white bandage. She wanted to record the shape of his ear, all those intimate whorls and cavities, the velvety lobe. In reality, Beech would never have done anything as attention-seeking as bringing out her drawing materials in public.

She wasn't to know that Jack routinely practised his charm on every woman under the age of forty that he met. Or that he had already told her two lies. She should have listened to Edward, but then, no one ever did. Beech still had a lot to learn about men. Instead of drawing his eyes, she should have looked at his mouth. You can tell so much more from a man's mouth than you can from his eyes. And that by observation only, before he even opens it to speak, to kiss, or to lie.

And anyway, Beech was a pushover for anyone like Jack, had been since she first fell in love with the boy who looked after the goats.

'What happened next?' asked Fergus.

'Jack insisted that I couldn't drive home. Edward drove my car while Jack put me in the front seat of his and took me back to Rita. Rita took one look at Jack and decided that he should join the family. She charmed him completely while I sat quietly in the background. She invited him back to drinks, and dinner and Sunday lunch and tennis. She had only two months and three weeks in which to land him for me, but she did it.'

'And did you have no say in the matter?'

'I was completely under Jack's spell. Why should I argue?'

Fergus sighed. 'I hope you can answer that question for yourself now.'

Later that day, while Beech was enjoying a solitary cup of tea in her own sitting room, the phone rang.

'Hello, may I speak to Beatrice, please?'

'Yes, Father. This is Beech.'

'I've been thinking about the Crabbe girl, and what happened.'

'Yes?'

'Have you asked her about Mrs deLyle?'

'No. I don't think they knew each other, did they?'

'I paid my debt. Tell her. Make her explain how I paid my debt. We owe her nothing now, because I paid. I thought she would ask for gold bracelets, but she wanted something else.'

Beech, mystified, said, 'Yes, Father. I'll ask her about it.'

'Good.'

Beech found Rita in the conservatory, drinking a gin and tonic and smoking one of her menthol cigarettes.

'Oh, there you are,' she said, when she saw her daughter. 'I've been sitting here on my own for *hours*.'

'Isn't Valma around?'

'That woman has discovered shopping. She's taken herself into Oxford with a brand new credit card and an acquisitive gleam in her eye. I expect she will come home when the last shop has shut.'

'Henry was on the phone just now,' said Beech.

'What did he want?'

'He mentioned Valma Crabbe, and if I understood him right, he said she had no reason to blackmail us.'

'What a ridiculous idea!' Rita's face had flushed. Beech watched her make an effort to remain calm. 'He's filled his head with some new nonsense, that's all.'

'Then why is she staying here, contributing nothing to the housekeeping, never offering a hand with the housework?'

'What a mean, ungenerous nature you have!'

'I'd like to know what hold she has over us.'

'I thought you'd learned years ago not to ask questions like this. This is none of your business.'

'But that's such a convenient reply when I want to know

something. And I think that if Valma is going to live with me indefinitely, then I should know the reason why.'

'She always got her own way. Don't you remember? She crept around with her downcast eyes and her demure manner, and you never knew what she was really thinking. There was the afternoon when Henry made me invite her to tea—'

'*Henry* made you invite her? Whatever for?'

'I didn't ask why. One didn't in those days. It was some favour for one of his friends at the Embassy. But then she minced into my drawing room with a smirk on her face and sat there in her modest, *inviting*, little-girl dress, like some horrible nymphet. You can't blame Henry, can you?'

'Blame him for what?' But Beech was remembering how uncomfortable she felt in those days when Henry got too close, and his hand rested heavily on her shoulder.

'Nothing. I'm sure Henry did nothing. He might have laid a fatherly hand on her knee, I suppose, but she didn't have to *insinuate* all those nasty things the way she did.'

'Recently, you mean?'

'Yes, of course. And then she went on to imply all sorts of other nasty things about dear Nicholas. I'm not even sure I understood what she was talking about. That woman can make my skin crawl with one of those knowing smiles of hers.'

'Perhaps we should call her bluff.'

'I can't have her ringing up Henry and upsetting him. Goodness only knows what effect it would have on him.'

'If she stays much longer, it's a chance I shall have to take,' said Beech with more conviction than she felt.

Rita stubbed out her cigarette with finality. 'I think I'll go for a walk in the park now. I feel in need of exercise.'

'Very well,' said Beech. 'I'll do a little work on Nicholas's book now, and I'll drive over to Chipping Hampton later this afternoon.'

'But you're not to go worrying Henry with all this nonsense, do you understand?'

'I'll do my best.'

Rita stared at her for a moment, as though working out what she meant.

Two of us can play at ambiguities, thought Beech.

Mrs deLyle, Beech murmured to herself, looking through the contents of the red box. Where are you hiding? She hadn't read all through Valerie Crabbe's diary. Page after page of that immaculate script mocked her. Very well, she thought. I'll plough through some more of the stuff.

Today I rose early in order to complete my essay on the poetic art of Racine. The classes on literature are the ones which I enjoy most, though the nuns do spend a lot of time instructing us in the subjects of morals, gospel studies, Church history and catechism, even when we are supposed to be studying history or geography, or even arithmetic. I know I should enjoy religious studies as least as much as the other subjects, but I am so curious to know more about the world. All I see of it is the interior of our shop, and the classroom at the convent. When am I ever going to escape?

The worst lessons are those given by Sister Norbert. She tells us always that if we are not good, pure, obedient girls we will end up in Hell, or at best frying like sausages for centuries in Purgatory. While she isn't looking I draw a picture at the back of my exercise book. In it her dour god sits in his heaven and pours down the summer fires. He is setting copper pans to heat on top of the furnace. He is roasting us in the glowing dome of his sky. He piles up his thunderclouds and flashes his wild anger across the mountains.

Unfortunately, Sister Norbert catches me with this

drawing. She makes me promise never to draw another. She tears it from my book and rips it into tiny pieces. I have an extra chapter of St Matthew to learn by heart as a punishment for my indiscretion.

Beech heard a key in the lock and the sound of the front door opening. The sound still made her feel apprehensive. Could it be Jack, home already?

'Hello!' called a female voice. 'It's only me!'

Valma. Beech pulled the door closed on her cubbyhole, but quietly so that she shouldn't be discovered just yet.

Much later, she put the notebooks away and went upstairs to change her clothes for the visit to her father.

'I'm off!' she called as she left the house.

Valma didn't bother to reply.

21

Alone in Beech's house, Valma floated in the bath, enveloped in scents of jasmine and tuberose, courtesy of Beech's expensive bath oil. She nudged the hot tap with her big toe to allow a little more hot water to flow in. Heaven.

It's easy for you to take this for granted, Beatrice Waring, she thought. You didn't see what I did. You should have been with me on the first Thursday of every month, in the afternoon, when we had no lessons at school.

On these Thursday, they followed Sister Wenceslas, their arms stretched with bags full of provisions. They walked down the sandy, dusty roads, smelling of undigested sewage, and entered the parts of the city that their parents never ventured into.

Sister Wenceslas was one of the smallest nuns, probably less than five feet tall, and slim in proportion. Her black gabardine habit, in that crushing sunlight, was immaculate. Her goffered white wimple surrounded her pinched, weatherworn face, with the yellow cheeks and the reddened chin, and her translucent black veil floated out behind her like a cloud of devilish smoke. It was impossible to imagine that there were legs under that billowing skirt and the large clicking beads of her rosary. Occasionally you might catch a glimpse of a child-sized foot in a tightly laced black boot, but otherwise it was as though she glided down those rough tracks on castors. Her pale blue eyes were fixed on some heavenly vision, her robust arms were laden with baskets of provender. Valerie, as the daughter of the city's most distinguished grocer, came immediately behind her, also laden with comestibles. Just behind, and slightly to one side, walked one of Stanley Crabbe's servants, sulky, kicking at the dust, wishing to be elsewhere. And then again, behind these two, came a gaggle of schoolgirls, giggling as schoolgirls the world over giggle, with provisions that they had begged from mothers and servants. At least, they thought, it was a day away from the confines of the convent, and they looked around them and wondered at the harshness of the outside world, and were glad that they did not belong to it.

The heat bounced off the pale dust of the track and clawed at their legs. They walked, this group of schoolgirls, in their cream shantung pinafore dresses and embroidered white muslin blouses. They wore Swiss straw hats on their dark hair, the deep brims tipped low over their foreheads to guard them from the harmful rays of the sun; they wore white leather sandals and short white socks. And gloves, of course, since no lady would be seen outside her house without them. Valerie's gloves were damp with sweat and had acquired grey smudges on the fingers that Sister Wenceslas would frown over if she saw. To begin with they chattered and laughed, but gradually, as the afternoon heat pressed down on the crown of their hats, and the light bounced off the pale earth and dazzled their eyes, they grew silent. All the colour was leached out of that landscape, and the creamy white earth and sky reflected back the harsh sunlight. They screwed up their eyes, they grumbled about the weight of the bags and baskets they carried.

'Enough!' said Sister Wenceslas, and they were silent. Only the Crabbes' servant, wilting under the weight of the provisions she carried, dared to pout and sulk and mutter about the uselessness of giving good food to people who knew nothing of such things, and who would anyway merely sell the goods in the market and spend the money on arak and . . . But at this point Sister Wenceslas silenced her with one of her looks.

'We will all say a decade of the rosary,' said Sister Wenceslas. And so, incongruously, the line of girls chanted the words of the prayers, in chorus, as they walked down that inhospitable road.

Much later in her life Valerie might have noticed the smell, but living in this city, she had long grown used to smells of all kinds. There was the particularly pungent stench of a dead dog that lay, fly-blown, in the gutter throughout the heat of the day. There was, here, the smell of an overcrowded shanty town with no sanitation and no running water. As the sun drummed off the mud walls, the ammonia made their eyes water, but they pretended not to notice, as they pretended not to see so many things.

Each form in the convent had to adopt a needy family. And three times a term they visited this family with food and clothing. If we had been less ignorant, we might have been patronizing, thought the adult Valerie, who now called herself Valma. But these girls were wide-eyed and innocent. They did not patronize because they recognized that here they, from their rich world of parents and servants, would not survive for a week. They were superior in wealth, perhaps in their education, but they were not wise in the ways of those who learned to survive in impossible circumstances.

As they entered the quarter where poverty and destitution pressed around them, the girls stayed silent with no prompting from the nun. Silent too were the women and children who peered at them from open doorways or played in the dust with twigs and pebbles.

Sister Wenceslas raised her right hand and her little caravan came to a halt. They had reached the hovel of their adopted family.

A few of the nice, clean convent girls crowded into the hut built mostly of corrugated iron, and with one small hole for a window. A woman, probably little older than they, sat on a chair and nursed a baby. The baby cried weakly, with a thin, hoarse, mewing sound. It was an odd colour, like sour milk, and flies had settled on the lids of its dark eyes. Its mother said little, as this crowd of young strangers pushed into her room, but sat rocking herself backwards and forwards, and sometimes brushed the flies away from the baby's eyes.

Sister Wenceslas gave orders and bags were unpacked and provisions neatly stacked against the metal sides of the shack. As they worked, the girls were surrounded by more and more huge-eyed silent children. Did they live here or were they neighbours' children? One of the larger girls, perhaps seven years old, offered them tea, or iced water, and cherry preserve. Where on earth had they acquired these things? Had the entire community been scoured for such delicacies? Did they keep them ready for visits from rich girls from the convent? They refused the offered sweetmeats, although Valerie thought it might have been more polite to accept. Who wishes to be a receiver without the possibility of giving in return? She remembered smiling at one of the scrawny children and accepting the glass of water. The heat was unbearable and the water welcome. For two or three days afterwards she waited for symptoms of some horrible disease picked up from badly washed glass or fetid water, but she survived her small generous act. Perhaps, after all, there was a God.

Before long the heat in the room became too much for her and the ammonia smell of long-wet baby and unwashed sweat stung Valerie's eyes. She wasn't crying, that she knew, but tears ran from her eyes and coursed down her cheeks. Sister Wenceslas looked at her with a sympathy that she knew she did not deserve.

'You may go outside, Valerie,' she said, in her cool, precise, voice.

Valerie left, pushing her way through the children in their long skirts and bare feet. They had scabs on their skin and snotty noses. They smelled. This, thought Valerie, is what poverty smells like. This is how it looks. And I am never going to be like this. I am going to marry and I am going to be rich. I will go to England and I will live in luxury.

When she remembered the scene in future years – it would creep into her memory, unbidden, unwelcome – the whole scene was imbued with the sound of the flies buzzing, a deafening noise, drowning out even the mewling of the baby and the chatter of the children. And she remembered the colour of the faces, pallid, greyish beige, as though they lived all their short lives in that metal shack, and never came out into the sun or walked through the flower-starred meadows in the hills.

'We shall go home now,' said Sister Wenceslas eventually, when Valerie thought that the sights and sounds of this visit would press down so heavily on her head that she would be forced to the ground, to lie there in the stinking dust.

'Home,' she repeated. And even the Crabbes' sullen servant smiled at the thought.

When Valerie walked through the door of Crabbe's Provisions an hour later, her mother looked up sharply from her post behind the till. Valerie stopped, and paused there in the centre of the shop, to give her mother the chance to inspect her.

'Yes,' said Mrs Crabbe, after the thorough visual inspection. 'You may go up to your room now. Take off all your clothes and put them in the laundry basket. I will tell Suha to wash them straight away, and separately from the rest of the laundry. You will have a bath, scrubbing yourself thoroughly with the red soap.'

'Yes, Mother.'

'Not a shower, mind. And you will wash your hair. Suha will help you to dry it and plait it again.'

'Yes, Mother.'

'You too, Fatin,' she said, turning to the servant, who stood a pace behind her daughter. 'You must wash yourself thoroughly and change all your clothes. Give the ones you have been wearing to Suha to wash.'

'Yes, madame.'

'Go, go now.'

And the servant bowed and left, not daring now to sulk.

'You too, girl. Go! Go!'

But as Fatin bowed her head and slid from the room she looked first at Valerie and gave her a crooked smile. *That's where you came from, you and your mother, and that's where you'll end up because that's what you are: rubbish. Poor, starving, nothing people, dependent on the goodwill of others for your livelihood, just as I am.*

And Valerie also bent her head in submission. This, then, was the meaning of poverty. This was the contagion which she must scrub from her skin and her hair, in case it stuck and held and pulled her down to its own level.

'Yes, Mother,' she said submissively.

And Valma left the shop and went upstairs to her clean white bedroom. 'Suha!' she called as she went.

Once in her room, she stepped out of her cream silk shantung pinafore, her white embroidered muslin blouse, her embroidered lawn underwear, her white leather sandals and socks, and wrapped herself in her bathrobe. 'Take these away!' she ordered. 'Wash them! Clean my sandals!'

And Suha, who was probably about thirteen years old, and whose family lived in just such poverty as the one Valerie had visited that afternoon, and who depended for their very survival on the tiny wage that Suha sent home each month, bowed her head, and gathered up the clothes, and took them down the back stairs to the servants' quarters, and placed them in the big stone sink next to the one where tomorrow the washerwoman would come to do the Crabbe family's laundry.

'Suha!' Valma shouted impatiently down the stairs. '*Dépêche-toi!*'

'*J'arrive, mademoiselle,*' Suha called timidly back. She returned up the narrow, uncarpeted servants' stairs. She went into the bathroom, her backless sandals slapping on the stone tiles, bringing in fresh white towels. She pushed down the brass plunger in the white porcelain bath standing on its curlicued legs in the centre of the room. Then she turned the brass dolphin taps and watched the steaming water gush out of their gaping mouths to fill the room with the scent of lavender oil.

When she had done this, she slipped out of the room, closing the door behind her, and returned downstairs, where she went into the washroom and filled the copper tub with water and put it to heat on the stove, for she didn't dare to use the water that was needed for the family's baths or showers. She pushed a couple of logs into the belly of the stove. It was stifling hot down here, but the water would not take long to heat in the copper tub, then she could allow the fire to die down again. She went to sit outside on the servants' balcony while she waited for the water to heat.

After she had bathed, Valerie put on her thin cotton dressing gown and sat in a chair by the open windows of her bedroom. There was a slight breeze from the sea, and the hot afternoon was cooling a little towards evening.

'And what are you doing here?' It was her mother.

Valerie rose to her feet to face her. 'I was waiting for Suha to bring me fresh clothes.'

'Can you find nothing more useful to do? Must you always wait for a servant to do things for you?'

Valerie met her mother's cross brown stare. What should I do while wearing my dressing gown? she wanted to say, but knew that such rudeness would bring a stinging slap on her bare leg.

'And what is that you're eating?'

'Just some dried fruit.' Something had upset her mother, she knew, and she would not be content until Valerie too was feeling unhappy.

'You do nothing but eat!' exclaimed Mrs Crabbe. 'Do you want to put on so much weight that no man ever looks at you?'

Valma pulled her dressing gown more closely round her plump thighs.

'Who do you think will marry a big, fat girl?'

And that is what it always came down to: her one object in life must be to marry, and to marry well. If she was to compete in the marriage market then she had to look after her figure and her face, and hide the fact that she had a mind that could add up a column of figures in a few seconds and calculate discounts of five or seven per cent without the use of pencil and paper.

'You're spoiled, you girls at that convent. I should speak to Mother Maria Dolores about it. You need more discipline in your lives.'

'Like you had in yours,' said Valma in a low voice. She had heard this complaint before.

'Are you being insolent?' challenged her mother.

'No, Mother,' said Valerie meekly.

However she fought against her mother she agreed with her that she must keep away from the poverty that she had seen that afternoon. That is where you ended up if you failed to catch yourself a rich man to feed you and look after you. Valma felt that there must be other ways of keeping out of poverty, but she had not enough experience of life to know them yet. She would learn, though, and meanwhile she would keep on the right side of her mother.

'Is it all right if I get dressed now?' she asked.

'Go! Go! *Petite paresseuse!*'

Valerie knew that this, compared with the other things that her mother might call her, was quite affectionate. When her mother had left the room she found fresh underclothes and a blouse and skirt, and dressed herself. Then she brushed her damp hair and twisted it up on her head. Only when she had done that, and put gold studs in her ears and a gold chain and medallion around her neck did she feel that she had removed the last scraps of poverty from her skin.

Valma up-ended the bottle of bath oil and watched the last few drops fall on to her round abdomen and trickle down to lie in a fragrant pool in her navel.

22

The spring was well advanced, with leaves appearing on the trees and in the hedgerows. The fields were losing their sodden, wintry look and were hazed with young wheat. As Beech drove north, away from Oxford and towards Chipping Hampton, she felt her spirits rise.

When she reached Rose Cottage and saw its grim gates and fence, the blind eyes of its windows, gloom returned. Henry was waiting for her. How long had he been there, watching out for her car? He stood by the gate, looking at her, a thin, bent man, with colourless hair falling back towards his neck, skin faded to a pale sand colour, eyes hidden in grey pouches. He wore an old woollen shirt with a green checked pattern that stood out from his scrawny neck, and shapeless corduroy trousers that fell in folds round his thin legs.

'Come in,' he said. 'You'd better come in, Beatrice.'

They went into the house through the kitchen door. The house smelled fusty, and she recognized the underlying odour of Gunter, but there were only one or two encrusted dishes in the sink, and a couple of mugs on the draining board. If Henry was incapable of doing the simplest household chores, at least he wasn't as extravagant as his wife in his use of crockery and pans.

'How are the compost bins?' she asked.

'I'm trying a new kind of worm,' he said. 'Up until now I have been concentrating on brandling worms, *Eisenia foetida*. But now I have a new kind, in a new bin. This worm is fatter, greedier.' He picked up a bowl of kitchen rubbish: a couple of cabbage leaves, the end of an old loaf, a heap of tea leaves. She wondered where it all came from. She didn't believe that Henry ate enough to keep a single brandling worm alive for a week, let alone anything fatter and greedier.

Henry opened the back door. 'I have to check,' he said.

'May I come with you?'

'If you like.'

And so they both went to visit Henry's shed.

'Here, boys,' he murmured, lifting lids, pulling up the squares of old carpet, watching as tails flicked down into the vegetation. 'Tea time,' he said, and gave them their kitchen leftovers.

'How are they?' asked Beech.

'Very well. Very well. But don't interrupt me.'

He shuffled over to a rough wooden bench and switched on a bare light bulb attached to the wall. He opened a worn hard-backed notebook and started to write.

'If you're to be scientific about it, you have to record *everything*,' he said. 'They can tell if you forget something.'

Beech watched him laboriously fill in a row of cells in a table, then he pulled over another notebook and started to write a paragraph or two of narrative. 'Log everything,' he said, as he finished and replaced the cap on his pen.

'Have you always done that?' asked Beech.

'Oh, yes. And so did the Crabbe girl. She wrote it all down, that one. Didn't miss a thing.'

'Have you finished out here?'

'Yes. We'll return to base now.'

Back in the cottage, Henry entered his study, Beech still following. 'Shall I make us some tea?' she asked. 'Is there anything else you'd like me to do?'

'I've already had tea. I'm going to write up the log now.' He sat at his desk, brought out another worn notebook and once more started to write.

'It's all here,' he said. 'I have it all.'

Beech stayed at her post for another ten minutes, not wanting to upset her father by moving away.

Once, he looked up at her, as though seeing someone else, then continued to write in his neat, crabbed hand. Beech went out to the kitchen to wash up the few plates and cups. When she returned to Henry's study he had put his logbook away.

'I shall take Gunter for a short walk. Then, I believe, it will soon be dinner time. I removed a packet of lamb chops from the freezer this morning, and I believe we have some fresh carrots in the rack.'

Beech sped through the preparations for supper. She washed up, swept and dusted. She ran a damp cloth over the kitchen surfaces and was just wondering whether to take out the Hoover, ready to remove Gunter's hairs from sofa and carpets, when she remembered what Henry had said. So, heart thumping, she returned to his study and took down the notebook and started to read from the beginning. Oh yes, he'd recorded everything all right. Every single visit to the shed, every cabbage leaf that he had dropped in the bin, every sighting of a worm. There was a record of every walk that he had taken Gunter for, every tin of dog food that the animal had eaten. She flicked through the pages to see whether there was any variation in his accounts, but could see none. She had been hoping to find some account of Henry's feelings, or perhaps even a muted reference to the afternoon of the picnic, but Henry's jottings were all of practical matters. She returned the notebook to the shelf and went to switch on the grill for their chops.

'Shall I pour you a drink?' she asked, when Henry returned. 'It must be well after six by now.'

'I'll have a glass of juice,' said Henry, opening the fridge and looking inside. 'Would you like one?'

'Thanks,' said Beech, prodding a potato. 'Anything but lime juice, please.'

'Of course,' said Henry. 'I won't have limes in the house, you know.' They both associated the smell with that dreadful time after Nicholas's death.

When their meal was cooking and could be left on its own, Beech joined her father in the sitting room and they sat on the now pristine sofas and looked at each other. She remembered her father as a huge man, tall and bulky, with fair hair, bristling eyebrows and a complexion as red and grainy as underdone mutton. His eyes were a very pale slate grey, his nose jutted out from his cushioned cheeks, and his mouth was red and fleshy. When he spoke, he revealed large white teeth, spoiled only by the splashes of dark metal fillings. She would watch his mouth, his lips pursing, opening, glistening, spewing forth the angry words like lava from a volcano. At least, that's how she remembered him.

We're all getting older, she reminded herself.

'Did you find out about the deLyles?' he asked suddenly. 'Did you ask Valerie about them?'

'No, I'm afraid not. I didn't have a chance to speak to Valma.'

'I know you're putting together an account of Nicholas's life,' said Henry. 'And I'm putting my version down on paper, too. It should be there, in black and white, shouldn't it?'

'I think so,' said Beech. 'Do you want me to include any of it in the book?'

Henry looked shocked. 'Oh, no! That would never do! This is for my eyes only. No one else's. You must never speak of it. Didn't I explain that to you when you were little?'

'Yes, yes, of course, I think our meal's ready. Would you like to eat now?'

So Henry was committing his memories to paper. She should let him complete his account, and then perhaps he would allow her to read it.

* * *

On the way home she wondered about calling in on Fergus. They regularly met for their coffee breaks, and occasionally for a rapid lunch when Rita and Valma were out. But she hadn't liked to ask what he did with his evenings. He might be entertaining. She turned left into Lewis Road and pulled up outside his house. Just one light on, in the sitting room.

She rang the bell.

He answered the door immediately. He smiled at her. He looked pleased to see her. He invited her in, offered her a drink.

'Anything but fruit juice,' she said. 'I am full to the ears with nonalcoholic drink. I can leave the car here and walk home, can't I?'

'It will do great things for my reputation to have it parked there all night. Please do,' said Fergus.

'Good,' said Beech, accepting a glass of Fergus's red wine.

For a while they talked of all sorts of things, the way she imagined normal people, ones who didn't have her peculiar family, talked. She managed to forget about Valma and Rita taking over her house, and Henry and his fear of limes. She forgot about the deLyles.

Then Fergus said, 'There is one thing I'd like to ask you.'

'Yes?'

'It's the goat. I can't understand why you drew so many pictures of the goat.'

To begin with, said Beech, I could only draw when the sun had gone down, in the warm, dark night-time. Then she sat at the desk in her room and put down on paper all the things she remembered seeing during the day. Sometimes she wrote in her notebook, but she found pictures easier than words. She wished that she could just take out a notebook and fill its pages while the sun shone in the long afternoons. There was nothing much to do, except read, or doze on her bed. It was too hot to swim, too hot to get in the car and ask the driver to take her somewhere. Too hot out on the metallic sea, even when a breeze was blowing. But even with the wooden shutters pulled close, she couldn't write or draw. She was always afraid that at any moment Rita or Henry would burst in and find her, and pick up her work and laugh at it.

'How's our little Michelangelo?' Henry would sneer, every time she came downstairs.

She had already been derided as the fourth Brontë sister when they had discovered that she liked to write stories for herself. She had given this up, but she didn't want them to take her drawing away from her too.

And then the servants let her sit out on their balcony, and listen to their conversations, and take her drawing pad and work away in the cool of the morning, before she left for school, and in heat of the afternoon when classes were over for the day. While the servants' noisy family life washed over her, she made drawings of all she saw. She could never see enough. She drew, in pencil or charcoal, in immense detail: a picture of the cook's youngest baby asleep in its cardboard box, flies settled on its closed eyelids. And she drew the goat that came to be milked every morning.

To begin with she could never complete it, since the goat was removed long before she ever got all the details down on to paper. But eventually, as she became more familiar with it, she worked faster and finished the drawing.

She got to know it well. The pale yellow goat, with its moth-eaten pelt, had dark, stick-like legs. Its knee joints were prominent. Its hoofs were sharp and mischievous-looking. Its mouth had an upward curl as though the animal was amused at what it saw around it. She had tried very hard to get the detail of its coat right. It didn't have long, silky hair, like an English goat. Its coat was short and scrubby and matlike. She had drawn every hair of that coat in her early efforts. Perhaps that was because she had wanted to draw Khalil but had not dared.

Or had thought that if she did, he would guess how passionately she felt about him.

'Who was Khalil?'

'The goat-woman's son. When she didn't come, he brought the goat in her place.'

'I remember now. He was the beautiful young man.'

'Like something out of a fairy tale.'

When the goat-woman noticed that Beech was trying to draw her, she pulled her shawl across her face, and held it in place with her teeth, while she continued to milk the goat. Then one day, the woman didn't come, and instead, the goat was in the care of the beautiful young man, son to the woman. His name was, she discovered, Khalil. Khalil was not tall, but square and muscular and with wavy dark hair, glossy brown eyes, and skin of a pale olive colour. He spoke a few words of English, but these were crude and simple, and she preferred to stay silent and invent conversations for the two of them that fitted in better with her fantasies. Khalil smiled at her, and wore a shirt with short sleeves so that she could see his muscular arms, with their silky black hairs and slight sheen of sweat. When he milked the goat, she turned away and pretended to be interested in her box of coloured chalks.

When Khalil was there, she drew the goat less, but its attendant more. She tried to catch the precise way that his eyelids drooped and his eyelashes brushed the skin of his cheek. She worked on the shape of his ear, with its minute whorls and its little tuft of hair. And she drew his mouth, with its full, sulky lips and the way they parted so that she could see the slight gleam of his teeth and the tip of his tongue, which appeared with the effort of his hands.

It was frustrating that her chalks were so thick, and even when she sharpened them into a wedge shape with her penknife, still there was an imprecision about her drawings that annoyed her.

'Oh, I don't know. They look pretty good to me,' said Fergus. 'Too much detail, if anything.'

When Khalil left, she drew the terracotta pots of setting yoghurt with their thick wrinkled skin, she drew the bougainvillaea that cascaded its purple, papery bracts over the balustrade. At this point she wished that she could use colour, so that she could capture the precise brown and purple of the plant, the ochre of the building, the dark transparent blue of the sky. Then she pulled off the sheet of paper and started again, drawing one of the chestnut cockroaches that lived in the kitchen cupboards, and went on to draw the folds in Amani's headscarf and the way they hid her hair and shaded her face when she went to the market. She drew the woven basket that Amani put over her arm, and how it bulged in certain ways, depending on what she had bought that morning.

'Can I go with you?' she asked.

'Better not,' said Amani. 'Your mother wouldn't like it.'

And Beech went back to drawing the palm trees in the garden, and the flea-bitten yellow dog that belonged to the caretaker.

'But what about this one?' asked Fergus, taking a drawing from her folder and passing it across to her.

'What?' She looked at the drawing in disbelief. Someone had taken a black graphite pencil and slashed across the picture, crisscrossing it with thick lines, many of which had scored the paper and torn it into holes.

'It looks as though it was done in a rage,' said Fergus.

'I don't remember doing it.'

'It's done using one of your own pencils. You used it for some of the other drawings. And here's another. Is this Khalil?'

'Yes. That's how I remember him.'

'Very flattering, I would say. But why did you try to destroy it?'

'Perhaps,' said Beech slowly, 'it had something to do with the picnic. Everything fades into a mess of black lines when I think of it. Henry told me to ask Valma about Mrs deLyle, so I shall do that, and maybe I'll learn more about it.'

'Why Mrs deLyle?'

'It was her picnic.'

'It looks like rather a nice goat. Nothing like the one you met the other week, when you looked so worried about it.'

'You were watching?'

Fergus sighed. 'Sad, isn't it? I couldn't wait to see you.'

'And now?'

'Now you come unannounced. I like that.'

'Good. I'll do it more often. But I ought to be getting back now. It is rather late.'

'Half-past ten. Is that late?'

'They'll be expecting me.'

'What for? Let them get on with everything by themselves. Ask Valma about Mrs deLyle tomorrow morning.'

'What do you suggest we do now?'

'Why don't we go to bed?'

'I think I'd like that.'

Fergus looked surprised, as though he had been expecting a direct refusal, or a long argument. 'It's upstairs,' he said unnecessarily.

Beech wondered briefly whether she was trying to get her own back on Jack. Just because he was having an affair, did she think she was entitled to one, too? But no, she thought, watching Fergus's long, thin back precede her up the stairs, it wasn't that. It was more to do with the way his hair curled over the back of his collar, and the lithe manner in which he mounted the stairs, and the extraordinary diversity of the mugs he used for their coffee, and the tireless attention he had paid to her and her concerns. Kindness, she thought, I reckon kindness is the most important thing in our relationship.

That, and the fact that I fancy him rotten, she thought a little later, when they had both removed their clothes with more haste than expertise, and were exploring the wonderful new territories thus revealed.

23

'What's the time?'

'What? Oh, it's ten past midnight.'

'I think I should be leaving soon.'

'Sod that. Sod your mother, sod your husband and sod your childhood friend Valma, if it comes to that. Stay.'

'That's the first time I've heard you swear.'

'I feel strongly about you and your family. *Stay*.'

'I am tempted. But I think I'd like to talk to Jack and Rita – sod Valma! – at a time of my own choosing. I don't want to slink in tomorrow morning and sound apologetic.'

'Don't slink. Don't apologize.'

'I must go.' She starts to untangle her legs from his. He buries his face in the hair on her neck. 'But I could see you again tomorrow.'

'Good.' His arms are still around her and he tightens his hold.

'Ten minutes,' she says. 'Ten minutes can't make any difference, can it?'

As a matter of fact, it was rather longer than ten minutes before she rolled out of bed and started to gather her clothes together.

Fergus sat up in bed and pulled the duvet straight. He watched Beech as she climbed back into her new cream silk underwear and then pulled on her sweatshirt and trousers. She was one of those people who looked better naked than clothed, though she had probably never noticed the fact. She didn't look at all gawky, and much younger than usual. 'I like you hair like that,' he said.

'A mess, you mean?'

'Yes. A lovely mess.'

'Very well. I'll leave it this way.'

Fergus was searching for his socks.

'There's one over here,' said Beech, handing it to him.

'Thanks.' He now had on a T-shirt, jeans and both socks. He found a sweatshirt of his own and pulled it on. 'Do you want anything before you leave? Tea? Coffee? More sex?'

Beech sighed. 'Yes, but I really have to go.'

'I'll find some shoes and see you home.'

'I'd like that.'

They ambled down the road, arms round one another's waists. The weather was surprisingly warm for the time of year and they didn't bother to hurry. Sometimes, indeed, they stopped underneath a tree and kissed. Mostly they smiled for no reason, and gazed fondly into one another's eyes and generally behaved in the witless way new lovers do.

'Jack's car's not here,' said Beech. 'He's probably with his woman and I couldn't care less.'

'You can creep in undetected?'

'I expect Rita is awake and lying in wait for me.'

'Tell her to sod off.'

'All right. I'll do that.'

They kissed again.

'I'm going in now.'

'Good night.'

Beech let herself into the house, then turned and waved goodbye to Fergus as he ambled back up the road. He had stuck his hands in his pockets and appeared to be whistling as he went.

'Is that you, Beatrice?'

'Yes, Mother.'

'Where have you been? I was worried.'

'Is Valma in?'

'Of course she is.'

'Well, keep your voice down. We don't want to wake her, do we?'

'I asked you where you'd been.'

'And I told you this afternoon that I was going to visit Henry. I cooked his dinner and tidied and cleaned the house for him.'

'But Mrs Allen is coming in to clean tomorrow.'

'You wouldn't want her to think that Henry had been neglected, would you?'

'Don't be ridiculous! And you still haven't answered my question. You must have left Chipping Hampton hours ago.'

'After I left Rose Cottage I called in to see a friend.'

'Couldn't you have telephoned to let me know where you were?'

'I didn't think of it. I'm sorry if you were worried, but as you can see, I'm fine. And I'm going to bed now. Why don't you do the same?'

'I think you're a thoughtless, selfish girl. And what about poor Jack?'

'Is he in? I didn't see his car.'

'He isn't in, as a matter of fact. But—'

'Well, that's all right then. Good night, Mother.'

And in the dark, lying alone in her bed, she remembered how it had felt with Fergus, and how very different he was from Jack, and how very much more imaginative and considerate a lover, and she drifted off to sleep, smiling.

'Good morning,' said Valma, yawning widely. She wore a plum satin dressing gown that was unkind to her natural complexion.

'Good morning,' said Beech, already bathed and dressed. The table was set, the coffee made, jugs of cranberry and orange juice ready to pour.

'Haven't you cooked anything?' grumbled Rita.

'Muesli and fruit is so much healthier, I always think,' said Beech.

Rita changed tack. 'You're looking tired this morning, Valma dear. Didn't you sleep very well?'

'I was woken a couple of times in the night,' said Valma. 'I thought I heard voices and movement.'

'It must have been the neighbours. They can be very noisy sometimes,' said Beech. 'You're subdued this morning, Jack. Are you feeling well?'

'Of course I am,' said Jack, who had acquired bags under his eyes and was picking moodily at his muesli. 'Could I have more coffee, do you think?'

'Of course.' He had arrived home in the early hours and crept into bed as quietly as he knew how. Beech had pretended to sleep all through his stumblings and shoe-droppings. How long could this go on? Was it possible for them to have a blazing row and agree to split up while Valma and Rita were in the house? By the way Jack was sighing into his coffee, he was thinking along similar lines.

After breakfast, Rita cornered Beech alone in the kitchen.

'I don't know what you think you're doing, Beatrice!'

'Have you had this conversation with Jack?'

'Don't avoid the issue. You disappear off without a word every day, you came home last night looking dishevelled and degenerate –' Beech laughed – 'and without a word of explanation for your behaviour.'

'Do you want me to explain? Do you want me to tell you everything? Would that really make you happy?'

'No! What I want, Beatrice, is for you and Jack to come to your senses and behave in a reasonable manner.'

'I think this is something that Jack and I will have to work out for ourselves. But we will try not to involve you in it. We shouldn't drag you into our quarrels, after all.'

'And, Beatrice . . .'

'Yes?'

'I see no reason to involve Valma in any of our discussions.'

'I can go along with that. Don't worry, I won't mention it to her.'

'Valma dear,' said Beech a little later. 'While I was visiting my father yesterday, he suggested that I should ask you about Mrs deLyle. You know what he's like these days, vague in the extreme. I couldn't get any more out of him than that, and it probably means nothing. But do you know what he was talking about?'

'Mrs deLyle? I remember her, of course. Anybody would.' She spoke slowly, as though giving out meaningless information while sorting out what she should reveal.

'Have you any references to her in your diaries or letters? I don't suppose it's important, but Henry was getting very upset about it.'

'I'll see if I have anything,' said Valma. 'I did bring some more of my things with me from the flat when I went up to London yesterday, and there may be something about her there.'

'I'll be in my office – well, cubbyhole – this morning, so if you find anything useful, please bring it along.'

'Of course, Beech dear.'

Later in the morning, Valma came and leaned against the open door of Beech's office. Beech looked up.

'Do you remember those *wonderful* parties we used to go to when we were teenagers?' said Valma.

'Did we?'

'Oh yes! Beach parties, treasure hunts on foot in the hills. Such interesting people! It was all so *wonderful*!'

Beech remembered Valma at that one party, on the edge of every group, using her sharp elbows to edge herself nearer the centre. Valma's imagination must have expanded the experience to fill a whole summer.

'And the *marvellous* picnics we used to go on, by the lake in the mountains, back in the old days.'

Valma too must have been thinking of the deLyles, for the famous picnics, the annual picnics, were hosted and masterminded by them.

'And the lovely teas your mother made us when I came to play at your house.'

As Beech remembered it, Valma came to tea once only. They had sat there with Rita, and eventually Henry, making stiff and unnatural conversation. She had felt that her parents wanted her to make a friend of this other girl, but she had managed to find nothing in common with her. They had come from different worlds, which might not have mattered, might indeed have provided a point of interest, but they were, too, headed in very different directions. Valma, even at the age of fifteen, had her sights firmly on marriage. A good marriage, amended Beech. And a good marriage meant a financially advantageous one. At fifteen, Beech had wanted art school and a wide experience of Life, whatever that might be.

But Valma had expanded this single picnic into a decade of glorious outings. Did she, like Beech's whole family, have such a conveniently inaccurate memory? No wonder she and Rita were getting on so well together. Fantasists the pair of them.

'Yes, there was certainly a picnic that last year, the year that Nicholas died.'

'Oh, don't talk about it! It was too awful!'

'But we'll have to talk about it if this memoir I'm editing is to have any meaning.'

'But you are so hard, Beech! Your mother and I feel things so deeply, you have no idea what it is like.'

'I feel it too,' said Beech in a strained voice.

'But you were just a child. Rita and I feel it as *women*. How could you understand anything that was going on? You were such a little innocent!'

From the bold expression on her face, Valma thinks I'm still the innocent, thought Beech.

'It will make sense to me eventually,' she said. 'I know it will.'

'I doubt it,' said Valma. 'And would you be any happier if it did?'

Old Mrs deLyle herself had presided that last year, in stately black silk jersey, which had probably come from Dior. A tight waist and lots of unpressed pleats, worn with sheer black stockings and toe-pinchingly narrow black kid shoes. So unsuitable for a picnic, Beech thought now, though at the time it had been impossible to imagine Mrs deLyle wearing anything else. Iron-grey hair in curls like cocktail sausages, and purple lipstick. But even a disrespectful teenager must fail to laugh at the old woman, for she was an awe-inspiring sight. And Beech had had the impression that Mrs deLyle did not like Valma, in spite of inviting her to the picnic.

24

The deLyles had been in the country for several generations and had married into other merchant families, so that they formed a network of rich, influential people throughout the whole Levantine area and into the Balkans. Their houses were old, expansive, full of wonderful, understated treasures. They spoke Arabic, French and Italian with ease, although they were never heard to speak anything but English among themselves when in the presence of other English people. What they did when they were on their own, nobody knew.

Blue-eyed, olive-skinned and variously red- or brown-haired, they were an exotic bunch, and Beech was rather overawed by them. Whatever they did, however they behaved, set the standard for behaviour among the British young. They never had to worry about being laughed at, like Beech, or looked down on, like Valma. Conrad deLyle had two sons, both a little older than Beech, called Edward and Harry. They were being educated in England at the moment, but were expected to go to university in France and to graduate school in the United States later. There were a dozen or so cousins in that generation. Daughters and younger sons were allowed to spend time at art schools. Doubtless, if they had shown talent, their elders would have encouraged them to study some musical instrument, but the deLyles were famous for their tin ears; tin ears, and money, also their excellent manners, and their charm. In the case of old Mrs deLyle, the charm had long ago been exchanged for an imperious bossiness, and a strong belief that anything she wanted should be done or acquired immediately. Oh yes, the deLyles were grand, there was no doubt about that.

So, old Mrs deLyle ordered the annual picnic to occur. This was not a simple alfresco meal in a nearby field, offering sandwiches and lemonade, but a grand expedition involving limousines and chauffeurs, and servants with tables and chairs, white damask tablecloths and napkins, and huge quantities of sophisticated food and drink. It was held some thirty miles away from the city, in the foothills of the mountains, on a grassy bank by a deep rocky pool. The Rainbow Pool, it was called. And when the sun shone out of the cloudless sky, up there in the clear air, in the shadow of the mountains above, the water was the dark blue, impenetrable colour of sapphires. When the sun disappeared into the canopy of the cedar trees, it darkened to pewter and then, with the arrival of dusk, to inky black.

The water was transparent, crystalline, and so deep that you could not see anything of the floor of the pool. The floor was probably of the same grey rock that thrust its points through the grass around them, but was it covered with swaying green plants, or inhabited by mysterious fish? It was impossible to tell.

The picnic took place in the summer, when those young deLyles who were usually away at school or university returned home and exchanged the pallor of European skin for the glossy olive of their homeland. The city was full of other European young, of course, also returned to their parents for the summer holidays, though in their case they did not usually think of the city as home in the way the deLyles did. Home for the Marklands, the Barrs and the Cottinghams was England.

Beech already knew the Rainbow Pool. She had been there with her own family earlier that summer, and for her too it was a special place.

* * *

Valma was sitting in the armchair in her bedroom. She had a blue notebook in her hand, but she wasn't reading. As a matter of fact, she was quite grateful to be away from the Warings, and on her own. She hadn't realized how tired of other people's company you could be when you had grown accustomed to spending so much of your time on your own. She tossed the notebook on to the table, rested her head against the back of the chair and closed her eyes.

So now your father wants me to tell you about it, does he? Well, why should I? It was bad enough when it happened, but why should I go through it again for your sake? You were a snobbish child in those days. You may have improved a little now, but I'm not going to humiliate myself again for you.

Stanley Crabbe's shop was an old-fashioned English grocery store. He stood behind the counter in a clean brown cotton coat, fresh from the laundry every day, and smiled at his customers. What he really thought of them, they never knew. They came in and bought his imported goods at inflated prices, instead of shopping in the local market. Cambridge sausages and Branston pickle; HP sauce and Cheddar cheese; Oxford marmalade, Portuguese sardines and Paxo stuffing mixes; Peak Frean's Christmas puddings, mincemeat and crackers. You could buy candles and paper frills for your birthday cake, tonic water to dilute your Gordon's gin, and Johnnie Walker whisky. There was a small discount if you ordered your gin and whisky by the case, and that is what most of his customers did. Stanley Crabbe was always polite, always helpful, and never by a flicker of his eyes indicated that, if the fancy took him, he might buy and sell many of the people who came to his shop and looked down on him as their social inferior.

Under his counter he kept, for favoured customers, various birth control supplies, forbidden by the Catholic and Muslim lawmakers of the country. These were smuggled in through

Customs every year by Mrs Roddis, Stanley's eldest sister, who packed them in her suitcases, underneath her pink bloomers and corsets, and her thick grey cardigans, when she arrived on her annual holiday from the Essex coastal town where she lived and where Stanley was born. No customs officer would dream of searching her luggage, for Mrs Roddis was both formidable and ugly, and they saved their attentions for young and attractive females, or scruffy Western backpackers. But what did the local chemist, in that conventional seaside resort in Essex make of her order of condoms by the gross box, of diaphragms in assorted sizes, of sponges and creams, jellies and pessaries? Did he believe that she had a secret and extravagant sex life? Or did he perhaps suspect her of running a brothel?

It was simple to see which of the English families patronized Mr Crabbe's shop and were treated to his store of prophylactics. He and Maria had only the one child, Valerie. The deLyles had two sons, with a neat two-year gap in their ages; the McCanns were childless; but the Barrs, who had fallen out with Stanley Crabbe some years before over a substandard order of patna rice, now had four children, and by the way Margot Barr was looking these days, there might well be a fifth little Barr on the way.

Maria Crabbe was of course the one reputed to have been picked up in Egypt by Stanley after the war. Found her in a knocking shop, as they whispered down at the club. In fact, she was a respectable Catholic matron, positively devout, in fact, who insisted on bringing her daughter up in her own faith instead of the tepid Anglicanism of her husband. Their daughter was named Valerie, because Stanley insisted on something steadfastly English. And then she was called Maria after her mother. Valerie Maria. Valma Crabbe. What could she be but a grocer's daughter?

Maybe just a grocer, thought Valma, but he was a very

successful grocer, and for a long time I was a lot richer than *you*, Beatrice Markland.

Crabbe's Provisions stood on a corner where the city's grandest shopping street was intersected by a small lane winding down into a fashionable square. The shop, with calculated humility, turned its back on the discreetly opulent boutiques of the avenue Bertrand, and put out a green striped awning over its mahogany door in the rue Arba'a instead. You entered from the brilliant sunlight and oven heat of the street into a dim, cool, spice-and-bacon scented interior. Valma realized now that this was achieved by efficient air conditioning, but at the time it had seemed like a magic trick that transported you over the oceans and continents back to a grocery store in an English country town. Mr Crabbe presided behind the wide polished counter with its brass scales and weights, while Mrs Crabbe sat behind the cash register and received the money. Mrs Crabbe was dressed in a respectable black dress, far removed from the Paris-designed one of Mrs deLyle, its very blackness an inferior imitation of the latter's. She spoke little, but her prune-dark eyes followed the customers as they browsed along the shelves and into the recesses of the shop. Mrs Crabbe at forty-something was built like a giant egg, with no neck visible to separate her face from her shoulders, no indentation for her waist; her legs descended like pillars into her stout shoes, with no apparent provision made for the possibility of ankles.

Valma, who was expected to help in the shop on Saturday afternoons, when she was released from her school, was quite different. When she was younger she had thin arms and legs, and a peaky, sallow face with hair that was inclined to be greasy. But her figure had developed early and she now boasted a well-rounded bosom which her mother insisted she should hide under high-collared stiff blouses, and hips and thighs which could well be described as powerful. She had her mother's eyes, which were improved in her case by long dark lashes. That year, she was trying out different ways of making her hair look more like a film star's. She washed it with egg yolk, she rinsed it with lemon juice, she wound it round soft curlers. For an hour or two after this treatment it looked wonderful, framing her face and bouncing healthily just above her shoulders, and you noticed what lovely eyes the girl had, and how delicate her bone structure was, but then the damp city heat would do its work, and her hair would descend into its usual sad rats' tails, and you remarked then that young Valma always had a sly look about her, never quite looked you in the eye, and was overeager to please. *Grocer's daughter*, they called her, long before someone else made the title fashionable.

So how was it that Valma received her coveted invitation to the picnic? People assumed that Mrs deLyle had had a sudden attack of compassion for the girl, or that someone else had put in a good word for her. Her parents certainly weren't asked, so she must have come with one of the other families. The Barrs, perhaps, the Pollocks or the Cottinghams. The old lady didn't address a single word to her during the day, but then she didn't speak to any of the young people apart from her own grand-children and that precocious little madam. Lyndal Barr.

It was late June and the summer holidays had started. Old Mrs deLyle entered the shop with one of her grandsons to inspect the latest arrivals of provisions and put in an order for any that took her fancy and suited her bulging, but firmly zipped-up purse. A chair was produced and placed in the centre of the shop, so that the other customers had to skirt round it and hide behind the shelves of marmalade and pickles, and the carefully stacked pyramids of tinned red Canadian salmon and jellied ham.

The old lady had in her right hand a rolled umbrella. In that climate rain rarely fell between the beginning of May and the middle of October, and yet she carried it the year round, as she had presumably been taught to do in some distant Edwardian summer on the other side of the world.

'Can I get you a cool drink, Mrs deLyle?' asked Valma, appearing at her side in demure blue and white gingham and sandals, with clean white socks. This was one of the days when her hair had fallen out of its curls and hung in damp, depressed strands.

'What? What? What are you on about? We were talking about coffee, I believe.'

'I thought you might be thirsty in this hot weather,' said Valma. 'And I have brought a cushion for your back.' She slipped the feather pad between the old lady's silk-clad back and the unrelenting wood of the chair.

'The Brazilian or the Kenyan?' said Mrs deLyle, shifting her hips a little to accommodate the cushion more comfortably. 'How am I to decide between them?' The umbrella stabbed the air in front of her, underlining the importance of her dilemma.

'The girl will make you up a pot of each to try,' came the voice of Mrs Crabbe from behind her cash desk. 'Valma, speak to Suha. Make yourself useful, young lady.'

Valma disappeared for several minutes while Mrs deLyle sat in state in the middle of the shop and Mr Crabbe brought bacon and tea, raisins and cloves, rice and tinned *petits pois* for her approval. A wave of the umbrella indicated that she would buy, a thump on the floor with the ferule and a downward curl of the lip indicated that she would not.

'Here,' said Valma, in her sly, soft voice. 'This is the Brazilian for you to try first. Milk? Sugar? No? Quite right, they would blur the taste.' She poured from the chased copper pot with the long spout into a tiny blue porcelain cup with a thick gold band around its rim.

'Aromatic, don't you think?' she said, whispering seductively into the old lady's pale mauve ear. 'Picked by pure young girls from bushes growing high in the thin, cold air.'

'Quite nice,' said Mrs deLyle, drawing the black liquid in with her long upper lip, and letting it roll to the back of her tongue. 'But on the bitter side, unfortunately. Are you sure that the maid allowed the water to go off the boil for a minute before pouring it on to the grounds?'

'Our servants have been well-trained by my mother in the making of coffee,' said Valma, and removed the cup from her hand. If Mrs deLyle knew that it was Valma herself, rather than the downtrodden Suha, who had made the coffee, she didn't mention it. 'But do taste the Kenyan now,' said Valma, 'once you have cleared your palate with a water biscuit.' And then she went through the whole oily, self-demeaning process once more. Valma bent close to the old lady, offering her sweetmeats from her own fingers, smiling at her.

'Yes, this is better,' said Mrs deLyle, handing back the second cup of coffee. The high ceiling of the shop soared above her like the roof of a cathedral. The other customers stayed silently in their recesses and hiding places like so many worshippers. 'You may put in half a pound of the Kenyan beans,' she added graciously. 'And bring me some more of these Damascus fruits. The apricots are the best. And a glass of water.'

'With ice?' asked Valma.

'But of course!'

Valma backed out of her presence as if from royalty's.

'How are you getting on at school?' asked Mrs deLyle, a few minutes later, sinking her large teeth into a third syrupy preserved apricot. 'I expect you'll be leaving soon and earning your living.' She looked pointedly at the bosom that Valma had failed to conceal within her unappealing dress.

'I have another year of studying yet,' said Valma. 'This is my last long holiday. Next year I shall certainly be working, as you say.'

'And you mean to make the most of this summer, I suppose.'

'Oh yes!' cried Valma, and the words 'annual picnic' could

be read in a balloon above her head by anyone with a shred of imagination.

'Well, you're a good girl, I suppose,' said Mrs deLyle, handing out the praise like a small tip, then struggling to her feet with the aid of her furled umbrella. 'And I believe you have friends in the English community.'

Valma opened her eyes wide, but Mrs deLyle offered no further enlightenment as to the identity of Valma's English friends. 'They have spoken well of you. So you must come to our picnic this year. I'll tell the Pollocks to bring you.'

'Thank you,' said Valma demurely. 'It will be a great honour for me.' And she went to hold the door open so that the old lady could make an exit as grand as her entrance.

'You must learn to stand up straight if you want to make something of yourself,' said Mrs deLyle. 'And try to do something about that accent of yours. It's all very well out here, but it wouldn't do back in England, you know. But apart from that I suppose you will do.'

Valma bowed her head meekly as if in acceptance of this advice and stood at the door until the old lady had entered her car and been driven away.

It hadn't been difficult to deliver the letter to Jarmila. The girl had been startled when Valma had pushed the white envelope into her hand one lunchtime, but she had soon understood what it was about, and had quickly slipped it inside an exercise book. Presumably the Intelligence community were playing their childish games with her help. She, Valma, really didn't care, except insofar as it helped her achieve her ambitions. And Henry Markland had kept his side of the bargain, she was pleased to see. She hadn't enjoyed the feel of his hand, hot and sweaty through the cotton of her dress that afternoon at the tea party. One day she would exact payment for that as well. Did that little innocent, Beatrice, understand what her father was up to? She doubted it. But Rita was a different person altogether. She imagined that Rita, too, received something in return for turning a blind eye to Henry's predilections.

'And now you will be asking for a new dress,' said her mother.

'In red,' said Valma. 'I've seen the material in the souk. Suha and I could go and buy a few metres of it later this afternoon.'

'Red? And what is the material?'

'A Swiss cotton, very fine, woven so that it feels like the softest silk.'

'I would prefer to see you in linen, and in some pale colour, but you will never listen to your poor mother. Take Suha with you. Buy your five metres of cloth. I don't want you looking like a poor relation at that picnic of theirs.'

'Thank you, Mother.'

25

July, and Beech had already been off school for a month, wandering about the house with nothing much to do, spending time with the servants, drawing what she saw on their balcony, going shopping in the markets with Munira. She had run out of books to read. She felt as though she was accepted in her own home on sufferance only. Rita didn't want her around when her friends were there, and certainly couldn't bear to take her to the sophisticated hotels and bars where she went at lunchtimes and in the afternoons. Where should she go? It was too hot to lie on the beach, and the tepid sea was unpleasant to swim in.

And then at last came the third week in July.

'I don't know why you want to come to the airport,' said Rita. 'There won't be room for you in the car, will there, Henry?'

'She can sit in front with the driver.'

'Well, don't blame me if you get hot and tired and we have to wait for hours because the flight is delayed,' said Rita, snapping the fading flower heads from the vase of carnations on the hall table.

Henry was clean and pressed in a silver-grey linen suit and a shirt that he had put on only minutes before, so that it was not yet patched with sweat. He smelled of Yardley's Lavender soap. He wore a panama hat, pristine as when it was bought from a shop in St James's. He stood by the door, waiting for Rita to finish her slaughter of the carnations. Beech tried to read the expression on his face, but even as she watched him he covered

221

his eyes with dark glasses, then drew a silver cigarette case from an inside pocket, extracted a cigarette and lit it with the lighter that Rita had given him for his last birthday: silver again, with his initials engraved on it. He had long hands and fingers, sandy-coloured from the sun, with dark brown stains on the right index finger from all the Player's Navy Cut he had smoked.

'You let that child do whatever she wants,' grumbled Rita, picking up her handbag at last and joining Henry at the door.

'I'm not a child,' said Beech.

'You're behaving like one,' said Rita. She caught sight of Henry's cigarette and the neat cylinders of ash in the cut-glass ashtray. 'I shall have to empty that,' she said, disappearing through the door to the kitchen. Henry and Beech looked at the lengthening ash on Henry's cigarette and silently hoped that she would reappear before it dropped on to the black and white tiles of the hall floor.

Childish, am I? Well why shouldn't I be? thought Beech, following her parents down the stairs and into the oven heat of the car. I'm only fifteen, but what about you? What's your excuse? She was glad that she was sitting in front with the driver. She could ignore the bickering in the back seat. Boutros was quite uninterested in her and her parents. He touched the Virgin doll that swung from the mirror and pulled away into the traffic. He then took no further notice of them at all, which meant that she could lose herself in her own thoughts and fantasies.

With the arrival of Nicholas the summer holidays could really start. It was as though the world had been in a continuous dark night since the last time he had been there. And now, with his arrival, the light would be switched on and everything would be visible and she could make sense of it. It was amazing how little sense she made of the world and its inhabitants as a general rule. They moved like wooden figures across the stylized landscape, with no apparent reason for their actions. If only they would stop and explain it to her sometimes instead of looking at her when she asked a question – an important question – and told her not to be so stupid. Sometimes, in an even more puzzling manner, they – Rita, usually – told her not to try to be clever. Or else she was told that she was too young to understand. And they shook their heads at her, and told her to get on with her homework. Or if she reminded Rita that it was the holidays, and consequently she had no homework to do, she was sent off to tidy her room. She must have the tidiest room in the Middle East by now.

Behind her the voices still murmured, the engine of the big car hummed under the shining bonnet and beside her Boutros glanced up at the swaying doll-Virgin as though she was the one who held the answers to all the questions of the universe.

Rita was right. The plane was over an hour late. They sat in the air-conditioned bar and sipped at iced drinks. Henry still wore his hat, but he had removed his dark glasses. This made his expression no easier to read. Did he practise in front of the mirror to get that particular dead look to his eyes? Just like a fish on the marble slab in the kitchen, before the cook took her thin-bladed knife and ripped a dark red line down its silver belly.

Rita tapped her scarlet nails on the table in an irritable tattoo. 'I don't know how you can drink that disgusting American stuff,' she said, scowling at Beech's Pepsi.

'It's better than gin,' said Beech.

'And how would you know that?' snapped Rita.

'Do stop,' said Henry, mildly. 'Remember that people are looking at us.' Rita composed her face into a superior mask then added a smile that lifted the corners of her mouth but did not expose her teeth. Henry gave a tiny nod of approval. 'And I believe that Nicholas's plane is about to land.'

They were allowed out past the passport and customs

controls, peaked caps dipping towards Henry as they walked. So Beech was there watching for some minutes as Nicholas came out of the plane and started to walk down the steps on to the tarmac, before he saw the group that was his family.

He had a suntan, Beech saw. He would not be one of those corpse-white English boys – men, she amended – who went lobster red and peeled and looked so awful next to the oiled brown skin of the locals. His hair was fair, and already streaked blond by the sun. He's grown, she thought. And he's got shoulders now, like a man.

Rita was moving forward, her arms rising in greeting. She is a humming bird today, thought Beech, watching the gauzy sleeves flutter in the breeze, the beak-like mouth open and start pouring out words.

'Nicholas darling! How you've grown! You make me feel quite tiny next to you. Let me look at you!' And so it went, as she enfolded him in her arms and pecked at his cheeks. Beech and Henry stayed where they were, waiting until it was over.

Nicholas took his mother's greeting in silence at first, his arms at his side, until he at last patted Rita awkwardly on the shoulders, as though she had been bereaved rather than reunited with her son. But he looked over Rita's shoulder all the while, and caught and held Beech's gaze. He smiled at her, as though the two of them were in a conspiracy. *You have to humour the parents; it's expected. Have to play the dutiful son. But I'm still the same person, really. When this is over, we'll talk, just the two of us.*

That's what his look said, or at least that's what she hoped it said. She stood placidly in the sunlight, awaiting her turn, but inside she was boiling with excitement, her stomach fluttering like a netful of small fish.

At last Rita's twittering stopped and she turned and led her son towards the others.

'Look!' she said, as though they hadn't noticed. 'It's Nicholas!'

'I'm glad to hear it,' said Henry drily. 'Hello, Nicholas.' And they shook hands.

Finally, Beech said, 'Hello, Nick.'

'Beech,' said Nicholas. 'Good to see you.'

They didn't touch. But they smiled. Nick's smile lit up her world, made sense of it all at last.

Rita said, 'Her name is Beatrice,' but no one took any notice.

Henry said, 'We can go straight through to the car. Boutros will pick up your suitcase later.'

'What about customs and passports and things like that?' asked Nicholas.

'Not necessary,' said Henry, and they walked past the peaked caps and silver braid and out into the oven heat of the car park, while Henry lit another cigarette and blew the smoke up into the hot air where it swayed and spread into a flat blue shape like a monstrous feather.

'What's that?' asked Nicholas, pointing to a crouched black form at the top of a concrete post.

'It's a bird,' said Rita.

'Some sort of predator,' said Henry. 'A raptor.'

'It's a vulture,' said Beech.

'Don't be disgusting!' said Rita.

'But it is,' protested Beech. 'They're quite common in this part of the world. It has a bald head, you see.'

The bird raised its wide, ragged wings and flapped its way up into the sky until it found a thermal strong enough to support its weight and it floated, wings motionless, in the soupy air.

'It will be looking for carrion,' said Beech, her urge to inform her family on the subject of vultures overcoming her discretion. 'There'll be a dead dog or something over there, I expect.' The vulture was moving out of sight, doubtless drawn by the smell of decaying meat.

'We really don't want to hear this,' said Henry, austerely, 'accurate as it doubtless is. Beatrice, you do not have to share your knowledge with the rest of us. We are simply not interested.'

Beech subsided, and remained silent for the rest of the journey back to the house. She knew lots more about vultures, as it happened, and she was sure that Nicholas wanted to hear it. She glanced up at him.

'Fascinating,' he said, and he smiled down at Beech from his new height. She liked this feeling of being smaller than her brother. Too often these days she towered over everyone, including most boys of her own age.

In the car, once more seated beside the driver, she heard behind her the snap and click and the indrawn breath that meant that Henry had lit another cigarette. The three voices wove in and out of each other as Nicholas answered his parents' questions about his life back in England. Beech didn't mind that she was out of it. She remembered the way he had smiled, just for her, and she hugged the memory to her. Later, when they were alone, she would tell Nicholas about the vultures, and he would listen and ask all the right questions. He wouldn't dismiss her the way Henry and Rita always did.

For when Nick was at home, everything changed.

It was as though a charge of electricity shot through the apartment. She wasn't the only one who noticed. They all felt it. Rita smiled. For a day or two, even Henry seemed happier. He didn't drink as much, just for that day or two. After that he grew angrier, as though he realized how he resented this strong young male who had moved into his territory.

'Be careful!' Beech wanted to cry.

But Nick took no notice. He couldn't understand why Beech should be so upset by Henry.

'Take no notice,' he said. 'You should stay cool. Let it slide over you.'

Beech couldn't. But she could watch in envy as Nick did what he said she should. And where did it get him? she wondered afterwards. How cool was he at the end? How much of the tragedy slid off his broadening, suntanned shoulders?

'We don't have to stay in the house, you know,' he said. And he called the driver and told him to drive them to the Poseidon Beach, or to the sailing club in the old port, where they would take Henry's boat out for the day.

'Let's go to the Rainbow Pool,' he said one day at breakfast. 'All of us, I mean.'

'I have to work. Haven't you noticed?' said Henry.

'I just thought you might take a day off for once,' said Nicholas.

'I'm not an irresponsible member of the *jeunesse dorée* like you,' said Henry.

'I'd never thought of myself like that before,' said Nicholas.

But Rita broke in and said, 'What a wonderful idea, Nicky! We can have Boutros to drive us, can't we, Henry?'

And Henry said, 'Yes.'

Henry left for work shortly afterwards, promising to send Boutros back with the car. And Rita immediately telephoned her friend Rowley, who apparently *could* take a day off work at a moment's notice.

'Who's he?' asked Nick.

'Her latest,' said Beech.

'Ah. She still bothers with all that, does she?'

In the hills, the weather was more like an English summer, warm and moist and green. As they climbed the hilly track towards the foothills of the mountains, the temperature grew cooler and the effort of walking was not so great. Once Boutros had laid a rug on the ground, and set out a couple of folding chairs and brought out the big Thermos box of mixers and ice,

Beech and Nick left the two adults to their gin and gossip and went exploring.

'Don't go too far!' called Rita after them.

Nicholas strode ahead, Beech followed more slowly, looking at every plant, every flower, crouching down to spy on insects in the undergrowth. She walked along a narrow path into the trees, following the sound of running water. Behind her head rose leaves as big as elephants' ears, swaying on thick stems, while other bushes pushed feathery, scented foliage towards her.

'Have you found the pool yet?' Nick had returned to find her.

'No, I was just watching everything.'

'Come on. I'll show you.'

There was water gushing down a cleft in the rocks. They followed it upwards, through vegetation and over rocks until they came to the place where a natural dam formed a large pool under the overhanging rocks. Trees soared above them filtering the sunlight through their foliage.

'Is the water cold?'

'We could try it and find out.'

Here, in this country during the summer, cold water was a luxury.

They took off their sandals and sat side by side on a flat rock, letting their feet hang in the water. Yes, it was very cold. Cold as England.

'I've got green feet,' said Beech, looking down.

'I'm going to swim,' said Nicholas. And he pulled off his shirt and shorts, leaving on only his underpants.

'Girls can't do that.'

'Why not? Oh, for goodness' sake, no one cares here. Rita's not going to come looking for us. She and the Rowley character are probably at it on the picnic rug by now.'

'Do you think so?' She wanted to ask exactly what it was they were doing, but was too shy.

'No. It would mess up her hair. She couldn't have that!'

They both laughed, and Beech pulled off her blouse and skirt. She was wearing the hated bra and her white school knickers. Last year she had been as tall as Nick. Now she was three inches shorter.

'How deep is it?' she asked, looking down into the smoky green depths.

'Very deep,' said Nick, and dived in.

Beech followed.

The water really was cold, and she felt her lungs contract with the shock as she went under the water. This was better than the warm seawater she usually swam in. Now that she was used to the temperature, she dived again and again, swimming deep under the surface, from one side to the other.

'Can you touch the bottom?' she called to Nicholas.

'No. It's too deep. Must be twenty feet or so.'

They swam slowly, side by side, from one end to the other, pulling themselves out to sit again on a broad, flat rock. Here a little sunshine reached through the vegetation and warmed their wet skin. In the distance, bells jangled and a goatherd called to his flock.

'Look,' said Beech. 'There's the line again.'

'The boundary,' said Nicholas.

At this end of the pool, the sun struck the water and turned it to turquoise and ultramarine. A dozen feet further on, and the shadow of the rocks painted a black line across the water. On the other side it was opaque, mysterious.

'When you cross that line, Nico, you can be who and what you want to be,' said Beech.

'That may be true, but I'm getting bloody hungry. Aren't you?'

As they pulled their clothes over their wet underthings, they heard a crashing and crackling of branches, and a thin brown goat appeared, pursued by a small boy with a long stick in his hand. The lad was dark-skinned and black-eyed and reminded Beech of Khalil. He smiled at them, shouted a greeting, and then scrambled after the goat.

'Come on!' said Beech crossly. 'I thought you said you were hungry.'

They scraped their fingers through their hair, and walked slowly back to the picnic place and Rita.

26

At the Warings' house in Enderby Road, they were putting on a play. Or so it seemed to Beech. They each had a part. They had lines to learn and to deliver, and with practice, and frequent rehearsals, they were improving. Word-perfect. They hardly needed the services of a prompter.

The play appeared to be one of those drawing-room comedies set in the 1930s, with happy, middle-class people tripping backwards and forwards through the french windows, laughing a lot. They were immensely polite to each other. Jack was charming, even if he often looked rather tired. Rita was gracious. Beech was cheerful and helpful to everyone, cooking meals, clearing up after people, working on the notes for the book of memoirs. When she disappeared off on her own for an hour or two every day no one mentioned the fact. Valma tried to exchange roguish glances with Rita or Jack when the front door clicked shut behind her. 'Off for another of her committee meetings, I suppose!' But she found herself met with bland, uncomprehending smiles in return.

Fergus didn't know how Beech could keep up the pretence.

'It isn't a pretence. We all know that I come here to see you, and that Jack disappears off to Kidlington to meet his lady-friend. Her name is Denise, by the way. I found it written on a scrap of paper and Jack looked so coy about it that I knew it was the one. We're just keeping off the subject. It can't be for long, can it?'

'How long are you carrying on like that?' asked Fergus,

frowning. 'Aren't you just adding to the cat's cradle of lies?'

Beech sighed. 'You're right. I know it. But just let me get through the anniversary with Henry's tenuous grasp on reality still in place, and I'll face up to it then. You and me, Jack and Denise: I'll bring it all out into the open.'

'And what happens then?'

'I'll face that when I get to it.'

'If you're so worried about your father, why doesn't Rita move back to Rose Cottage to look after him?'

'Because she's a coward. She hates to see him pottering around the place, getting dottier by the week. She likes to see herself as the centre of a brilliant social set, and it's difficult to do that when Henry's in this state.'

'Will he get better, do you think?'

'Yes. In September. He'll be a different person then.'

'And even if Valma has to stay at your house, why can't Rita move back to Rose Cottage?'

'I think she has to keep an eye on Valma. She doesn't trust her, though she's better at hiding it than me.'

Indeed, it feels as though Rita and Valma have moved into her house and will never be shunted out of it again. The house is even less her own than it was before. Her bathroom smells of exotic oils, the thickness of her towels has been criticized. Rita has imposed some of her own ideas on her cooking. Beech has started to draw up lists, and a rota of chores, and is considering how to introduce these duties to her guests. They have all learned their new parts so well that she thinks they will adapt to these extra lines with no trouble at all. She has not yet found the right moment to open the subject, however.

Next morning at breakfast, Beech looked across at Jack as he scratched the top of his ear while puzzling over the *Telegraph* crossword. He filled in a clue, then frowned at the letters he had written in. Got it wrong again, thought Beech. You should have used a pencil.

'I think I'll be going back to Rose Cottage today,' said Rita into the silence.

It was hard to ignore the way Beech and Jack looked at her with ill-concealed delight.

'To pick up a few more clothes, and one or two other things I need,' she added.

Jack and Beech subsided again.

'Valma can come with me.'

Jack rubbed at the crossword letters with his finger, smudging the Biro ink. He scratched the top of his ear again, transferring the ink from finger to ear.

'Why don't you stay in Chipping Hampton for a day or two?' said Beech. 'Wouldn't Valma like to see that part of the county? You could show her the Cotswolds.'

'I don't think so,' said Rita dismissively. 'You wouldn't want to see all those dreary picturesque villages and elbow your way through the crowds of tourists, would you, Valma dear?'

'Well . . .' said Valma, then saw the bored expression on Rita's face and decided not to push her luck. 'Of course not. But I *should* like to see your lovely home.'

For three glorious days Beech had her house to herself. Even Jack made himself scarce. But all too soon Valma and Rita were back.

When they walked through her front door and into her house as though it was *theirs*, Beech felt fury welling up inside her. She wanted to shout at them to go back to Chipping Hampton and stay there. *Why don't you do it?* But she knew why. Rita, with her impossible behaviour, was, in spite of everything, still her mother, and against all reason she still loved her. She couldn't allow Valma to destroy her. And she couldn't let that dreadful little woman needle and provoke Henry until he lost his precarious hold on reality and ended up in a nursing home, or worse. Rita, with her ridiculous snobbery, adored her life at the centre of the Chipping Hampton social round. She didn't want to be seen as an object of pity. Pity would demolish Rita. No, she couldn't risk it. She would have to grit her teeth and hold her tongue and do all those other English things that protected you from the pain of reality.

'How is it going, Beech dear?' Valma had opened the door to Beech's cubbyhole and stood there like a scarlet balloon in her latest outfit.

'I believe I've nearly finished. Just a few more reminiscences to type out, just another handful of photographs to paste in. Do you like the green leather?'

'Quite beautiful. Really, though, I was wondering how far you had got in your delvings into past history. I've never really known what a hidden agenda was, but don't you think this must be it?'

'I don't believe there is anything hidden,' said Beech. 'Nicholas, a pleasant boy of seventeen, drowned accidentally and tragically during a mountain picnic. He wasn't the great love of your life, or you of his. He had years, he thought, to make up his mind about things like that. He was still trying out all the different people he might have been. I don't believe he had made any major decisions.'

'While I was staying in your parents' lovely home this week, I had the chance to talk to dear Henry.'

'My father is not always quite himself. You must know that.'

'Why so defensive about him? I found him a delightful old gentleman. He remembered me, I must say, very well. He and I got on like a house on fire. He introduced me to dear old Gunter –' she inadvertently wrinkled her nose at the memory – 'and showed me his compost bins. All those worms burrowing away in the fertile soil, working their magic in the dark.'

'I'm glad you've found an interest in compost.'

'And he kept telling me that something terrible had happened and that he blamed *you*, Beatrice.'

'As I said, he's getting muddled in his old age.' She stared resolutely at Valma, who tried a different tack.

'And your mother with her wonderful social life! I hadn't realized how positively feudal the English countryside still was. And those delightful neighbours – all so conservative! Don't you call it the old-fashioned charm of England?'

'Very charming, if you like that sort of thing,' said Beech guardedly.

'And Rita does, doesn't she? And with her so-respectable background in the Levant, she is accepted right into what you might call your county families.'

'I think they're quite robust,' said Beech, catching Valma's drift. 'I think you'd have to do something quite spectacularly vulgar, and in a public place, before they would take any notice of you.'

Valma gave a little, tinkling laugh. 'I do so hope you're right, Beech dear.'

The red balloon detached itself from the doorframe and bounced slowly away into the kitchen.

Bitch! The sanctimonious, blackmailing bitch!

She opened another notebook.

27

'Why are you mooching around the house all day?' asked Nicholas.

'I'm not supposed to go out on my own. They say it isn't safe,' said Beech. 'If I go out into the town, I get whistled at.'

Nicholas laughed. 'I don't think that's very life-threatening.'

'I don't like it much. People look at me. Men.'

'Well, you're not on your own any more. I'm with you.'

That was what she had been waiting to hear all summer. 'Where shall we go?' she asked.

'We could take the boat out.'

'I'd like that.'

'Bring a swimsuit. It's much nicer swimming out in the bay than it is from the beach.'

'Is it safe?'

'Stop worrying about being safe! Live a little. And anyway, there's practically no tide, and no dangerous currents. Just acres of smooth blue sea. Your only threat is from the sun. Bring some of that white stuff with you: if you get burned, Rita will give me hell.'

It took her only a couple of minutes to bundle together swimsuit, towel and sun-stick, and shove them in a bag with the identity card that would get her into the port. With Nick she needn't wait until her father's car and driver were free. They could walk together through the town, looking at stalls, even wandering into shops if they wanted. With a young man beside her she was safe from catcalls and whistles.

Out in the bay there was a breeze, and the deep water was cool beneath the surface. They took it in turns to swim off the boat, diving into the turquoise water, climbing back over the side and flopping down on to the deck like oversized, beached fish. Back on the coast the temperature would be climbing over a hundred and the humidity would make every exertion a torture. But out here in the bay, Beech could lie on her back with her eyes closed and enjoy the feeling of hot sun on her wet body.

'Put a shirt on, you'll get burned,' said Nico, when she climbed back into the boat for the last time.

'Look!' she said, pointing at an area of sea a hundred yards away. A long, oval stretch of water boiled white in the sunlight. The smooth blue of the bay was broken by a shoal of fish. The tunny had arrived.

Nico had taken out the oars, fitted them into the rowlocks. He rowed towards the tunny very quietly and gently, without sending shock waves through the water. Beech could hear the fish hissing as they rose from the water, arching back into it with a slapping noise. Under the surface they moiled and circled, their bodies moving fast, upwards and sideways, slicing silver and black through the blue of the water.

'Time to go back, I suppose,' said Nico reluctantly. 'Rita will make a fuss if we're not back in time to be polite to all her boring cocktail guests.'

'There's time for one more swim,' said Beech. She was wearing her new swimsuit, with its jagged stripes of black and silver. As she dived and turned in the water she looked like a fish herself as the sun caught the silver of her costume and turned her wet hair to molten copper.

'Black or silver. Do you know which you are?'

'What? Yes, of course I do, Nico. I'm me. And I'm going to be a famous painter,' said Beech.

'When I've got my degree, I can be your legal adviser.'

'You're laughing at me.'

'No. Really, I'm not.'

Nico shipped the oars and Beech trimmed the sail, then she swung the tiller over and put the little boat about.

'We're coming up to the boundary again,' said Nico.

It was the line that divided the brightly sunlit half of the bay from the shadowed part. This time they were passing out of the sun and into the shadow.

'Now we can be whatever we want,' said Beech, as they moved from one to the other. 'You don't have to be a lawyer if you don't want.' For a few moments, as they moved out of the light, she was blinded and couldn't make out her brother's face. He seemed a stranger, his features unknown. Then, as her eyes adjusted, he turned back into her familiar Nick.

From out in the bay the town had been a vague jumble of white bricks scattered among the green of its palm trees. As they moved closer, she could see the individual buildings, the toy cars and trams, and finally the matchstick people. And the familiar smell of sewage and charcoal-cooked food wafted over the water towards them. From an open café door came a high, sad love song.

On the way home, as they walked up through the dusty lanes towards their own part of town, the clouds massed overhead and blotted out the sun. Seconds later, the rain came down in glassy rods and they ran for the shelter of the market. They stood in a small shop, hung around with swags and swathes of coloured, embroidered silks. Beech stood against a length of white and silver silk, sewn with little stars and moons and swirling lilies. She shook her head, scattering raindrops in a shower of diamonds, and letting the pearls of water drip down her face.

'Shall I buy it for you?' asked Nick.

'What?'

'I've got my allowance. I can buy some of that silk for you.

It suits you. That, or the blue and green one over there.'

The shopkeeper approached and pulled out bales of cloth, draping them over Beech's shoulders as she stood, laughing, in front of the long mirror. She laughed because it was a ridiculous idea that she should have the material she wanted for a dress. It never happened like that.

'That's the one,' said Nick.

It was the simplest of all the patterns, just a dark blue silk with a shiny green spot.

'You can't buy it!' exclaimed Beech.

'Yes I can. How many metres do you need?'

'Three? Four?'

'We'll have four,' he told the shopkeeper.

'You should argue about the price,' said Beech as he handed over a bundle of notes.

'Should I? Yes, you're probably right. You must have it made up in a very simple style. Don't let Rita bully you into flounces. A high neck and sleeveless, cut in to here –' he indicated a point on her shoulder – 'and a short skirt. Everyone in England's wearing them.' He tossed the package of silk over to her. 'Here, you carry it. Men don't carry the shopping in this town.'

When they arrived back at the house, still wet from the sudden downpour, and holding their bundles of damp towels and swimsuits, they found that Rita and Henry were both at home. Beech hid the parcel of silk under her towel and hoped that the sea water wouldn't seep through the paper wrapping.

'Where have you been?' asked Henry.

He's been drinking, thought Beech.

'We took the boat out,' replied Nicholas.

Nicholas doesn't understand, thought Beech. He doesn't know that we should be staying quiet, keeping out of Henry's way, pretending we don't exist. *Now we can be whatever we want*. How ridiculous we were to think such a thing!

'Just the two of you?'

'It's quite a small boat,' said Nicholas. 'There's no room for a crowd.'

'Why didn't you ask permission?'

'We didn't go far. We could see the shore all the time we were out.'

The whites of Henry's eyes were suffusing with red, a mixture of anger and whisky.

'I don't like clever young people who answer back,' he said.

Nicholas opened his mouth to reply.

Shut up, Nicholas, prayed Beech.

'Really, we were quite safe,' said Beech quickly. Henry turned towards her, as she knew he would.

'Another clever young person. And what do you know about danger and safety? You've made yourself an expert on the subject, I suppose.'

It's not just his eyes that are bloodshot, she thought. His lips, too, are suffused with blood. At any moment they might burst and purple gore would spill down his chin.

'Well? You consider that you've been showing proper judgement in your actions, do you?'

She wasn't sure what he was talking about. She did know that she had done something awful and that, eventually, she would be allowed to know what it was.

Henry walked across to the table and picked up a sheaf of papers. He held them up in front of Beech's face. 'An expert on danger, just as you've made yourself an expert on art.'

'Not an expert. I'm just practising.'

'Be quiet! I'm not interested in your excuses.'

'Why should she make excuses?' put in Nicholas. 'They're only drawings, aren't they?'

'Only drawings. How innocent. And what are these, eh?'

'Nothing,' said Beech.

'Goats,' said Henry, holding one of them up. 'What a talented little girl you are.' He leafed through the drawings, letting them drift to the floor as he discarded them. 'And not so little, either. We shall have to keep an eye on you. Who's this?'

It was one of her drawings of Khalil. She could see now that it flattered him, idealized him even. In her drawing his hair was thicker and wavier, his eyes darker and larger, his smile more alluring. He looked like a young film star. All her adoration was there on the page.

'Well? Who is this? What's been happening while your mother and I have been out?'

'Nothing. Really. It's just the boy who sometimes comes with the goats. He's the goat-woman's son.'

'First of all you study goats. Then you extend your intimacy to the boy who looks after them. How long did these drawings take? How long have you been spending in the company of servants and randy young peasants?'

It was best to say nothing now.

'I'll speak to Munira,' said Henry. 'He won't come here again. I won't have it.' He turned on Nicholas again. 'And I won't have you taking Beatrice off alone in a boat. She can't be trusted!'

'That's unfair!' said Nicholas.

'Unfair? Life is unfair, and the sooner you learn that the better.' He tore the drawing of Khalil into small pieces and threw them on the floor with the other drawings. 'I won't have that little slut making an exhibition of herself,' he said. Beech saw the beads of spittle on his bottom lip. She guessed that he wanted to pour himself another whisky and she started to leave the room. Nick hesitated a moment as though wanting to argue with his father, but finally followed her.

'Munira!' shouted Henry. 'Come and clear up this bloody mess!'

'I think we can go now,' said Beech to Nicholas as they hovered by the door.

'Is he often like that?'

'Yes. Mostly. Didn't you know?'

'I've never seen him quite so nasty.'

Nicholas went off to find some books. On her way upstairs Beech met Rita. 'What have you done to upset your father?' she asked.

'Nothing,' said Beech.

'And why are you always hanging around Nicholas? He doesn't want to be bothered with his little sister, you know. He wants to make his own friends.'

'He wanted to go sailing with me. He asked me himself.'

'That's only because he feels sorry for you. But I'm sure he'd rather be with some nice girl of his own. Lyndal Barr, or that plump little daughter of the Cottinghams.'

'They're both horrible. And boring.'

'I don't wish to hear your opinion. And I do think you should watch your behaviour, Beatrice. It isn't very nice for me to be shouted at by your father, you know. Well, make sure you're showered and changed in half an hour. I have a few friends dropping in for drinks.'

That night she could tell there would be a thunderstorm, for the sun shone copper behind a cobalt haze, and the heavy clouds pressed upon the flanks of the mountains until the air was squeezed flat and filled her nose and lungs like noxious jelly. She could feel the weight of the sky and all the universe beyond lying on her head, pressing her into the dust of the city. She went alone on to the empty balcony to watch. And then the rain began. Drops the size of her palm, stinging down on to the dust, hitting her skin. Hot rain, slapping against her shoulders and arms. She ran for cover when the raindrops changed to hailstones as big as the eggs of some exotic bird. White, compacted, heaping up like snow drifts until they melted in the tropical heat. The lightning shimmied down the hills, illuminating the sky all around the bay, like a fireworks show for the gods. Thunder blocked out the sound of radios, blanked out the call of the muezzin. Oh yes, the skies are more powerful than your gods. Bars of water rolled down off the mountain and fell from the skies.

And just as suddenly, it was all over.

'Here,' said Nicholas. 'I've rescued these for you.'

He gave her the drawings that had been flung on the floor. Only the full-face detailed portrait of Khalil was missing, but then that one had been torn to pieces.

'Thanks.'

She leafed through the drawings. 'What's wrong with them? *What?*'

'Nothing. Some of them are rather good. I like these two. Is this really the boy who comes with the goat?'

'Yes, of course. His name's Khalil. He's a friend of mine.'

'Can I take a couple of them for myself?'

'Of course.' She knew he was only being kind, trying to make up for the way Henry had made her feel.

When she was alone, she picked a graphite pencil from the box and scored through the top page, over and over again, until the pencil point tore holes in the paper. She stuffed them all into her chest of drawers. That was the last of her ambitions to be a painter, she told herself.

The summer passed in a brilliant stream of outings and parties. Beech remembered seeing Valma, always a bit of an outsider, but doggedly attending every entertainment organized for the young. She stood on the outskirts of every group, listening, noting, *spying*.

Beech tried hard to enjoy herself, to gain her parents' approval, but never quite managed it. If she tried to be vivacious and amusing, she felt her father's eyes on her, glowering, disapproving. She seemed to shrink inside, as though everything she was trying to bring into flower was shrivelling and dying. The only one who was always on her side was Nicholas, her brother. He was the only one she wanted to dance with and the only one too who found her amusing. But then she was in trouble again.

'Go and talk to someone else,' Rita hissed. 'You're cramping his style like this, Beatrice.'

And Beech was reduced to talking to her parents' friends. All those hot, perspiring men with their heavy hands and hairy ears! She dreamed of long-haired, dark-skinned lovers. Lovers that looked a lot like Khalil, though they would know all about books and poetry and the latest sort of painting.

And then, finally, as August burned itself out and the new school term loomed on the horizon, came the greatest, grandest party of them all: the annual picnic given by the deLyles at the Rainbow Pool.

28

'What shall I wear?'

It was the morning of the picnic. Beech had asked, unsure how dressed-up an occasion it would be. In previous years she had been one of the children, running around in shorts and sunhat. This year she was determined to be one of the adults, but she still wasn't sure what she should wear.

'The blue Swiss voile,' said Rita.

'I've grown out of it.'

'I don't know how you do it! Go and try on your green.'

A few minutes later Rita turned to look at her. 'Is that really the best you can manage?' she asked.

Beech stood before her in pale green tulle, the taffeta bodice pulled into creases across her growing bosom. She looked down at the scuffed toes of her apple-green satin pumps and scowled. Rita prodded at Beech's shoulders, tried to lift her chin from its place on her chest.

'Stand up properly, do. I'll have to lend you something of mine, I suppose.'

Beech's heart sank further. She and Rita were completely different shapes.

'Or some sort of corset might do the trick.' But Beech's expression was so mortified, so rebellious at this suggestion, that even Rita hesitated before pushing through this particular humiliation. It was obvious that the only answer was to get Beech a new dress, something grown up, but simple, in a plain, bright colour. But Beech's clothes came out of Rita's dress allowance, and she was unwilling to forgo some outfit of her own to provide Beech with a dress for the party. Beech, groomed and appropriately dressed, might even provide competition for her. Rita forced the lines and folds of her face into an upwards direction. Ageing was to do with willpower, she believed. And Beech was still a child and could be dressed as one.

'It's too late to get you anything new.'

'I have the dress Amani has made for me. It's very simple, but it's silk.'

'What dress is this? I don't know what you're talking about.'

'I'll show you.'

Plain dark blue silk with a woven green spot. Rita rubbed it through her fingers. 'Very nice. Where did you get it?'

'It was a present.'

'From whom? You can't go accepting presents like this! It simply isn't done. Don't you know *anything*?'

'It was from Nick. A present for my birthday,' she improvised.

'But your birthday is in October.'

'He'll be back in England then, so he gave it to me now.'

'It all sounds most odd. Whatever made him think of giving you a present like this? It's much too grown-up for you.'

'I like it. It's mine.'

Amani had made up the material from a sketch by Beech, following Nick's instructions. The dress was just the right length, neither so long that it looked dowdy, nor so short that she looked like a schoolgirl. There was really nothing Rita could object to. She contented herself with, 'Well, you'll grow out of that soon enough, and how on earth are you going to lengthen it?'

Washed and dressed, Beech presented herself at her mother's dressing table. Rita was sitting in a plain white gown, her hair drawn back from her face with a pink bandeau. Her skin was dotted with white cream which she was gradually blending in with light strokes.

'Always work upwards,' she told Beech, following her own instructions. The cream melted in the heat and formed a shining layer on Rita's skin as though she were excreting some exotic, scented oil.

'What is it you wanted?' she asked, her gaze still fixed on her own mirrored image, not on Beech.

'I was wondering what to do with my hair.'

Rita brushed it for her into an overelaborate pageboy bob, which made her face look even longer and thinner than it really was.

From beyond the bedroom came the sound of water gushing out of taps and being vigorously relayed to Henry's head and torso. Henry sang, something from Gilbert and Sullivan Beech recognized, while simultaneously splashing water over himself. Rita turned slightly towards the extrovert sounds and an expression of distaste crossed her face. Steam curled in swathes out from the open bathroom door, hiding Henry from view. Beatrice was afraid that at any moment he might emerge, naked, from his ablutions.

'He will be ready in time, won't he?' asked Beech.

'Of course. Your father is never late. Now, let me look at you.'

She inspected Beech from shining head to polished foot.

'Very nice, I suppose. Now do try to behave properly when we get there. Remember, keep your mind on other people's comfort, not your own. You won't go far wrong if you do that.'

Rita removed the white gown. Underneath it she was dressed in hyacinth blue linen with drawn-thread work across the collar and down the buttoned front. She looked cool and very chic. She waved Beech away and proceeded to apply her lipstick.

On the way back to her room Beech met Nicholas. He was dressed in white shorts and dark blue, open-necked shirt. Both went well with his tanned skin and sun-bleached hair. He also look cool and appropriately dressed for a picnic.

'How do I look?' she asked him. 'Is this all right?'

'You look very elegant,' he said. 'But couldn't you do something to your hair? It makes you look like a depressed pony.'

'Yes,' she said.

Back in front of her own mirror she pushed her hairbrush roughly through the stiff pageboy bob. Once she had got rid of the artificial waves, she pulled her hair back and lifted it experimentally on top of her head. Better, but she didn't have time now to fabricate some sort of topknot. She could hear Rita yapping like an irritated poodle downstairs. She would have to hurry. She took a piece of green ribbon and tied her hair in a pony-tail high at the back of her head. An enormous improvement. She hardly recognized her reflection now. It would be better if she had some make-up to wear, but she could hardly rush along to Rita and Henry's room and steal some from her mother. Anyway, during a day in the open air, make-up would look artificial and would probably melt and run and disappear anyway. She thought about using charcoal or one of her dark crayons as eye make-up, but decided this wasn't the time to experiment.

Henry's voice boomed up the stairs. 'Beatrice! Come down immediately!'

She went downstairs.

'What on earth have you done to your hair?' asked Rita. She had perched a pale straw hat on top of her red curls and looked like a picture in a fashion magazine.

'Your hair. It's a great improvement,' said Nicholas.

'Stop arguing and let's get going,' said Henry, leading the way. 'Come on!' he shouted. 'Time to go!' He herded them out of the house and into the car.

'Very well, Boutros. You know the way to the Rainbow Pool,' he said.

* * *

The heat in the city sat on top of the buildings like a steaming wet duvet. It burned down on the metal roof of the car and heated its interior like a furnace. It was so hot that it hurt Beech's lungs to breath in the air. It was like moving through a building on fire. This was what it must be like to burn to death, with your lungs getting tighter and tighter as you walked through the flames. The sun struck down on the dome of the cathedral so that it shone like copper. It lit white sparks from the minaret, so that Beech scrabbled in her bag for her sunglasses and wished that they had darker lenses. Sitting in the front of the car, next to Boutros, on the roasting hot beige leather seat, Beech felt as though she was sitting inside the copper saucepan that the maid used to make coffee in. Someone had put the lid on top and then lit the charcoal underneath it.

As they rose gradually through the foothills and into the mountains, the air thinned and cooled, and it seeped into the car and calmed and soothed their lungs and tempers. A sense of relief came over her. The cathedral and the mosque gradually grew smaller and less important as the car rose through the dusty grey palms towards the dark green pines.

'Is that child all right?' Rita's voice cut through her daydream. 'She's not going to be car sick, is she?'

'I can hear you,' said Beech. 'You don't have to talk about me like that. I am a person, you know.'

'Don't be silly,' said Rita. 'And you look quite green. You mustn't be sick in the car, you must let us know if you want the driver to stop and let you out.'

The cars, most of them black Humbers, with the occasional sand-coloured Buick or Chevrolet, had parked at a distance from the picnic site. The drivers had produced yellow or white dusters and removed the dust of the journey from burnished paintwork, and rubbed at chrome until it shone again, and were now enjoying a cigarette in the shade of some cedar trees. All had removed their jackets and hats except for the elderly man who always drove old Mrs deLyle, and who kept on his dark green jacket and cap all afternoon. Mrs deLyle had ridden alone in her Humber Super Snipe, insisting that any other occupant would make it unbearably hot for her. No one dared to suggest that she should remove her hat or gloves, or wear a lighter dress. She had been the first to arrive, after the servants with the food, chairs and tables, and a small platform had been put up for her, with a green and white striped parasol and a folding canvas chair that gave the impression of being a throne. She had overseen all the arrangements, calling out instructions in her cracked but still imperious voice and pointing her displeasure with a furled umbrella.

Now the guests were arriving, driving in a procession from the city, for the instruction on arrival time had been issued in the manner of a royal edict. The black cars, with their fillings of guests in frothy dresses or well-pressed casual clothes, stretched up the winding mountain road like a convoy of rich refugees. It would be no surprise to see them accompanied by armed outriders in Land Rovers. Or perhaps they should be preceded by priests in ceremonial robes and sung to their destination by celestial choirs, thought Beech, sitting sweltering in the leather interior of the Marklands' car. For we are surely about to take part in some solemn sacrifice. Why else have we dressed and ornamented ourselves in this way, like the goats and calves that were hung with garlands before having their throats slit with a silver knife? No doubt it was the heat and the way the family was squashed together in a small space for an hour or more that produced such morbid thoughts. And still, once they arrived at the picnic place, there was more discomfort to endure before they could relax and enjoy themselves.

The air up here was cooler than down in the city, but it was still too hot and the light too brilliant to enjoy standing in the sun for more than a few minutes. Beech's skin began to itch and she knew that she would start coming out in a pink heat rash in a few more minutes.

'Why can't we go over there?' she asked, pointing to the other side of the clearing.

The trees up here were some sort of conifer. Thin, bright green needles lay on the floor of the open space and pierced the blue air with their scent. Down in the city the gardens were filled with palm trees – tall, swaying grey trunks and untidy tops, the central broad leaves pointing towards the sky, the lower ones, discouraged, drooping towards the pale earth. Here in the foothills, they were in a different country.

They walked across the clearing, crossing the line between the glaring white of the dusty ground and the green shade under the trees. After the sun's glare the grass looked black, the trees nearly so with their leaves shivering slightly in the lightly moving air. Here it smelled earthy, elemental. Not so much what the smell included, thought Beech, but more what was not there: no smell of unwashed hot bodies, no sewage, no cooking smells. No noise, either, yet, for everyone stayed silent until they had walked in their shuffling line past the chair where Mrs deLyle sat. Only after they had shaken her hand and thanked her for their invitation could they feel free to turn to each other and exchange greetings and the sort of small talk that they all felt at home with.

The site chosen was a grassy clearing, sloping gently down from Mrs deLyle's podium to a stream, which trickled like a leaky tap in the summer sunshine. Behind her, trees clustered into a small wood, and higher up stood majestic cedar trees, black against the brilliant blue sky. Up here in the foothills of the mountains, the air was clearer, cooler than it was down in the city and on the burned brown coastal strip. The grass and the leaves were green. Not the green of an English meadow, nor an English woodland, but still lush compared with the tropical gold and bleached biscuit colour of the plains. And to hear the sound of water, however feeble, was a balm to the soul in this land of summer drought.

'I thought there was a lake,' said Valma Crabbe, coming to join them, her voice taking on a petulant whine. 'Why do they call it the Rainbow Pool if there isn't one?' She had already examined the dying stream and found it didn't match up to her fantasies.

'Follow the stream round that bend, behind the hill, and climb up towards the cedar tree,' said Nicholas. 'That's where the pool is. I expect we'll all go and look at it later.'

'Why did you tell her about it, Nico?' asked Beech, hurt. 'It's our pool. Our place.'

'I think we have to share it with the rest of the picnickers,' said Nicholas. 'It doesn't just belong to us.'

'Oh, of course! You came here once with the dreadful Caroline,' said Beech. 'Caroline Cottingham.'

'She wasn't dreadful,' said Nicholas. 'Or not very, anyway.'

'Yes she was, and she still is. And she's over there, by the way, wearing a horrible green dress and pointing her bosom at Rowley Lacoste.'

'I don't think I'm very interested,' said Nicholas. 'One has to find out the hard way what one's preferences are. And she's playing with fire if she thinks she can lead Rowley on without delivering.'

'I think she's really pretty,' said Valma, who appeared to have attached herself to them. 'And I wish my mother would buy me a bra like that.'

'You really shouldn't make quite such vulgar remarks,' said Simon Barr, who joined them now. 'People might think your parents are shopkeepers or something.'

Valma flushed.

'I don't see the difference between owning a shop and selling oil,' said Beech, who felt sorry for her. 'Except that Valma's

254

father actually owns all of Crabbe's Provisions, and your father isn't exactly the owner of Levant Oil, is he?'

'You're being stupid. And even if you don't see the difference, I can assure you that everyone else can.'

'Have I told you my orchestra joke?' interrupted a boy of about ten.

'Oh, go away, Nigel,' said Simon. 'This is my young brother,' he said to the others.

'No, but you do want to hear my orchestra joke,' insisted Nigel.

'Let's go and get something to drink,' said Nicholas, pulling Beech away from the other three, who looked set to squabble throughout the whole afternoon.

'You can't leave her alone with the awful Simon,' said Beech.

'She'll survive. And anyway, we'll join up with them again in a few minutes.'

'And what's the orchestra joke?'

'You'll have to ask Nigel.'

Drinks were being served from round silver trays by menservants in tight white tunics. The one who gave each of them a tumbler of Pepsi Cola had liquid brown eyes and a smooth skin. Beech thought he looked far more interesting than most of the other males at the picnic, but she knew that it would be considered too bizarre of her to stand and talk to him instead of to the English schoolboys standing around in their crumpled khaki shorts and going pink in the sun. As he moved away from them, she could smell the oil he had used on his hair, like orange flowers, and the soap he had washed with. She thought that when he looked at her, there had been a smile of recognition, but then they had both looked away.

Conrad deLyle was announcing the events of the afternoon.

'Just like the church fête,' said Rita, but only loudly enough for her immediate neighbours to hear her.

Conrad was dressed in clothes that looked uncomfortable for a picnic, and on such a hot August day. His face was going red and the sun gleamed on his oiled hair. But he had so much confidence in his own looks and charm that he almost convinced others that he was as attractive as he thought he was. His face in childhood had doubtless been very pretty, with large soft dark eyes, a broad brow and a small chin. But the small, pretty features that are so attractive on a child can be insipid on an adult, and so it was with Conrad. His face seemed too big, too fleshy, for his delicate features: the little button nose, the mouth with the strongly indented upper lip, the pointed chin with the hint of a dimple. The dark hair was thinning and receding from the broad brow, and even by lunchtime there was a blue shadow around his jowls. He had small feet in soft white kid shoes, and his shirt was made of a heavy silk. He drew people's attention by raising a small brass horn to his full red lips and blowing into it.

'Looks like a hunting horn,' said Harvey Barr. 'Though goodness knows what that particular call was.'

Conrad's wife, Mena, moved to stand beside him. She was wafer-thin and it was well known that she flew to Paris for her haircuts. She was wearing pale olive green, which was just a tone or so lighter than her well-oiled and anointed skin.

'That's how I'd like to look when I grow up,' said Beech.

'Not a hope,' said Simon Barr, to whom this remark was not addressed, but who answered it anyway. 'You'll be the fair, milkmaid type. You should wear flowery dresses and smile a lot.'

'Oh, piss off, Simon,' said Beech. 'I'm going to be tall and slim and elegant, and never smile at anyone, just like Mena deLyle.'

'You might end up with a mother-in-law like old Mrs deLyle,' said Simon, unabashed. 'Would it be worth it?'

'Conrad's pretty dishy,' said Beech, who in fact always addressed him as Mr deLyle.

'Conrad has girlfriends,' said Valma, whose red-adorned figure had just joined them and who was listening avidly to their conversation.

'I don't believe it,' said Beech.

'Mena would knife them if he did,' said Simon. 'And probably kill him too.'

'He keeps them well away from the city and from Mena,' said Valma. 'I expect old Mrs deLyle knows about them, but she probably approves. He can do no wrong in her eyes.'

'Whereabouts?' asked Simon, who liked the idea of a man keeping a series of mistresses instead of staying at home with his own wife and children. 'Where does he keep them?'

'He has one in Damascus,' said Valma. 'And one in Alexandria.' She saw their eager expressions, and started to extemporize. 'One in London, of course, and one in Los Angeles.' These were the two most glamorous places that she could imagine. 'And two in Italy,' she ended.

'I don't believe it. How would he have the time?'

'He's always travelling,' said Simon. 'I suppose he visits them in turn. You know, "If this is April it must be Damascus and Angelina." He'd have to have some system so that he got their names right.'

'Perhaps he calls them all "darling",' said Beech. 'And how does he remember all those birthdays, as well as his wife's and children's?'

'I expect that his secretary deals with all that,' said Simon.

' "Order me a dozen silk scarves from Hermès, and distribute them as you see fit," ' said Beech, imitating Conrad's resonant baritone.

They started to giggle. 'Perhaps his secretary blackmails him,' said Valma, looking consideringly at Conrad as he stood in front of them, raised a little on a small knoll to give him

257

importance. 'I think I should like to be secretary to an important man.'

'I can see you'd be good at the blackmail,' said Nicholas.

'Yes, she would, wouldn't she?' said Beech, with no hint of irony.

'I would slip in and out of meetings, pretending to take notes, or hand round coffee,' said Valma. 'And I would listen to everything that was said.'

'I expect that a lot of it would be very dull,' said Nicholas.

'And I would listen in to telephone conversations,' said Valma. 'That would probably be the most interesting. And I would take copies of any letters that looked useful. But the meetings would tell me what was important and what wasn't.'

'When would you get your own work done?' asked Nicholas, with interest. He liked to sort out the practical details of a problem.

'I would be a super-efficient secretary,' said Valma. 'I would get all my work done in the lunch hour if necessary, and then I would spend the rest of my time watching and listening and learning.'

'Spying, you mean,' said Simon, nastily.

'I wouldn't be working for anybody else,' said Valma. 'It would all be for myself.'

'But when would you live your own life?' asked Beech. 'All that superfast typing, and then listening in to other people, you'd have no time to be yourself and do what you wanted to do.' She could not imagine a life that had no space in it for painting pictures and reading books.

'That would be my life,' said Valma. 'That's what I want to do. Like that I will be able to have power over people and control them.'

Nigel reappeared and pulled at Nicholas's elbow. 'What's the difference between a buffalo and an orchestra?'

'What? How should I know?'

'What's old Conrad got to say?' asked Simon, who had grown tired of a conversation that did not focus on himself.

'You've got to hear my orchestra joke,' insisted Nigel.

'Go on,' said Beech kindly.

'What's the difference between a buffalo and an orchestra?'

But at this moment Conrad lifted the hunting horn to his lips and blew a convincing tune. They all turned to hear what he had to say.

'Swimming first,' he informed them. 'I expect that it will be mainly the young people who want to avail themselves of the pool. For their elders –' polite laughter from the audience – 'drinks will be served. Oh, and changing facilities –' more polite laughter – 'the boys can change behind the rock on my right, the girls behind the outcrop on my left.'

'Simon!' called Margot Barr crisply. 'How about fetching us all another drink? Something long and cool, please.' Margot was not keen on her eldest son socializing with the Crabbe girl.

'Well, are we going to swim?'

'When are they going to serve the food?' asked Valma.

'Greedy pig! You're supposed to work up an appetite in the pool, then you can attack the groaning tables of food.'

'I think I shall stay and talk to people. My mother would not approve of mixed bathing,' said Valma.

'You must be joking! This isn't the nineteenth century any more, you know.'

'Here, in my community, it certainly is,' said Valma. 'But I shall escape from it eventually.'

'Using extortion and blackmail, no doubt,' said Nicholas quietly.

Conrad blew another fanfare. 'After swimming, we shall eat!' he announced. 'And after our meal, we shall have the Great Treasure Hunt.'

'I'm looking forward to that,' said Simon, who had evaded

his mother and rejoined them. 'They give a really good prize, and I'm going to win it this year.'

Nicholas caught Beech's eye and smiled. They'd see about that!

'Time to change into swimsuits,' he said. 'Are you coming, Simon?'

Even the laughing and jostling crowd of young people couldn't entirely destroy the magic of the Rainbow Pool. But still it wasn't quite the atmospheric spot of her last visit, alone with Nico. Someone jumped in, splashing water over the others, screaming at the jolt of the cold. Beech moved a little away from them. At this end of the pool the water was a murky olive. It was odd the way it changed like that, from the clear sapphire colour to the muddy green, as though some invisible underwater animal had moved through the silt at the bottom of the pool and stirred it into this viscous soup. She could see odd fronds of reddish vegetation suspended in it, indistinct and unidentifiable through the opaque water.

'Come on!' shouted Simon Barr, beside her. 'I'll race you to the other end.'

So Beech too jumped in and swam, turning the whole pool from its mixed blues to a rusty green.

Filemot, she thought. That's the word that describes this colour.

And after their swim came the food.

The centrepiece of the feast was a whole tunny fish, poached and garnished with chopped peppers and cucumbers. Beside it sat a big silver bowl of lemon mayonnaise. Was this one of the monstrous, vital fish that Nick and I saw from the boat? Just yesterday it was out there, in the foaming white sea, jumping and flying with its shoal. And now it was tricked out as a fat morsel to tempt the palates of these overfed people. What was she thinking? Wasn't she one of them? She looked around at them: fair hair, red faces, large knees, fat bottoms. Loud voices and braying laughs. Oh no, I am not one of you. I am a person apart.

She helped herself to cold chicken and green salad and left the fish for the others.

'Old Mrs deLyle must have emptied Crabbe's shop for this spread,' said Harvey Barr to his wife.

'I don't think so,' said Margot, looking over at Valma. 'She only uses Crabbe's for a few of her groceries. For the rest, she has her own suppliers. But isn't that a whole roast pig over there? And they must have slaughtered a flock of chickens and at least three cows.'

Nigel Barr left his mother's side and came over to Beech.

'No one wants to hear my orchestra joke,' he said.

'We're both outsiders then,' said Beech. 'Go on, tell me, what's the difference between a buffalo and an orchestra?'

'A buffalo has its horns at the front and an arsehole at the back, whereas an orchestra—'

'Come over here, Nigel!' ordered Margot Barr. 'That's quite enough of that sort of language.'

Beech picked at her green salad and waited for the treasure hunt.

29

'You're not eating much,' said Nicholas, who had piled his plate high and was tucking into the food with a healthy appetite.

'I'm not very hungry.' She couldn't explain about the tunny, and how Margot Barr's comments had put her off the rest.

'They've flown in strawberries from somewhere or other, and there are all the usual melons and kumquats and apricots and so on over there.'

'Thanks. I'll think about it.'

'Well, and what are you two doing, skulking in this corner on your own?' It was Henry, and he had been drinking. Beech and Nicholas said nothing.

'And you, Beatrice? Did you enjoy making up to that spotty Barr youth? Or the adulterous Mr Lacoste?'

'Leave her alone,' said Nicholas quietly.

'Really? You're standing up for her, are you? Well, that makes sense. It's all you're good for, feeling up your own sister.'

'I'm not sure I understand you.'

'Oh yes, you do. I've watched you all summer, looking at her, touching her, the two of you disappearing off on your own to God knows where.'

'You're jealous, that's your problem. And drunk. You don't know what you're saying.'

'Stop it,' Beech whispered.

'It's a pity you didn't say that sooner,' said Henry.

'He's done nothing wrong. Really. You're making a mistake.

Please stop,' said Beech. Her voice had no substance to it. It sounded as though she was standing a very long way away. 'You're characters in a play. You're not real.'

Nico laughed without humour. 'That's the story of our family, isn't it? We're all great actors. We pretend not to notice what's happening. Henry doesn't want to know about Rita's other men. He doesn't want to know he's attracted to his own daughter. Rita's seen but she doesn't want to know either. She manages to hide her fear behind all the put-downs. And why do you think she buys you such dreadful clothes?'

'I suppose she doesn't want me to grow up.'

'She doesn't want anyone to fancy you, most of all Henry. And me, of course.'

'You're talking filth.' Henry rejoined the conversation.

'It's the truth. You and I are the most important men in Rita's life, in spite of all the Billy Echevins. She can see what's happening, and she's jealous of poor old Beech.'

'She's not jealous of her. She has no need to be. But she wishes that this stupid little girl would stand aside and let you make some other friends. If you could manage it, which I doubt.'

Henry stood with his lids half-closed, watching his son and daughter. At this moment Conrad deLyle blew another jaunty tune on his hunting horn, and Henry melted back into the crowd.

'Don't worry, it's the whisky talking. He didn't mean anything.' Nico's voice was urgent in her ear, then they were separated by a laughing knot of young people.

'Time for the treasure hunt! Find yourself a partner, and then line up over here to be given your first clue. Good luck, everyone!'

'What's the prize?' called someone from the back of the crowd.

'The latest in water-skis for each winner, and lessons from

the professional at the Poseidon Club,' replied Conrad.

Simon Barr appeared and grabbed hold of Beech's wrist, dragging her to the front of the group. 'You're good at these clue things, aren't you?' he said.

'Am I? What clue things?'

'If I'm going to win the treasure hunt, I need you to solve the clues. I really want those water-skis, so I need you to do the brain-work. Someone said you're always sitting around with a book, and so you must be good with words.'

Beech wished that she was really good at words like 'no' and 'piss off', but the unbearable politeness of old Mrs deLyle hung over the picnic like a pall, and she found herself saying 'all right', when she didn't mean to.

'I'm not going to let those foreigners win.' said Simon, scowling in the direction of Didier and Serge, Nadia and Agnès, children of various ambassadors. 'We've got to show them who's best.'

Simon was not tall, he was slightly built, and had fuzzy, pale reddish-blond hair. Harvey, his father, had hair that had receded into deep Vs and had a bald spot on his crown. Simon would soon look the same.

From behind them, Didier and Serge, pressed white shorts setting off their deep golden tans, laughed, and sprang effort-lessly to their feet, and offered gallant hands to Nadia and Agnès. Didier's eyes were black and shiny as olives, Serge had eyes of a dark slaty blue; both looked as though they had spent the summer in swimming and diving and lying on the beach. It was obvious to Beech that Simon truly hated them, and not because they were foreigners.

'Here,' said Simon, handing her a crumpled slip of paper. 'Here's the first clue. I managed to get hold of one. You can work out what it means and then when the treasure hunt starts we can get a head start on the others.'

'Isn't that cheating?'

'What?'

'And won't they just follow us, instead of working out the clue for themselves?'

'Good point,' said Simon, believing that at last she understood the problem. 'You work out the clue quick, and then we'll position ourselves so that we can slip away from the others without their noticing where we're going.'

Unwillingly, Beech unwrapped the paper slip and looked at it.

'Search for the twisted deer trace, and look for me at his eye's height,' she read. That was simple enough. Only a Simon Barr would have much trouble with that one. Or a foreigner, perhaps.

'Well?' asked Simon impatiently. 'I thought you were supposed to be brainy or something.'

'Hello, Simon,' said a voice behind them. 'I'm afraid you can't partner my sister, you know.' It was Nicholas.

'Why not?' squeaked Simon. Nicholas was a head taller.

'Because we agreed ages ago to work together,' said Nicholas. 'She solves the clues, and I do the running. We'll be unbeatable. And we've always wanted to water-ski. But don't worry, I do believe that Valma Crabbe is still looking for a partner.'

'Oh no!'

'Valma!' called Nicholas. 'Over here!'

Valma, in her scarlet dress and with her hair still neatly braided, came walking over. She looked as though she had never exerted herself to run in her life. It was probably against her religion, thought Beech.

'Are you looking for a partner, Nicholas?' she asked, and behind her cool manner, Beech could feel her eagerness.

'No, not me. But Simon is. You two know each other, don't you?'

And he and Beech left them to join the laughing, shrieking group around Conrad.

'Simon's scowling, and Valma looks pissed off,' said Beech. 'Will they ever forgive us?'

'Do we care?'

'No.'

'You're still looking upset about that stupid scene with Henry. Forget about it. He was drunk and saying the nastiest things he could think of. It didn't mean anything. None of it was true. Let's concentrate on winning these water-skis.'

'I've still got the first clue that Simon tricked out of one of the deLyles.'

'Let's take a look at it. Well, that's not going to keep people puzzling too long, unless they're as thick as Simon. Let's get away to the other side so they can't follow us.'

The cedar tree, its umbrella-shaped canopy black against the crystalline sky, stood a few hundred yards above them.

'The clues will get harder as we go on,' said Beech.

'And will take us backwards and forwards over this hill for miles. The crumplies want a quiet hour in the shade with their gin bottles and their gossip,' he said.

Even as he spoke they could see their parents and the Cottinghams drawing into a group at one table and signalling to one of the servants to bring them more drinks.

Conrad deLyle was speaking.

'Very well, everybody! You can open your first clue now!' He lifted the hunting horn to his lips and blew a short blast.

'They're off!' shouted somebody, and laughed.

She and Nicholas were away like hares, up through the short brown grass and into the shade of the trees.

'A cedar tree,' said Nicholas.

'And a message at eye height,' said Beech. Behind them they could hear heavy footsteps thudding through the undergrowth.

'Here it is!' cried Nicholas. 'This way!'

And they were off again.

* * *

The hunt was breaking up into small groups, scattered all over the hillside and along the bed of the stream. She and Nicholas had slowed down at last, in possession of most of the clues, but not really caring whether they won water-skis or not.

Beech knew this was how it should always be: not in the everyday world, perhaps, but in their own private world, the one where Nico and Arrie lived. They needed no one else. Rita and Henry could go off to their eternal cocktail parties and she and Nico would drift forever along the pathways on this hillside, solving the final puzzle, searching for treasure.

For a moment she saw a flash of red skirt between the trees and heard Valma's urgent voice calling, 'Wait for me!'

But Nico and Arrie waited for no one.

'I only tried to win in order to annoy Simon,' said Nicholas eventually. 'Aren't you bored with this game by now?'

'I'm hot,' said Beech, using her arm to wipe the sweat from her forehead. 'Let's sit down. It's cooler here.' They might have been alone on the hillside.

She could hear a distant sound of bells, the syncopated clanking of the dull brass bells that the local goats wore. She heard the sound too of a boy's voice as he called to his flock, and soon he appeared, a thin brown sprite of about twelve years old, a long stave in his right hand, his unenthusiastic flock of goats straggling behind him. The animals were so thin that she could see the long flat skulls under the meagre fur, a dirty white and brown colour, and their ribs showed through their taut sides. Their spindly legs ended in tiny, delicate hooves, which scuffed the white dust and clipped a staccato rhythm down the track. One or two made their *mnyeh mnyeh* noise, and the others took it up, until the boy-shepherd turned and shouted at them again, and set a faster pace down the hill to their evening pasture. The white dust threw its heat up through the soles of her sandals, burning the skin of her feet.

Beech raised a hand in greeting, and smiled, and called 'Mahaba!' She watched until the last white and brown goat had disappeared out of sight around the rocky outcrop. For a time she could hear the flat notes of the bells and the boy's high voice calling the goats to follow him. She closed her eyes against the glare of the sun.

The sound of a goat-bell close by must have woken her. The scrabbling sound of its hoofs. She was alone on her rocky seat. Where were the rest of the treasure-hunters? Where was Nico?

She thought of the pool, of the shade under the trees. She could dip her hands in the cold water and rinse her face. She followed the narrow pathway out of the sunlight and into the dark cavern of the trees. She kneeled by the edge of the pool and leaned over it. Her reflection, dark and slightly wavering, rose to greet her. She dipped in her hand and it broke into a thousand fragments.

At first, with the water running down her face and misting her eyes, she didn't see him. He was sitting at the other end of the pool, his feet in the slate-blue water. Her heart gave a lurch as she recognized him. It was odd, that. It was no figure of speech: she felt the jolt, felt her heart move in her breast as she saw who it was.

'Nico!' she cried. She shook her head to free it from the veil of water. 'It's me!' It was only then that she saw he wasn't alone.

Slim legs, round arms, long fingers, sly brown eyes, shining black hair. 'Who is it?' she asked, knowing that no one would answer. Why did he need anyone else when he had *her*? Nico and Arrie: brother and sister. They were a pair. They were all she needed. Weren't they complete enough for him?

'Go away,' said Nico, lazily. 'Push off, little sister. Go and play with the other children.'

'No!' She could feel her face going red, she knew she was about to cry like the child he thought she was. And then another figure joined them, approaching from the path behind her and through the undergrowth from the track to the village.

Behind Nico the boy was pulling on his shirt. Nico himself just stood there, naked in the sunshine. His body was burned brown, except for the white strip where his swimming trunks usually went.

'Hello, Father,' said Nico.

'Get dressed,' said Henry. 'And tell your catamite to come over here.' He sounded dangerously angry, but not drunk any more.

Mnyeh mnyeh. She hadn't noticed the goat, just a young, skinny thing, chewing at the leaves on the lowest branch of a nearby tree.

'I don't remember any more,' said Beech stubbornly.

'Of course you do,' said Fergus. 'Just keep looking at the picture in your head. Don't turn away from it this time.'

But Beech was gazing at her shoes as if the answers lay in their polished toes.

'Come on,' said Fergus. 'Nico, the boy, the goat. Henry. Look up. Tell me what's happening.'

Unwillingly, Beech raised her eyes from her feet.

'The boy can go,' said Nico.

'Be quiet.' Henry had taken a roll of banknotes from his back pocket and started to peel several away.

'There's no need for that. He has already been paid,' said Nico.

Henry took no notice of his son, but beckoned the boy across. 'Here,' he said. 'Take this, and forget what you saw. Forget everything that happened.' His Arabic was inelegant but adequate, and Beech could follow it easily. 'What is your village?' The boy replied with a name Beech didn't recognize. He had a high, childish voice.

'So you are a Christian,' said Henry. The boy shook his head, meaning yes. 'And you know this thing you did was very wrong.' The boy gave a quick grin, then saw the expression on Henry's face and looked frightened. 'You must not speak of it. Ever. Or you will be in great trouble with your parents and with your priest. You will go to prison if people learn of it. Do you understand me? Perhaps you will hang. You will die, and when you are dead you will burn in hell.' The boy looked back at Nico, but Nico's Arabic wasn't good enough to follow. 'Forget him, he is not important. Listen well to what I say.' Henry held out the notes. The boy took the money. 'So keep silent if you wish to live. You must keep this secret for the rest of your life.'

The boy looked at the bundle of notes and then again at Henry. He said something Beech didn't catch.

Beech stopped again.

'It's no good. I just can't remember any more.'

'Nothing?'

'I was told to leave the pool and go back to the picnic. Nothing else. Except for what happened afterwards.'

You will never tell anyone what you have seen today. You will forget all about it. Kill it. Bury it. Never even think about it again. As far as you are concerned, nothing has happened.

'You have to lift up the lid of the compost bin,' said Fergus. 'Remove the square of old carpet and look into the mess of cabbage leaves and potato peelings. The answer has to be there somewhere.'

She followed the stream out of the wood and into the clear expanse where the picnic was held. The crowd of guests was clustered around Conrad deLyle and he was handing large, colourful packages to a flushed and cheerful couple. Beech didn't recognize who it was, but it wasn't Simon Barr.

271

'Can we go home soon, do you think?' asked Nigel Barr, who was once again at her elbow.

'I do hope so,' said Beech, who had a throbbing headache and a feeling of disaster so intense that she thought she might have to be sick in the bushes.

'Are you feeling all right?' asked Nigel. 'Shall I tell you another joke?'

'I don't think I'm in the mood,' said Beech.

'I'm bored,' said Nigel. 'I want to go home.'

'I want to leave too.'

What had happened back there after she had left the pool? Would anyone ever tell her?

'Beatrice!' called Rita.

'Yes?'

'Have you seen Nicky?'

'No.'

'Henry! Have you seen Nicholas?'

'What? Oh, I'm sure the lad's all right. He's probably making up to the Cottingham girl. Is it time we left?' Henry's face was set in a mask of unbaked brick. Only his eyes, hot and angry, moved.

'No one's allowed to do that until Madame deLyle has left,' said Rita. 'Anyone would think she was royalty.'

'Stop fussing,' snapped Henry, then stamped on his irritation, retiring back behind the mask.

But where is Nico? wondered Beech. Did Henry send him home in disgrace? She refused to think about the scene with the goatherd. What had it meant? Nothing. Nothing at all. She closed a steel shutter on her memories and connected it to the mains. Now if she was tempted to pull open the shutter and look, she would be electrocuted. There, she was already starting to forget what happened.

Over by the cars there were people moving about. Someone came and fetched Henry away. 'We'd better go and say goodbye to Mrs deLyle and thank Conrad and Mena for making it all such a wonderful success,' said Rita to Beech. 'Then we'll be ready to leave as soon as your father gets back.'

Conrad deLyle had joined the group by the cars. He was shaking his head.

Eventually Henry returned.

'I'm afraid there's been an accident, Rita,' he said.

'What do you mean? What accident?'

'It's Nicholas. It's serious, I'm afraid.'

'No,' said Rita. 'I don't believe it. Is he injured?'

'It's worse than that. I'm afraid he's dead.'

'No,' said Rita again. 'It can't be. It can't.'

They had found his body floating in the Rainbow Pool. He was easy to recognize with his fair hair spreading like weed in the water, and wearing white shorts and navy shirt.

'But how could he have drowned? He was such a good swimmer.'

Rita's question was never properly answered.

'I don't believe it. There's been a mistake. It isn't Nicky.' She was holding on to Henry's arm with both hands, pleading with him.

'I'm afraid there's no mistake.'

'How can you be so calm?' Rita's make-up had melted in the sun and now mixed with her tears, smearing her face.

'We have to stay calm,' said Henry. 'All these people . . . they mustn't see us break down.'

'Get rid of them!' screamed Rita. 'Just get rid of the people.'

Henry looked at her as if at a loss what to do. She had pulled away from him and was crouching on the ground, her arms wrapped round her knees, rocking back and forth as though her pain were physical. 'Nicky, Nicky,' she moaned.

Henry, stiff as an automaton, offered her his outstretched hand. 'Get up, Rita,' he said at last. 'We'll get through this together.' Every drop of emotion had been drained out of him at the Rainbow Pool and all he was left with were these meaningless, wooden phrases.

Rita was on her feet again, but swaying against him. 'Take me to him. I have to see him.'

Only after she had seen the body, lying on the ground, covered up to the neck with a navy blue blanket, was she finally convinced that Nicholas was dead. She kneeled with his head in her arms and kissed his cold, wet face.

30

For days Rita stayed in her room, lying on her bed in the exhausting heat, with the shutters closed on the view of the mountains.

She smoked, she drank iced water, she turned away the trays of food that Amani brought for her, but mostly she just lay beneath the tent of her mosquito net and stared at its translucent white walls. She lost weight until it seemed that her bones would poke their way through her pale skin and she would transform herself into skull and bones and join her son in his lead coffin.

Beech kept to her own room, remote from the friends she had seen over the previous weeks. *You will forget everything you've seen. You will never speak of this to anyone*.

She saw Henry, briefly, at meal times, when they sat at either end of the dining table. They didn't talk. The only sound in the room was the shuffle of the maid's sandals as she brought in the dishes, the clink of the ice in Henry's glass.

Henry arranged for the funeral at the English church. Beech tried to recommend a favourite hymn, but had her suggestion brushed aside. Nico's funeral would be conventional and impersonal: the minister had never met him and would mouth generalizations over the coffin. Rita wouldn't rouse herself from her torpor even to add her own contributions to the arrangements. To every suggestion she just nodded her head, as though she didn't care what happened.

There were thirty or forty of them in the bare church with its blond wooden pews. They sang their two hymns, they listened to the readings, and then they laid Nicholas to rest in the English churchyard with its sparse brown grass and the tumble of wild purple bougainvillaea over the wall.

Afterwards, having dispensed dry sherry and drier biscuits to an awkward group of mourners, Rita returned to her darkened bedroom.

Beech took out crayons and drawing pad, but could think of nothing she wished to record, and put them away again.

September crept forward. No one mentioned Beech's future, or her education. Now that Nicholas was gone, it seemed irrelevant to them. Rita gradually rose from her bed, joined in, in a desultory way, with the life of the house. Beech and her parents exchanged a few words on everyday matters. It was at this stage that Beech stopped thinking of her parents as Mother and Father, and called them by their names, at first only in her mind, but soon also when she addressed them aloud. They accepted it without comment.

Gradually, from apathy, Rita moved to anger.

'It's all your fault!' she cried, when she saw Beech.

Maybe she was just looking for someone to blame for the death of her son. It was natural that she couldn't accept that it was a simple accident, just one of those dreadful things that happens. It had to be someone's fault.

'Why Nicholas?' she wailed. 'And why *me*?'

There were no answers.

Beech could hear her parents, always in the next room, or below her on their balcony, talking, talking, in those last days of August, into the first week of September. The murmur of their voices would rise to a wail (Rita's) and then drop back to a gravelly monotone (Henry's). Perhaps he did explain to her something of what happened, the subject of that last argument between father and son. Certainly Beech found herself the object of all her parents' guilt and blame. She could hear them talking on the balcony beneath her bedroom window. She picked up the odd word or phrase, and knew that they were blaming her.

'She tagged round after him all summer,' she heard Rita saying.

'She kept him away from the girls he might have flirted with,' said Henry. 'It was unnatural, unhealthy, the way she clung to him. And she showed him those drawings of the goat boy. She put ideas into his head.'

'What ideas? I don't understand?'

'Never mind,' said Henry. 'It's too late now.'

It was too much. She had lost the one person on earth she had loved the most, and now she was being blamed for his death. What had she done? She would have given anything, done anything, sacrificed anything to save Nico's life. Why had no one given her the chance? The whole house was so full of her parents' despair that there was no room for her own.

She watched her father sideways from across the room when he came into the house that afternoon. She didn't dare let him know that she was watching. He had changed, she saw. His face, only last week at the funeral, it seemed to her, had resembled coarse brick-red sandpaper so that if you dared to rub your fingers down his cheeks it would abrade your skin. But now his cheeks had fallen in and at the same time become puffy, so that his skin was smooth and unhealthy-looking. His eyes, before, had bulged with rage, the whites suffused with red, the pale grey irises transparent as the sea, but now they were hidden by his lids, which he held half-lowered at all times. His bristly lashes were pale against the dark skin of his eye-sockets.

'Get me a drink,' he said in an exhausted voice, sitting in the corner by the window, not even bothering to pour it for himself.

'Vodka and lime. And put in plenty of lime.'

Always, afterwards, she associated this time with the smell of limes. The whole house was suffused with it. The servants were constantly squeezing out the juice from the small green fruit, grating the rind, steeping it in sugar lumps to make the lime cordial which Henry drank with his vodka. Why? Did he believe that their smell disguised that of the alcohol? Or was he trying to cover up some other, more noxious, odour that existed only in his imagination?

She poured vodka over ice cubes in a tumbler, added lime cordial, took the glass over to her father. He accepted it without a word.

'You've got to do something about that girl.'

'I can't. I'm tired.'

'She has to go away. I can't stand seeing her around. Every time I see her drooping about the house, I want to scream.'

'I'll talk to her.'

'It's all her fault.'

Rita and Henry sat in their usual chairs on the balcony, underneath her bedroom window. This part of the terrace faced west and they could watch the orange and scarlet streaks of sunlight fading as they were swallowed by the sooty sky. Why do they do this? wondered Beech. *For fear that you might argue with them. In case you contradict them.*

Beech could picture them even if she couldn't see them. Rita had taken to wearing dresses that, while keeping her reasonably cool, still suggested mourning. Today it was a black linen halter-necked dress with a full skirt and a very short jacket. Her smooth white legs were bare, but her sandals too were black. She had drawn her hair back from her face in a severe, backswept style. Her face was white, with a dab of rouge to bring out the line of her cheekbones, dark red lipstick, sticky and shiny as sealing wax, and the pencilled eyebrows giving her an air of permanent surprise. Even her hair had been tinted a darker brown, instead of the golden colour she had favoured earlier that year.

Henry, on the other hand, perspired constantly. His grey linen suit was crumpled and damp. What had happened to the elegant, tall Englishman?

'Do change your shirt, dear,' came Rita's voice, echoing Beech's thought. 'And that is a very horrid tie. Where on earth did you get it?'

Beech's heart bled for him, but she was quite incapable of closing the gap between them, of breaking the silence that lay like an impenetrable jungle that neither of them could hack their way through.

On the other side of the house a door opened and closed again and she heard footsteps on the hard tiles, and the voices, louder, clearer.

'You must send her away.'

'You want to send her home to school?'

'Those places are so expensive. Can we afford it?'

'We've got the money. I don't suppose it will be as expensive as that place of Nick's. How old is she now?'

'Nearly sixteen.'

'Then it will have to be a school. She's too young for any sort of finishing place yet. I'll ask around,' said Henry. 'Someone must know of a suitable place.'

Escape, thought Beech, from her listening post. I can get away from this place, from Henry and Rita. I will be able to mourn Nico in my own time and my own way.

Beech was putting on weight. It was as though she wished to grow a thick shield against the accusations around her. She felt as though all the world was pointing a finger at her: 'That's the girl whose brother died, and *it was all her fault*.' If she could understand the street Arabic, the Armenian, or whatever it was being spoken around her, she would hear them jeering at her. She heard the sharp laughter, the aggressive consonants and knew that they were all talking about her.

When Henry finally told her that she was to go back to England to school she felt only relief. Part of her knew that England in late autumn would be cold and dark and wet, but she wanted to escape to somewhere where no one knew who she was and what she had done. She wanted, most of all, to be anonymous.

'Fatlands. That's the name of the school,' said Henry.

Rita laughed.

Beech blushed. 'Stop it!' she said foolishly.

'Learn to take a joke,' said Rita. 'Or else stop eating like a little piggy.'

'They say it's a good school,' said Henry.

Only long afterwards did it occur to her that neither of her parents had visited the school or met its headmistress before she was packed on to a plane and sent thousands of miles across the world.

'I suppose we'll have to buy her this hideous uniform,' sighed Rita, reading a typewritten list.

And so Beech was met by an Agency Aunt at London Airport and given tea and then taken by taxi to an impersonal department store where large quantities of shapeless, ugly garments, many of whose uses were obscure to her, were bought and packed into her new suitcases. They followed her like improvident relations into taxis and on to trains.

'They've spared no expense,' remarked the Agency Aunt approvingly. She wore an auntly tweed suit and a professionally friendly smile. Beech felt that her blue eyes never really saw her properly, and she was grateful for that.

Resounding in her head all the time were the phrases from the last conversation she had had with Henry. She hadn't understood all of it, but she had taken in the anger behind his words.

He had spoken of the nature of homosexuality, and how it could always be laid at the door of the women of the family. It was a mark of degeneracy and had no place in his own family, the Marklands. 'Neurasthenia' was what they called it when they were being polite, but everyone knew that it was a filthy practice, and a deadly sin.

'Don't let all this talk of changing the law fool you,' he told Beech. 'In the eyes of all decent people this will always be a crime. And so you must never talk about it. You must never mention it to anyone. And you must take your own share of the blame for Nicholas's behaviour.'

'What about Rita?' asked Beech, wondering whether her mother would explain the situation more clearly.

'Rita must never be brought into this. Your mother would be devastated at such a disgusting thing associated with her own son. She's too highly strung.'

'What about *me*?' asked Beech.

'You have a coarse streak in your nature. Perhaps it's your generation. But your mother is to be protected from this knowledge. As far as she is concerned, Nicholas was drowned while swimming in the Rainbow Pool. Perhaps it was too soon after our substantial meal. I expect he had a sudden cramp. There was no one else present. The water is deep and he failed to swim to the edge and haul himself out.'

'Is that what really happened?' She wanted to ask him about the goat boy but she didn't know how.

'Truth is a funny, slippery thing, you will find. For our purposes, the truth is that Nicholas drowned. It was an accident.'

Beech didn't understand. Either Nicholas drowned or he didn't. If he didn't, what had happened at the pool after she was sent away? 'But—' she began.

'No "buts", Beatrice. I've told you all you need to know. From now on you will concentrate on helping your mother to come to terms with her grief. You will forget your own, selfish little desires.'

'Will Rita believe our story, do you think?' Already, she noticed objectively, it was 'our' story, not just Henry's.

'She will if we are firm in our resolve. Make sure that you are, Beatrice.'

'Of course we will miss you, darling,' wrote Rita that November. 'But it's not worth coming all the way out here just for Christmas.'

Beech wasn't as disappointed as she expected. Christmas was an unnatural time of year in the Levant. The city had a half-hearted attitude to such a Christian festival. Even the various Catholics kept their festivities for Easter. Only the Anglicans, the Americans and a few other Protestants took Christmas seriously. In the city the night came early, dark blue sky weeping down on to the gold-spattered pavement. In the main European shop there was a Christmas tree in the window, a small symmetrical object, much hung about with knobbly gold baubles. A nativity scene sat in the front of the window. The rain fell relentlessly, a warm, sticky drizzle that never seemed to have a beginning or an end to it, unlike the sudden, vicious rains of autumn and spring.

So Beech decided to enjoy her English Christmas. She supposed that she would be told where she would be sent to spend the four weeks of holiday.

'I don't believe you've ever met my Aunt Laura and her daughter, Catherine,' wrote Rita. 'We haven't seen much of each other in the recent past, but they have most kindly offered to take you for Christmas and the New Year. I know that you will be properly grateful when you meet them. I enclose a cheque which your headmistress will cash for you, and you will use the money to buy them some suitable presents. Hand-kerchiefs, perhaps, or a bottle of lavender water. Nothing too showy. They are quite modest people.'

Compared to Rita, Laura and Catherine may have been dowdy, but they were welcoming enough to her daughter. And there was an elderly gentleman in attendance, who appeared to be some admirer of Laura's, but whose exact relationship to her great-aunt Beech never quite fathomed. They all happily called her Beech, rather than Beatrice, and seemed quite satisfied with their mean little presents.

'Do come and spend Easter with us,' called Laura, as she waved Beech off on the train back to school.

'I will! Thank you!' called back Beech, as certain as Laura and Catherine that she would not be welcomed by her parents for that festival either.

I enjoyed that, she thought with surprise when she was sitting in her third-class seat, sucking on home-made chocolate fudge. It had been more like what she imagined a normal family to be. And no one had lost their temper and made her feel an idiot.

She was only sorry that Nico couldn't have been with her.

I've been getting out and about a bit more recently, wrote Rita, the following April. *Eva Bishop, from the embassy, has been taking me along with her when she does her charity work. But you wouldn't believe how horrible it all is! Those nasty, fly-ridden babies, the smell of the open sewers, the malicious way the older children stare at one! And they don't even seem to be grateful. I tried to talk to Eva about it, but she didn't appear to understand. Luckily, the good old St Maroun is still the same as ever, and I manage to get down there two or three times a week*

Le pipi, c'est le parfum des Tanakés, thought Beech, and read on.

Of course we're delighted to hear that you have such firm ideas about your future. If Nicky had lived, we all know what a wonderful success he would have made of his career in law. I can understand that you would want to take over this ambition and live it for him, but please, darling, don't be too disappointed with yourself if you find you can't quite manage it. We know you will do your best, and that is all any of us can ask, isn't it?

But she did do it. The teaching of the Misses Hapsted had left her a long way behind her contemporaries, but Fatlands was used to coaching children who had spent part of their education abroad and so she passed a respectable number of O levels. Working so hard at her studies kept her mind off what had happened at the picnic, and soon it faded into a memory that seemed rather less real than the films she watched on Saturday evenings in the assembly hall.

She took her A levels and applied to universities. She was accepted and, despite Rita's protests about the expense, she went to read Law.

I know that Nicholas wanted to be a barrister, she wrote to her father. *And I would have liked to fulfil this ambition for him, and make you proud of me – and of him through me. But I don't really think that the Bar is quite right for me, and I should like to become a solicitor instead. Please don't be too disappointed. I shall do my very best to make a success of it, even if it isn't quite as much as you had hoped from me.*

'So that's what I did,' she told Fergus. 'I became a solicitor.'

'Why aren't you doing it now?'

'I was working part time for the council after I had Alice and while she was still small. When she went to secondary school I returned to work for a firm in Banbury. I specialized in divorces for put-upon women. I ended up with quite a reputation. But I haven't got the ambition and push that you need to bring in the new clients, and I gave it up again a couple of years ago.'

'What do you want to do now?'
'I want to learn to paint. I should have done it years ago.'
'Shall I tell you that it's never too late?'
'If you did, I might even believe you.'

31

A stretch of hot, dry weather has set in. Jack exclaims with pleasure at the arrival of summer and flings off most of his clothes to lie in a reclining chair in the sunshine to encourage his suntan.

Rita is nervous about her complexion and the possibility of gaining further wrinkles. She is sitting in the conservatory, smoking and sipping cold fruit juice. Valma is keeping her company. Beech is free to walk to the shops and take a bus across town to call on her daughter. She might also visit a friend on her way home.

She is wearing a fine Indian cotton dress in a pattern of olive green and turquoise leaves. It is cut like a smock and reminds her of the dresses she wore in pregnancy. To be frank, it does not really suit her rather angular figure, but it is cool, and there are no tight waistbands or armholes to chafe and collect the sweat that trickles down her back as she walks.

She tries to walk more slowly so that she will not arrive scarlet in the face, with her hair stuck to her scalp, but pace is a question of geography, she finds. In the Middle East she could float around, choosing just that slow speed that kept her from puffing and sweating. In the open air, at midday, it was a languid pace. She tries to slow down in Enderby Road, but finds that she has got into her energetic English stride again, ignoring the sticky heat.

Alice looked clean and quite cheerful when she opened the

door, and her usually dull hair was pulled back from her face and tied with a green ribbon. When she saw it was Beech, she called over her shoulder, 'It's all right. It's only my mother.'

'May I come in?' asked Beech.

'I suppose so,' said Alice, and stood aside for Beech to walk past her and into the house. It was an old semi-detached council house that had been bought several years ago by its tenants and was now let to Beech and Francesca.

Outside was grey pebble-dash, but the inside was freshly painted and there were bright new curtains at the windows. The house did not smell like an old garbage pail, or even a three-day-old ashtray, as all Alice's previous places had done. Someone had been baking – *baking* – and someone – perhaps even the same someone, had hoovered the ratty piece of carpet in the hall.

'Hello, Francesca,' said Beech. 'You're looking well.'

Francesca stood waiting for them in the sitting room, a tall, madonna-like figure with long dark hair drawn back from a serene face, holding a red-faced infant.

Beech went across and looked down into the sleeping face. 'He's quite like you were at that age, Alice,' she said. 'I can see it now.'

She had met her grandson, briefly, in the maternity ward the previous week. But even after so short a time he had gained a little weight and looked more human. When she had first seen him he had reminded her, with his fuzz of blond hair and large blue eyes, of Nicholas.

'Here, I've brought you a few oddments.' And she handed over a bulging plastic carrier.

'You can sit down if you want,' said Francesca, and took her own place, with the baby, on an upright chair. Beech moved a packet of disposable nappies and sat down on the sofa. Alice planted herself in an old armchair at right angles to her.

'I suppose you know you've ruined my life,' said Alice.

'Why's that?' asked Beech. Alice was sounding more like Rita than ever. 'I thought you were managing to ruin it quite satisfactorily all on your own.'

'You were always horrible to me,' said Alice. 'But now you've gone too far.'

'I don't know what you're talking about,' said Beech.

'Shall I get you a coffee?' asked Francesca, handing the baby to Beech.

'Thanks. Has he got a name yet?' she asked.

'We're calling him Ash,' said Francesca.

'That's unusual.'

'It's no one else's name. Just his. He doesn't have to grow up to be like his father or his dead uncle or anyone else. He can be his own person with a name like that,' said Francesca.

'That's good,' said Beech.

'You've got to stop it, Mum,' interrupted Alice.

'Stop what?'

'It's that man of yours. That boy. He's hardly older than me. It just isn't fair.'

'Where did you hear about him?'

'I bumped into Lizzie Barton from school and she told me all about it. You've been seen around north Oxford with this toy boy, apparently.'

'He's a lot older than you,' said Beech. 'In years, nearly fifteen.' In maturity, an infinity.

'Everyone will laugh at me,' said Alice.

'Rubbish,' said Beech. She could hear the kettle groaning and puffing in the background, and the clink of mugs. She hoped that Francesca would soon return to keep the peace. 'And do you really think that I am going to stop seeing the man I love just because you believe that people are laughing at you? What people, for goodness' sake? How many of your friends know or care what I do?'

'You've always been a selfish bitch.'

'I've made you both a coffee,' said Francesca, putting the mugs down on the table.

'You can hardly insist that Ash should be his own person and then refuse me the chance to live my life the way I want.'

'You're not even trying to understand how it is for me,' said Alice.

'I wish you two would stop fighting,' said Francesca. 'It's not good for Ash to be brought up in a negative atmosphere.' She took the baby back from Beech.

'Sorry,' said Beech. 'At least, I'm sorry if we upset you. I'm not sorry for what I said to Alice.'

They drank their coffee in silence for a few minutes.

'Have a biscuit,' said Francesca. 'I made them this morning.'

'Thanks.' They looked delicious, full of dried fruit and with crunchy oat pieces. Beech chewed while the silence lengthened. The baby burped.

'What I really came to ask about was your grandmother,' she said at last to Alice. 'She still doesn't know about her grandchild yet, and I hate all this secrecy. You know she'd be thrilled. You said you were going to tell her months ago. Can we arrange a lunch or something?'

'We'll have to bring Ash,' said Alice. 'We're not going out without him.'

'What about Rita and Henry? I suppose you're leaving it to me to tell them about Ash.'

'Yeah. But don't get in a state about it. I bet Granny'll be really pleased. And Henry won't remember what you've said two minutes later, so that's all right.'

'I'll do my best. Just so long as you come and show off the baby. I'll fix a day with Rita and give you a ring.'

'Don't worry, Mum. We'll be there. And we'll wear our best frocks and put Ash in a clean nappy.'

Which was the nearest to a joke that Beech had ever heard from her daughter.

Now all that remained was to break the news to Rita.

'What do you mean, my granddaughter has a baby son? Why have you been keeping this from me, Beatrice? You're so secretive. And so selfish! I should have been with her. The poor lamb has been going through all this anguish on her own.'

'Not entirely on her own.'

'Has the father taken responsibility? Is she getting married? Who is he? Do we know him?'

'No,' said Beech, which was an accurate answer to most of her mother's questions. 'And she isn't on her own. She has a close friend, Francesca, with her. I believe she spoke of her to you once? Yes, it's the same Francesca, and they're sharing a house on the Goldfinch estate and looking after the baby quite beautifully.'

'When am I going to see them?'

'How about this weekend? Why don't you all come to lunch with me on Sunday?'

'Must I wait till then?'

'It's only a few days.'

'Very well then.'

Beech took a deep breath to calm herself and then said, 'There's something about their relationship I should explain.'

'What's that? What's wrong?'

'Nothing's wrong. It's just that Alice and Francesca are . . . together, if you take my meaning.'

'What on earth are you on about, Beatrice? You're not trying to tell me there is something unnatural about this relationship? What nonsense!'

'It depends how unnatural you think homosexuality is.'

'I simply don't believe you.'

Try a little harder, Rita, thought Beech.

* * *

Beech had cornered Jack at last as he sidled in from one of his unexplained absences.

'This is ridiculous,' she had said. 'Why are we both pretending that your Denise doesn't exist?'

'Denise?' Jack had tried to pretend that he didn't know what she was talking about, but Beech was tired of the pretence.

'Denise. Your lover.'

'Well, what about you?' Jack had blustered.

'You're talking about Fergus?'

'Is that the man's name?'

'Yes. And as soon as our house is free of Valma and her flapping ears, I suggest we sort out what we're going to do about the situation.'

'Divorce, do you mean?'

'I do indeed.'

She had left Jack looking stunned. Had the man really thought he could carry on with dear Denise while she turned a blind eye and consoled herself with lovely Fergus? When Valma finally left they could have a vulgar, shouting row about it, she thought, and then they could decide to go their separate ways.

Rita, at least, had returned to Rose Cottage for much of the previous month. Valma was a different story. Although she made the occasional trip to London, and Beech hoped each time that the sight of her own dear little flat would induce her to remain there, inevitably she returned, carrying with her a few more possessions which she stowed in various rooms in Beech's increasingly crowded house. Somehow, each time Beech tried to raise the subject it appeared that Valma understood entirely how dear Beech felt and was just on the point of returning to London, or to Rose Cottage for a stay with dear, dear Rita. She had been away for as long as a week on one occasion, and a couple of times for five days. And all the time she managed to indicate, without ever exactly saying so, that dear Beech had so many of life's good things, and poor Valma so few, that it would be churlish to throw her out on to the pavement with her purple suitcase and piles of plastic carrier bags.

And underneath it all, unspoken, was the threat that Valma might reveal dreadful scandalous happenings in the Markland family to all and sundry. Rita might have to pay exorbitant nursing home fees for Henry, and her own social life would be ruined.

At least with the Alice problem solved for the moment Beech could get on with other areas of her life.

She went down to her office and frowned at all the material she had collected for the anniversary book. It was amazing how much she had amassed. Perhaps she should buy some archive boxes and pack everything away for a future generation. With Ash on the scene, who knew how many more generations there might be? The book itself was on her desk, safely enshrined in tissue paper inside its box.

'So beautiful,' said Valma from the open doorway. 'You must be proud of what you've achieved, Beech dear.'

'I feel a great sense of relief now that it's done,' said Beech.

'May I look at it? I have just washed my hands.'

The cover was dark green, with dark blue quarter calf. The title page gave simply Nicholas's full name – Nicholas Henry Markland. Beech had managed to steer Rita away from any references to Arrie, or to their undying love. There were photographs of Nicholas from birth to young manhood, pasted into their places and surrounded by cuttings and extracts from his diaries and the reminiscences of his family and those of his friends she had managed to track down. Very tasteful. Very restrained.

'Wonderful,' said Valma, closing it and placing it reverently back in the box.

'The anniversary is in a week's time. Rita and Henry are

coming here, of course, and I may manage to persuade Alice and Francesca to bring Ash, though they seem more interested in the future than in the past. After that is all over, I will be able to get on with the rest of my life. And what about you, Valma? What are your plans for the future?'

Valma opened her eyes very wide. 'I have very few more of my belongings to bring down from London,' she said.

'You don't mean that you want to stay here permanently?'

'But of course. The lease on my flat expires at the end of this month and I have told my landlord that I do not wish to renew it. Now that dear Rita has returned to Rose Cottage, I thought that I could take over Alice's old room and turn it into my bedroom, and use the other upstairs room as a private sitting room. We'll have to get rid of one of the beds, of course, but I'm sure we can find enough bits and bobs around the house to furnish it quite adequately.'

'No,' said Beech. 'No, Valma.'

'What?'

'You can't move in here with Jack and me. You will have to find yourself another flat, in London or Oxford, I don't mind which. But in eight days' time you will have to go.' The final word came out more forcefully than she had intended.

'I don't think so,' said Valma.

'What?'

Valma picked up the anniversary book again and leafed through the pages.

'It is quite lovely,' she said. 'But there is so much missing, isn't there?'

'What do you mean?'

'This.'

She held up a couple of blue notebooks. She must have had them concealed about her ample person. 'I don't believe you've seen these. But I don't think you would really want your friends and relations to read them. It does put a slightly different light on your dead, sainted brother.'

'I thought you were supposed to be in love with him. You said you were going to marry him.'

'You and I know better than that, even if it is a fairy tale that Rita enjoys.'

'And the letters? The other journals?'

'The letters are quite genuine, but not written to me, as I'm sure you know. I'm afraid that I did a little creative work on the envelopes.'

'I guessed as much. And what about this one? Have you done some creative work on this, too?'

'I didn't need to. Read it. You'll soon agree with me about it.'

'Let me see!'

'I've photocopied it for you. You can read the copy at your leisure, but the original stays safely with me.'

'And what about the other?' She pointed to the second notebook.

'This is one of my own. It includes my observations on the day of the picnic. Just one relevant observation, in fact, but it can be made to mean so much. And no, Beech, you can't see it just yet.'

'How did you get hold of these things? Where have they come from?'

'You were such a careless family. You would leave things lying around, knowing that a servant would put them away for you. Such bad training for children, I always thought.'

A memory of the picnic came back to her, and Valma Crabbe saying, in so many words, that she wanted to be a spy when she grew up. Not a spy, thought Beech. We got that wrong. She wanted to be a blackmailer.

Beech stared at the photocopied pages of her brother's writing, unable to bring herself to read the words.

Come on! You have to go across the line, out of the sunlight into the darkness, if you want to find the truth. But when you've done it, you can be anything you want. Remember?

Black and white. Light and dark. All right, Nico, I'll read.

Today we took the boat out and swam in the deep water out in the bay. Arrie was wearing her new swimsuit that shimmered in waving stripes of black and silver.

'I can see you!' shouted Nico. 'You look just like a fish.'

Diving down, swimming under the surface until you reached the darker, icy water. Then, when at last you shot up into the air, in a shower of silver water drops, you were reborn. New people. Nico and Arrie. Wonderful Nico.

Why had they chosen those particular names? Nico was easy: Henry called him Nicholas, so they had to find something different. Rita called him Nicky and that made them both puke. So, Nico. Cosmopolitan. Cool. The private name they kept for one another. It had been one of those days when they had been the victims of Henry's rage, and all they wanted to do was get away from their parents, into their own world.

'No one can seriously think of you as a Beatrice,' he said, out there in the bay. 'You need to be at least eighty before you can be called that.'

'What about calling me Bice?' She pronounced it Beechay.

'To rhyme with mice?' he laughed.

'Well, what about my middle name?'

'Beatrice Harriet Markland. You want me to call you Harriet?'

'Call me Harry.'

'I'll call you Arrie.' He spoke with a mock-Cockney accent.

'Wouldn't she just hate that!' They both knew she meant Rita.

And so Arrie she became. Just for the two of them, when

they crossed the boundary out in the bay, and could do and be what they wanted.

They had to make their own world, somewhere where they could be safe. It was the only way they could escape. If they had included outsiders, then some of the family secrets might have slipped out. Rita's drinking. Henry's rages. Henry's drinking. Rita's adultery. The spitefulness. Henry's possessiveness towards his daughter. Henry eyeing up her young friends. The whole lying edifice might have crumbled. So they kept it to themselves.

Dearest Arrie . . . All my love, Nico.

He was so very beautiful.

She had noticed it for the first time at the Rainbow Pool. She shivered as she thought about that cold, dark water, and the way they had thrown their clothes off and dived in. Rita and Rowley hadn't been interested in them, or in what they were doing. They were stretched out on the picnic rug, out of sight of the ever-discreet Boutros. The three adults were half a mile away from the pool.

That day was the first time she saw just how like Henry he looked. Tall, broad-shouldered, with fair hair that flopped over his forehead, and Henry's eyes and eyebrows. But Nico was young, and fit, and attractive. He didn't get drunk, and frightening, breathing whisky fumes in her face, like Henry.

She reread Nico's version.

Today we went to the Rainbow Pool with Rita and her latest. Arrie and I got away from them, followed the stream up to the pool itself. It was so shady and green under the trees. I can't describe it. I haven't got the right words. And I can't draw like Arrie. Then the water. The darkest of sapphires, I recall. And the way we dived in, just the two of us, and the cold was so intense, although the heat below on the coast was so heavy, that we could hardly breathe. For a moment, I remember, it was as though my heart stopped beating. An icy hand gripped me around the chest. I couldn't draw in any breath. It wasn't like drowning, it was as if I was frozen for an instant in time. Time stood still. Isn't that what they say? I don't know how long for. It must have been several seconds. Silence. Then it had all gone again, and I could inhale and move, and swim. And Arrie was there. I saw her face with the blue water streaming down it, hanging in mercury drops on her lashes and in her hair. Like a water nymph. Like a fish. A grey and silver fish, turning, diving, swimming.

If only all girls were like her, maybe I could be interested in one of them.

If only she were a bit older, or understood more about life, I would be able to talk to her about how I feel. I thought I could try.

But then the lad with the goats turned up, so like the one that Arrie had been drawing, and he smiled at me. He knew, but I knew that Arrie was too young to understand. This was what I wanted. He was what I wanted. I knew. But I couldn't explain it to Arrie.

Oh, Nico, I wish you'd tried. I wish we'd had the time. I'd have understood, really I would. At some level I knew about you, in any case. It wouldn't have been such a great shock, I promise you. I pretended not to understand that last time, at the pool, when I saw you there with the boy. I turned my back and walked away.

They were right. It was my fault. I should have stayed, and then I might have prevented whatever it was that happened to you. How could you have drowned, there, with Henry and the boy standing by? But I walked away. This time I'll stay. This time I'll find out the truth.

I must open up the compost bin and take a look inside.

* * *

'Well now, Beech dear, what did you think of Nico's diary?' Valma had once again tracked her down to her office.

'The usual adolescent jumble of fact and fantasy, don't you think?'

'No. I don't.'

'So you think it's going to provide free board and lodging in my house for the rest of your life, do you?'

'When you're ready, I'll show you my own account of the picnic. Just tell me when you would like to see it.'

'I don't think that will be necessary.'

'Wouldn't you like to know what I saw?' Valma looked teasingly through mascaraed lashes.

'I can see you're dying to tell me.'

'What an appropriate word.'

'I don't believe you were there. I don't think you saw anything at all.'

'Let me convince you. After the treasure hunt, I was slipping away into the woods, answering a call of nature.'

'Having a pee?'

'If you must put it so. I did not wish to be seen, naturally, and I walked some way into the woods, until I was quite sure that I was out of sight, and I found myself quite close to the Rainbow Pool. When I had accomplished that which I had come for, I joined the path back to the others. And then I saw Henry.'

'What was he doing?'

'How startled you sound! It was a little odd, I agree. He had a knife in his hand, a long, thin blade, and he was cleaning it, quite carefully, with his handkerchief.'

'That doesn't sound very sinister. He could have used it for anything.'

'Oh, but it was sinister, very sinister, I assure you. He was cleaning blood from the blade. I could see it on the white cloth quite distinctly.'

'And where had the blood come from? Nicholas was drowned, if you remember, not stabbed.'

'Of course. That is what they all said. But there were whispers.'

'What whispers? I didn't hear them.'

'No, but then you didn't speak to the undertakers, did you?'

'What did they say?' Beech was drawn into this unlikely story in spite of herself.

'That there was a puncture wound, on the left side of the chest, such as might have been made by a thin, sharp blade.'

'But there would have been blood everywhere! People would have noticed!'

'Not if the knife-thrust was accurate. That sort of wound, straight to the heart, would bleed very little. And what little blood there was would be washed away in the pool.'

'And you're telling me that Henry stabbed his own son?'

'How should I know what Henry would do? He was a very different man in those days, don't you think?'

But surely not so different that he could kill Nico. She refused to believe it. And why should Valma be telling the truth?

Valma's expression, however, was so smug and self-satisfied that Beech could do nothing else but believe her story.

32

After Valma left the room, Beech sat and thought for a while. She couldn't run away this time. She couldn't turn and leave the scene, pretending that nothing nasty was happening. She would have to go to see Henry. Surely, somewhere in the cobwebby depths of his mind there must be the truth of what happened that afternoon. But first she had to deal, finally, with Valma.

She had come to a decision.

'Valma!' she called.

'Beech, dear, how very loud you are!'

'I want that notebook of yours. And Nico's. And any letters of his that you're still holding on to.'

'Really? What for?'

'I think I know most of the story now. There's nothing you can tell me that will surprise me, nothing you can do to us. I'm going to find out the last few fragments and then I shall bury them for ever. You can give up. You can start to pack your things.'

'How very positive and assertive you are being! Are you absolutely sure about this?'

'Yes. You stole those notebooks and letters. You forged the envelopes. You wormed your way into this family and hoped that we would support you for the rest of your life.'

Valma raised an eyebrow. 'I was thinking only of you and your family, especially at such a sensitive time, on the thirtieth anniversary of this sad occurrence. A betrothal to a respectable young woman: wouldn't that silence any gossip and provide such a soothing memory for your dear parents? So much nicer than ugly rumours at their time of life.'

'Just go and fetch down the notebooks and letters. If they belong to anyone, they belong to *me*.'

'I thought we were going to be such friends,' sighed Valma, disappearing upstairs to do her bidding.

Beech bundled the letters and the notebooks, with their mixture of fact and fantasy, into a plastic carrier bag.

'Start packing!' she called to Valma, and she set off in her car, northwards.

'Henry!' she shouted, when she arrived at the house in Chipping Hampton.

'It's me! It's Beech!'

'Hello?'

It was Henry, peering round the gatepost. 'What is it you want?' he asked. 'I wasn't expecting you.'

'Is Rita here?'

'No. She's gone to the shops.'

'Good. I wanted to find you on your own.'

'What is it you want?'

'I want the rest of the letters and notes that Rita has been sorting through. And I want to look in Nicholas's room,' she said.

'Oh no, he wouldn't like that,' said Henry. 'It's private.'

'There's nothing private there any longer. It's just the toys and fantasy world of a child,' she said, and went into the house. Upstairs in Nicholas's room, she took down the model planes, the child's books, the battered model cars and small heaps of written pages, and bundled them into yet another plastic bag. This one was large, and she needed a second one before she had finished.

'What are you doing?' asked Henry as she came downstairs and opened the back door, releasing its wooden bar and pulling back the bolts that held it shut.

'Destroying the lies of the past,' said Beech, walking into the middle of what would have been a lawn if Rose Cottage had such a thing. 'It's about time it was done.' She dropped the bags of rubbish – yes, *rubbish*, she thought – on to the parched stubble of grass and weeds. If the truth was to be found at all, it was in Henry's memory, not in these pages.

'Do you remember that afternoon?' she asked him, desperation in her voice. 'At the Rainbow Pool, when you told me to leave? The day that Nico died?'

'Come indoors,' said Henry. 'I've tried so hard to forget.'

'That afternoon at the Rainbow Pool.' Henry paused and pushed his hands through his thick, fair hair, finding to his surprise that his fingers encountered papery dry skin and sparse soft tufts of hair over his ears. He smoothed these down, then dropped his hands to his lap. Their backs were spotted with the liver marks of age. What had happened to all the years? These hands, these fingers were the ones that had found pleasure in the feel of a young girl's skin, the softness of her dress, the sensation of the peachy hairs clouding her arms. He leaned over to pat the top of Gunter's head and to massage the old, waxy ears. Gunter grunted, perhaps with pleasure, perhaps just to remind himself that he, too, was still alive.

'You're still here, boy, aren't you? You and me both. Ailing but alive. Unlike Nicholas, of course.'

He was silent for a few minutes, then seemed to rouse himself again. 'Do you remember Rita when she was young? She was always such an upright figure, she had such a good carriage, such a straight back. Until it happened. It was the first thing I noticed about her afterwards, the way she was curled up with misery. A crescent of grief that rocked and wailed and unravelled. I hardly recognized her.'

'And what about the day it happened?' asked Beech gently.

'He made me so angry. He had that insolent look on his

face, defying me. He stood there and drawled, "I have a horrid feeling that you're going to shout more nasty things at me." That was when I ordered you to leave. I didn't know what I might say. Or do, if it came to that. "I told you to get dressed," I said to Nicholas. He obeyed me, but with an air about him, oh, as if he felt no *shame*. He didn't even bother to turn his back, he just pulled on underpants, white shorts, blue shirt, sandals. He took his time.

' "Have you a comb I can borrow?" ' he asked.

'I ignored him and went to pay the boy with the goats. He was a knowing little bastard, and he argued with me over the price. I could hardly look at him, I was so angry. I refused, and the stupid boy pulled out a knife. I don't suppose he really meant to use it, but he threatened Nicholas with it, you see.

'I should have tried to disarm him. I shouldn't have left it to Nicholas. What did he know about knives and fighting? That's why it's my fault, you see. *I* should have been decisive. But Nicholas and the boy were scuffling, and then Nicholas fell to the ground and the goat-boy dropped the knife and ran. I let him go. I didn't care about him. I could see that he had killed my son.

'And what I remember most clearly is the short, sharp, pang of relief. Can you believe that? But it's the emotion I remember above all. Yes, Nicholas's death would solve all my problems. Death would take away this son who would never live up to my expectations for him. I had such plans for that boy. Such ambitions.

'I'll never know why the goat-boy did it. I've always been afraid that he read something in my face that urged him to thrust the point of his knife between Nicholas's ribs. Something in my eyes, perhaps, that willed him to kill my son, since I was too much of a coward to do it for myself. But that was it.'

'Did you never tell anyone about it?'

'Why should I? I couldn't face the scandal. It would all have come out, don't you see? But I did try to revive my boy. I tried, but there was nothing to be done. And no one had seen. There was so little blood, and it seemed kinder to make it look as though he had drowned. Just an accident, do you see, instead of a sordid little crime.'

My son! He felt again the sharp pain of loss. But he had taken his grief and wrapped it up and locked it away in a dark corner of his heart where it had rested, cold, unresolved, hidden. Sometimes he thought that this cold grief was the only authentic part of him, that and his affection for Gunter.

What had happened to the old, flesh-and-blood Henry? The man who had enjoyed the sight and feel of young female flesh, the one who drank, far from Rita's watchful eye, at the Cricketers. *You buried him with Nicholas in the leaden box.*

There was no way to reconcile these two halves of himself, he reasoned. Not until death spliced them back together.

'Henry?'

Beech's hand was on his arm. Perhaps he had drifted off to sleep there for a moment.

'Did no one notice that he had been stabbed?'

'I made sure that no one made it public, even if they had noticed. There was a man at the embassy who owed me a favour or two. He fixed it for me.'

Did I kill him? He still wondered about it. Had the thought gone from his mind to the boy's hand, guiding the knife to that vulnerable spot between the ribs? The thought would have haunted him down all the years if it weren't for his other interests. Come to think of it, it must have been about then that he started to buy his books about gardening.

He had stared at the lush scenes of clipped box and mown grass and tried to lose himself inside them. He had wandered in imagination the green paths and sniffed at the lavender that lined them, the roses that scrambled up the walls. They were so far removed from the parched brown landscape of the Levant and the torrential rains that arrived in October. He bought a notebook and made plans for the garden of his dreams. This country is too dry, he thought. There'll never be enough water to cultivate a proper lawn.

The image of Nicholas, floating face down in the Rainbow Pool, faded as he read of roses and wisteria and made his plans in his new notebook.

'Come on,' said Beech. 'It's time to get rid of it all. Come outside with me.'

The stalks crackled in anticipation of the flames to come as they walked across the dry grass.

'Sticks,' she said. 'Kindling.' And she toured the garden, finding anything that would burn. She opened the shed doors, ignoring the mewing sounds of distress from Henry. Gunter ambled out into the sunlight, blinking his grey lashes. She found broken kitchen chairs, and a table with three legs, riddled with woodworm, and she picked out a pile of old newspapers.

She built her pyre in the middle of the garden, rising six feet or more from the ground, and then she set fire to it.

She watched the small orange flames licking at the chair legs, and the spiral of blue smoke creeping up through the twigs and the crumpled newspaper.

'Why?' cried Henry. 'Why are you doing this?'

'I told you. I'm setting fire to all the lies,' said Beech. 'You don't have to hide in your house any longer, Henry. You don't have to spend your days producing compost that will never be used to grow anything at all. You can stop being frightened of your dreams. They are all going up in flames. *You can stop pretending.*'

Henry looked at her in incomprehension. 'We could have composted all that paper,' he said. Beech ignored him.

She tossed the torn cover on to the fire and started on the second notebook. She crumpled up the crisp grey pages of the letters. She threw them away and watched them blaze and die.

Small grey flakes rose in the currents of air and fell like snow over the garden. She threw more lumps of wood on to the fire to help consume all the paper.

'Be careful,' said Henry. It was true that the fire was getting very hot now, with a pale yellow heart and long thin flames reaching up to snatch at the books and toys, the old furniture and the decaying clothes that Beech flung into them. The flames leaped higher than the roof of the shed, and the heat was so intense that she could no longer stand so close to it.

A sudden volley of sparks shot into the air and Henry and Beech took a step backwards. Hot air buffeted their faces and pricked their hands. Beech could smell burning, singeing. She put a hand up to her hair and felt it dry as tinder, ready to burst into flames. She looked over towards Henry's sheds. The door of the first was smoking. Some rubbish on the floor of the second was starting to catch.

Beech came to her senses at last. She had destroyed all that she had set out to get rid of. She hadn't meant to demolish any of Henry's property.

'Where's Gunter?' she shouted.

'Indoors. I put him in my study. What are you going to do?'

'Buckets! Water!' she called. 'Where's the hosepipe?'

'I haven't got one,' said Henry, watching as the flames licked across the shed floor towards his compost bins.

Beech left him there and ran for the house to telephone the fire brigade.

Two fire engines arrived fifteen minutes later and one of the firemen led the frail old gentleman into the house and left him to sip hot, sweet tea in the kitchen.

'Got a bit too enthusiastic with his bonfire, did he?' he asked Beech, sympathetically.

'I think that was my fault rather than his,' she said.

Beech stared out at the devastation that had been her father's garden. Blackened debris covered everything and the water ran off in rivulets, failing to soak into the parched ground but gushing in streams and rills, dripping on to the concrete paths along the sides of the house. The sheds were in ruins. She hoped that the worms hadn't suffered too much: it must have been a rapid end.

At last she went back into the kitchen.

'How are you feeling?' she asked.

'I shall have to start all over again,' he said.

'I am very sorry. I intended to burn the letters and notebooks, maybe some of Nick's old childhood belongings, nothing more, really.'

'Have you seen Gunter?'

'Don't worry. He's still in your study. He's fine.'

'Oh, good. Good. I think I shall go back to the brandling worms. I do believe they were the most successful. Thank goodness I still have my log books.'

'You don't have to go back to making compost. Not now.'

'Oh, but I must. You don't understand. It's the most important thing.'

'Do you mind if I use your phone?'

'Please do.'

Beech went to the telephone and dialled.

'Hello? Fergus?'

'What's wrong? You sound strange somehow.'

'We've had a bonfire out here at Chipping Hampton and it got a little out of hand. Do you mind if I come and stay with you for a day or two? I don't want to go back to Enderby Road.' She waited, holding her breath, for his reply. Now she really was taking a risk. Barriers raised, fences down, sheds burned.

'Of course,' said Fergus. 'Stay as long as you like.'

'I only want to stay until I've found a place of my own,' said Beech, later. 'I'd like to live on my own for a while, just to remind myself what it's like.'

'And Jack? Not that I care about Jack.'

'He can have the house in Enderby Road. I've always hated it. He'll have to pay me half its value, but he can afford to do that. He can move Denise in as soon as he likes. I really don't care.'

'And now that you've sorted out your own family's past, maybe you could help me with mine.'

'Do you need my help?'

'You could sit on the sofa and make encouraging noises as I load stuff into plastic bin liners.'

'I think I could manage that.'

'We're going to be all right, aren't we?'

'Oh, yes.'

Beatrice Waring and Fergus Burnside walk hand in hand down Lewis Road. They are talking and laughing and caring not at all for the rain that falls from the leaden sky.

Two crows flap their ragged wings and fly away.

If you enjoyed this book here is a selection of other bestselling titles from Headline